RECLAMATION

Look for other books by Chuck Black

The Kingdom Series
Kingdom's Dawn
Kingdom's Hope
Kingdom's Edge
Kingdom's Call
Kingdom's Quest
Kingdom's Reign

The Knights of Arrethtrae
Sir Kendrick and the Castle of Bel Lione
Sir Bentley and Holbrook Court
Sir Dalton and the Shadow Heart
Lady Carliss and the Waters of Moorue
Sir Quinlan and the Swords of Valor
Sir Rowan and the Camerian Conquest

The Wars of the Realm
Cloak of the Light
Rise of the Fallen
Light of the Last

The Starlore Legacy
Nova
Flight
Lore
Oath
Merchant
Reclamation
Creed
Journey
Crucible
Covenant
Revolution
Maelstrom

www.ChuckBlack.com

Author's Commentary

It is with much prayer and extreme carefulness that I present this story to you. Today, our lives are immersed in worldly entertainment, from the innocent to the blasphemous. But rarely, if ever, does the secular entertainment industry point us to Jesus Christ as the exclusive author of our salvation. Therefore, it is my heart that the Starlore Legacy books might entertain while heralding the inerrant Word of God as true and acknowledging that there is no name given among men whereby we can be saved other than that of Jesus. As Jesus taught through parables, allegory, and metaphor, this is my attempt to likewise inspire people of all ages to search out the Holy Scriptures and follow our Lord and Savior.

These books are not intended to replace, distort, or confuse God's Word. These books are also not intended to teach theology or doctrine. Therefore, please do not make the mistake of rigidly applying this loose allegory to such and thus misunderstanding its intent. I am grateful and humbled to be able to share my passion for serving God through literature with you. Thank you.   ~Chuck Black

P.S. As a bonus feature for Episode Six, I have full color images of significant characters, scenes, and technology to help illustrate the story. I recommend reading the entire chapter and then viewing the corresponding images for that chapter. Don't look ahead or you'll find spoilers. You'll find the images by chapter at **www.chuckblack.com/reclamation** or you can also scan Rhett Stryker's com band below. Enjoy!

Praise for
The Starlore Legacy

"Wow! The Starlore Legacy series is amazing! I must say that as someone who has been making a living in the creative industries my entire career with lots of ideas and very innovative concepts for movies, projects and media, I am continuously blown away by the level of allegorical stories with incredible biblical symbolism that Chuck produces. I absolutely LOVE this Starlore series! And of course, I can already picture the movies!"

> ~JESS STAINBROOK, Executive Producer, *Seven Days in Utopia* featuring Academy Award winners Robert Duvall and Melissa Leo; Exclusive Adviser, *The Bible Series* by Mark Burnett and Roma Downey

"Greetings from Ireland. We have been journeying with your books for over 10 plus years. We fell in love with the *Kingdom Series,* and we've read and re-read them several times. We came across them at a local Christian bookstore as we were seeking a series to read aloud as a family. Our children were young but old enough to grasp the content and meaning of the stories and what they truly represented. We were thrilled to learn about the *Wars of the Realm* books, and we snatched up the series as quickly as we could. I still read aloud, and our youngest son, 17, who lives with us in Ireland, still enjoys our reading times. I am often nudged for "just one more chapter, Dad." When I saw that *The Starlore Legacy* series was available, again we jumped for joy. We cannot wait until the release of the fourth book. The characters are great, and your writing style always has us captivated. It's amazing how often we'll refer back to something the characters are going through and compare it to real life. On behalf of my wife and our three kids, we want to say thank you for answering the call to write good, godly, Christian books. You have become a part of us, and we are so grateful for how you have influenced our family over these many years. Please know that you are making an impact and that your mission is certainly a success. God's blessings on you and your precious family, and may the Lord grant you wisdom and insight as you continue to weave the tales for the *Starlore* books."

> ~ SCOTT CHATTERSON, Missionary, the Republic of Ireland

THE STARLORE LEGACY

RECLAMATION

EPISODE SIX

CHUCK BLACK

PERFECT PRAISE
PUBLISHING

Contents

CHAPTER

1

A Body to Heal

Ruah – a dimension outside the existence of humanity. It is the abode of powerful beings that can see and interact in both dimensions.

Malakian – the race of beings in the Ruah that serves Sovereign Ell Yon and his Son, the Commander. The First Admiral of the Malakian Aurora Galactic Fleet is Admiral Halem.

Torian – the race of beings in the Ruah that serves C'fir Dracus. The Torians are the archenemy of Sovereign Ell Yon. They are also commonly known as the Scourge.

The first time that Jeshu revived from teetering on the edge of death, the stifling stench of Haleo was still very much evident. Exhaustion, starvation, and dehydration had pushed him beyond the ability for a human body to function, yet life had not completely abandoned him. He fought to recover his mind and memories. Cool liquid was soothing his swollen lips and tongue. The sensation pulled his mind forward out of the darkness of unconsciousness. He allowed himself to stay for a moment, resting in the slightest comfort of a drink of water. He swallowed the few drops of water and yearned for more. He dared not open his eyes for perhaps this dream would stop. More drops of the life-giving liquid touched his tongue. Slowly...ever so slowly, he drank. Hanging on to the edge of life, time was irrelevant, so he patiently waited for more to come. It was the sound of a strong voice that pushed his eyelids upward.

"My Lord."

The words were hardly more than a whisper. Jeshu opened his eyes to see the murky face of a gallant warrior. He tried to form a word, but his parched, split lips constrained him.

"Don't speak...we have you. Drink and rest."

Jeshu closed his eyes, allowing the strength of his companion to hold him. He didn't know how long he was unconscious, but the cool water in his mouth and belly was the first step to being made alive again. He tried to lift his arms, but the gravity seemed twice what it should be. He relented, then fell back to sleep.

The next time Jeshu awoke, Haleo was gone, and he was glad for it. His fight to recover was easier than before, but there was still no strength in his body. The cruel jagged ground of Haleo had been replaced with the comfort of a soft pad. A soothing cool breeze wafted across his face and arms. The beams of a yellow sun danced in the sky above him through the shifting leaves of lofty trees that formed a delightful canopy of green and amber.

"Commander...here...drink."

Jeshu turned his head to see his admiral kneeling beside him, a cup of water in his hand. With the help of Kalem, Jeshu lifted himself up on one elbow and took the cup. He drank heavily, once more feeling the spirit of life slowly reviving his body. Kalem refilled the cup, and Jeshu drank again. After catching his breath, he looked up at his first admiral.

"How long?" he asked in a raspy voice.

"Two days since Haleo, my Lord."

Jeshu thought for a moment. "And what of Daeson Starlore?"

Kalem frowned. "They've killed him. But the young Brae Starlore lives."

Jeshu took a deep breath. "What of his transference? Was it successful?"

"Admiral Galec saw to it himself, Commander." Kalem reached for a bowl to his right. "You must eat."

Jeshu nodded, then allowed Kalem to feed him a meat broth, its savory sweet and salty taste teasing his stomach. The flow of the warm liquid down his throat was a delight he would not soon forget. After a bowl of the broth and another cup of water, Jeshu was exhausted. He fell back to sleep once more.

The third time Jeshu awakened, he was able to sit upright and eat a meal that was more than just liquid. He peered over at Admiral Kalem, who wore a dour look on his face. Jeshu glanced at his surroundings. The place was unfamiliar but as beautiful as any he had ever seen. At the peripheral of this haven, Jeshu spotted twenty to thirty sentries standing guard.

"Kalem, thank you," Jeshu said, his gaze falling back to his admiral.

Kalem continued to look worried.

"Are you certain, my Lord...certain that this is the only way?"

Jeshu allowed a gentle smile. "When I enter into my mission on Rayl, your men can't be there to protect me," Jeshu said with a nod to two of the closest sentries.

Kalem shook his head. "But as a mortal you're so vulnerable and subject to the whims of evil humans."

Jeshu looked at Kalem, waiting for his valiant admiral to lift his eyes to his own.

"I didn't come to this realm to be protected, Kalem. I came here to save the galaxy. I'll leave no space for Dracus to claim that this victory over his kingdom was won by any other hand than that of the frail, mortal Son of Ell Yon."

Kalem's silence testified to his submission to Jeshu's command. "I understand...as you wish, Commander. But when the day comes, should you utter one word of help, I will be there with all twelve fleets of Ell Yon to come to your aid…I so swear!"

Jeshu reached out, placing a hand on the arm of his noble servant. "Come, Admiral, help me up. It's time to strengthen this body. I have much work to do."

CHAPTER

2

A Soul to Mend

For eight days, Brae Thornton was so utterly despondent that the will to live had altogether abandoned her. Her vision of Jeshu's triumphal ascension to power as heralded by her father, Daeson Starlore, had been shattered in a moment. The image of Daeson's Starcraft exploding haunted her with relentless persistence. The darkness of those few days following the tragic end of the Magnifical Festival seemed to choke the very life from her soul.

Brae had never known her mother. The bond she shared with her father was her anchor, mooring her to everything she cherished in life. Since she was just a little girl, Daeson had been there for her, teaching and loving her with such purpose and depth. Now he was gone, and it felt like her entire life was made pointless.

As she struggled to breathe again, one sliver of light repeatedly pierced her prison of darkness, and it emanated from the most unlikely place. Rhett Stryker, in his stubbornness, would not leave her alone. At first, after awakening to the reality of her calamitous condition, she was angry and annoyed that he had pulled her from the death that would have ended her misery. Her frustration with him revived to fullness once she realized she was condemned to live. Eight days she wallowed in self-misery, her severely wounded leg contributing but a fraction of her gloom. But each day Rhett came to her, coaxing her back to life. Slowly the years of bitterness toward him began to dissolve until the truth of his heart reached into the mire of her depression and firmly held on to her soul.

Here, in the depth of her sorrow, Rhett sat beside her and dared reach into the darkness to hold her. He was all she had. As she held tightly to him, his embrace revived the ember of life. She finally allowed herself to see Rhett Stryker for who he was...a true and loyal friend. She had misunderstood him and his actions all along. Her own pride and selfishness had blinded her to the character of the man. Now she clung to him as if her life depended on it.

She held on to him a long while, letting a portion of her despair melt away. He seemed strong enough to bear it, and she was grateful. In that moment of deep understanding, the fabric of her being was altered forever.

"Thank you," she whispered through her tears.

Brae could feel Rhett nod his head as he continued to hold her. For the first time in years, she felt safe with him...completely safe.

When Rhett stepped away, returning a few moments later with food, she devoured it ravenously, not realizing how famished she was until that first morsel awakened her body to its dire need for sustenance.

"Be careful, Thornton," Rhett warned. "Too much and you'll have to start over."

Brae offered a slight smile between bites, trying to temper her intake, but it was hard.

Now that the few shared moments of tender healing had passed, Brae wondered how the new understanding would affect their future interchanges. Rhett, having just called her by her last name, offered a helpful cue, a strategic move to help them carefully navigate this budding friendship.

Brae reached for a glass of water. First sipping, then gulping, she stopped long enough to look over at him. He was sitting on her bed once again, a demonstration of his continued pledge to help but far enough away to honor the boundary of friendship.

Brae swallowed. "There are a few things I need to be honest with you about," she said, wondering how he would react to her name actually being Starlore. That would be a large first step.

"Finally," he said with a smile.

"I know," Brae responded. "But even now it will take some time to get it all out."

Rhett looked down at her leg.

"Based on what the medtech tells me, you're going to need some time anyway. And I'm not going anywhere." Rhett looked back at Brae. "Is it painful?"

"Yes. But I'm ready to start working on it."

Rhett nodded. "Unfortunately, we can't start here."

Brae tilted her head, questioning.

"Prefect Terrok is on a mad hunt to find anyone associated with the insurrection at the Magnifical. Partisans are being hunted and executed every day. He's also looking for you."

Brae's eyes widened. "I guess that only makes sense. He's ruthless. Where are we, by the way?"

"Zareth," Rhett said. "Too close to Terrok. We need to get you out of here."

Brae thought for a moment. "I suppose I'll never see my home again." She looked up at Rhett, hoping there would be a glimmer of hope, but instead his countenance fell.

"I'm sorry, Thornton. Terrok is scorching the homes of anyone who's associated with the so-called insurrection."

Brae's heart sank. The image of her childhood home in flames was painful. Anything precious to her would have been within its walls.

"Where do we go then?"

"I have an idea. Will you trust me?"

Brae had to quell her initial reaction to do the exact opposite. This would take some time.

"Yes, Stryker...I'll trust you."

It took much longer than it should have to get Brae into the speeder. The pain from the wound in her leg was severe. Rhett said that the medtech had mentioned nerve damage that was impossible to repair. Surely this nerve damage had something to do with the extreme pain that came with movement of any kind.

When they arrived at the Zareth spaceport where their shuttle, *Aviel*, was hangared, Rhett left Brae sitting on the steps of the shuttle to coordinate with departure and the launch crew. When he returned, he looked anxious.

"What aren't you telling me, Stryker?" she asked as he hurried to get her on board.

Aviel at Zareth Spaceport

"I overheard the port manager issuing orders to the mechtech launch crew after I left them. Terrok's henchmen are coming to inspect the spaceport. We need to get out of here now!"

Rhett hopped into the left cockpit seat and began whipping through the preflight checks. Two mechtechs approached, giving him the "SHUT DOWN" signal at the same time that a radio transmission blasted over their com channel.

"Attention, all craft. By order of Prefect Terrok, all departures will standby for inspection from a detachment of Royal Guard personnel."

Rhett turned toward Brae. "We can't let them scan you."

Brae's heart began to race. Terrok would show no mercy.

"Strap in, Thornton. We're launching," Rhett ordered as he initiated engine startup.

Brae reached for her harness straps. "You sure about this?"

"Oh, yeah!" Rhett said with a wink and a smile. He pushed the throttles forward and the mechtechs took cover as the *Aviel* lurched upward. The launch initiated a flurry of activity at the spaceport, but Rhett and Brae didn't stay to watch. In no time they were passing beyond the spaceport's terminal space. Rhett turned off the repeated orders to stop that bellowed from the spaceport's com channel.

Brae finished strapping in then went to work monitoring their sensors and transponder readings.

"I'm picking up two Royal Guard patrol craft bearing 1-6-5 and coming up fast," she reported.

"Those are P-88s—faster than us. We don't have enough of a lead to break orbit and get to a slipstream gateway," Rhett said, as he flipped the shuttle upside down and pulled back on the stick. Brae's stomach churned at the unexpected aggressive maneuver.

"What are you going to do?" she asked.

"We're going to lose them down in the dirt," Rhett replied.

Within seconds, they were skimming the tops of the trees and hugging the rolling hills of the terrain. It was reminiscent of times when Brae would fly with her dad on geomapper missions.

"They'll still be able to track us," Brae acknowledged.

Rhett set a flight path toward the densely forested Crystal Woods region. Here the terrain was nearly mountainous, and the thick vegetation offered occasional opportunity to lose visual contact with their pursuers, but it did little to hide them from the radar lock both patrols had on them. Brae had to hold tight as Rhett yanked and banked to match the rugged terrain. She was duly impressed but knew it would not be enough.

"They're gaining, and this isn't going to lose them, Stryker." She looked over at Rhett, his countenance as determined as she'd ever seen.

"What's their distance?" he asked.

"Three miles and closing," she replied.

"We have to try to lose them in the canyon up ahead," Rhett stated as he adjusted his course.

"I'm showing two missiles in the air and locked on!" Brae exclaimed.

"Uh-oh," Rhett said, glancing at the radar signatures of the missiles Brae was pointing at. "P-88s carry the high frequency Harpoon homing missiles. They have their own active radar system—very maneuverable and very deadly."

"Please tell me you have a plan," Brae pleaded.

"Hang on," Rhett said, as he pitched the *Aviel* up thirty degrees, then rolled inverted and pulled back on the stick.

Brae grabbed tightly to a hand-hold bar as the shuttle dove inverted into a rocky canyon nestled in the Crystal Woods, their canopy skimming the top of a tree hanging precariously close to the edge of the rocky wall. The visual was frightening, taking Brae's breath away. Three seconds later, Rhett rolled upright and pulled back on the stick again to keep from impacting the floor of the 500-foot-deep canyon. Brae thought for sure the bottom of the shuttle had kissed the raging waters of the river that flowed through the canyon. She glanced at the radar tracker.

"The missiles have broken lock," she reported.

Rhett shook his head. "Not for long. As soon as they cross that ridge, they'll pick up a lock again."

Before he had finished his sentence, the radar signaled a lock by both missiles. They were coming in fast. Brae could feel the adrenaline pulsing through her arms and legs, the pain of her wound momentarily masked by the intensity of the missiles' deadly pursuit.

"Stryker!" Brae said, still pleading for a miracle of some kind.

By the closing velocity of the missiles, Brae knew they had less than fifteen seconds before impact.

"Hang on!" Rhett said, as he accelerated to full power while setting his course directly toward a cluster of towering rocky columns.

Brae watched as both missiles inched closer on the radar. Ten seconds...five...four...three...

All of a sudden, Rhett cut power to fifty percent then banked the shuttle ninety degrees, executing a hard 12-g turn around the largest of the towering spires. With just seconds to impact, the maneuver positioned the rock column between their shuttle and the missiles.

WHAM! WHAM! Both missiles slammed into the rocky column with a thunderous collision. Brae saw a deadly splay of rock fragments fly in every direction. Were it not for the fact that their position was on the opposite side of the column, the fragmentation alone would have taken them out. The massive, towering spire began to topple, and Rhett had to reverse his hard turn in the other direction to avoid being crushed. After narrowly escaping two episodes of calamity, Brae caught her breath.

"Great move, Stryker, but those P-88s won't be far behind."

"Yep. I need to find it fast," he muttered cryptically.

"Find what?"

Rhett was scanning the terrain ahead, apparently ignoring Brae's question. She stifled her annoyance and let him concentrate. Five seconds later...

"There you are," Rhett said to himself. "Here we go."

Another series of towering rocky spires rose up from the canyon floor, the river encompassing their bases. Beyond the spires, Brae could see that the walls of the canyon narrowed, then veered to the right. Rhett flew straight at the spires then pulled another tight turn, dodging between two of them. On the other side, Rhett banked hard right to avoid colliding with the canyon walls. When he rolled out, he was flying just a few feet above the canyon's raging river. A 125-foot waterfall was just ahead.

"Any radar contact from the patrols?" Rhett asked as he headed straight for the waterfall.

"Not yet," Brae reported. "But—"

"Perfect," Rhett interrupted as he slowed the Aviel to half its original speed but continued straight at the waterfall.

"Stryker," Brae declared as their canopy began to fill with the mist of the falls.

"It's okay, Thornton—just hang on."

Brae's eyes widened as Rhett flew their shuttle right into the falling wall of water. She braced for impact as she heard and felt the weight of thousands of gallons of water hitting the *Aviel*. A couple of seconds later, they were through the edge of the waterfall and inside a dark cavern. Rhett slowed the shuttle further then flipped on the exterior lights to illuminate the cavern.

"We need to go deep enough so they can't pick up our radar signature," Rhett said, as he scanned the path ahead.

"Remarkable!" Brae said after catching her breath. "How did you know?"

"My brothers and I discovered this place on a hunting expedition a few years ago," Rhett said without breaking his concentration as he continued to maneuver the shuttle through the cavern. The further they went, the deeper and larger the cavern became. "You haven't even seen the best part yet," Rhett added with a grin.

Brae stared in wonder as a luminescent glow began to light the cavern. Ahead the path narrowed, but as they continued, the cavern opened up to a massive, hollow rocky world of glowing streams and brightly colored flora. The ceiling illuminated the cavern with a soft green glow that made Brae feel as if she were in a dreamworld. Watery columns seemed to lift up from the ground in a gentle swirling vortex that ended in the large glowing section of the ceiling.

"What is this place?" Brae asked in awestruck wonder.

"I don't think it has a name," Rhett said, as he focused on setting the shuttle down on a large, flat rock, smooth enough for the shuttle's landing struts. Though the surface of the rock was at a slight incline, the struts auto compensated to keep the shuttle level. "Any hits on our radar?" he asked.

Brae was so enchanted with the aura of this magical place, she had nearly forgotten about the pursuing Royal Guard patrols.

"Oh...sorry." She scanned the readings. "All clear. Looks like you lost them." Brae looked over at Rhett. "That was some stellar flying, Stryker."

Rhett glanced toward Brae and shook his head.

"What?" Brae asked.

"This is weird...us not fighting and you even giving a compliment."

"Oh...that. Well, I'll try harder not to let that happen again," Brae responded with a sly grin. "Can we get out? I want to see this place up close."

Rhett hesitated, then nodded. "Sure, but we should stay close to the shuttle just to be safe."

Rhett helped Brae to the shuttle door where she hung on to a side support. Brae noticed that Rhett checked his blaster's charge level then reached for the access panel to open the door.

"Why did you hesitate when I asked if we could go outside?" Brae asked.

"There could be critters," Rhett replied. "But if we stay close, we'll be fine."

"What kind of critters?" Brae asked.

Rhett pulled his hand back from the door access panel. "I don't know all of them, but there's one that my brothers and I tracked here. It's how we found the place. We were hunting big game, and my youngest brother, Kase, swore he saw a large white zefflyn."

"You and your brothers were hunting zefflyns? Are you crazy?" Brae exclaimed. She had never seen a zefflyn in person, but she had heard stories. The zefflyn was a four-legged predator that was nearly as tall as a man and twice as fast. Its muscular form, a ferocious mouth framed by sharp three-inch teeth, two short curved horns, and an ability to stalk its prey in absolute silence placed the zefflyn at the top of the food chain on Rayl.

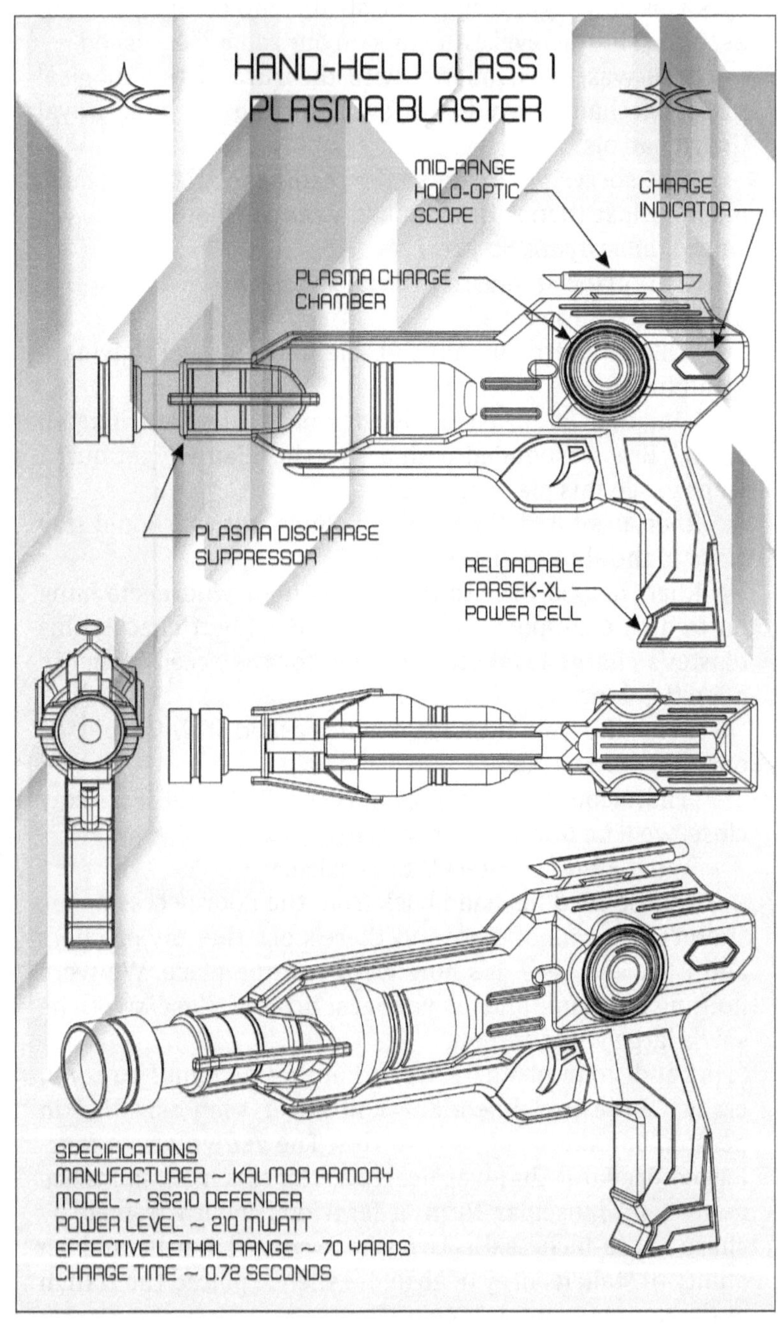
HAND-HELD CLASS 1
PLASMA BLASTER
MID-RANGE
HOLO-OPTIC
SCOPE
CHARGE
INDICATOR
PLASMA CHARGE
CHAMBER
PLASMA DISCHARGE
SUPPRESSOR
RELOADABLE
FARSEK-XL
POWER CELL
SPECIFICATIONS
MANUFACTURER ~ KALMOR ARMORY
MODEL ~ SS210 DEFENDER
POWER LEVEL ~ 210 MWATT
EFFECTIVE LETHAL RANGE ~ 70 YARDS
CHARGE TIME ~ 0.72 SECONDS

Typically, the zefflyn's fur was gray with black streaks about its neck and hind section. Brae had never heard of a white zefflyn.

"No, we weren't hunting zefflyns. But we did track one into this cavern. We never found it, and I think all of us were silently glad about it," Rhett said with a grin. He tapped in the code to open the shuttle door that immediately began to split open from the middle.

Brae felt the cool humid air of the cavern flow across her face and arms. The sensation triggered a wave of chills that added to the feeling of stepping into a magical place. Brae hung on to Rhett's shoulder as he helped her hobble down the steps until they were standing on the floor of the cavern. With his support, Brae was able to stand, engulfed in awe at such untouched beauty. Her eyes immediately were drawn to the spiraling columns of water that terminated at the ceiling 100 feet above them.

"Is that a lake of luminescent water on the ceiling?" she asked.

"As near as I can tell...yes," Rhett said. He pointed to the side closest to them where ripples caused from the vertical columns were lapping up against an upside-down shoreline. "See the waves there? There must be a concentration of anti-gravitons arranged in some configuration I've never seen before. With the rock ceiling of the cavern, we have an inverted lake."

"But the water glows!" Brae said.

"Phosphorescent algae," Rhett replied. "I've seen this off the isles of Napar."

"This place is incredible!" Brae whispered as she tried to soak up the mystical magnificence of the cavern. The gentle sound of the water created a constant soothing ambience. She gazed across the expanse of the cavern, spotting intricate geometric crystalline formations that shimmied brilliantly in the luminescent light of the glowing lake. On one side of the cavern, stalactites and stalagmites reached toward one another from ceiling and floor. Besides the mosses and fungi that carpeted various portions of the cavern, the light from the luminescent water fostered the growth of a few species of broad-leafed vegetation.

Brae's gaze finally fell on Rhett. He was looking at her, a subtle smile on his lips.

"This is the same look I saw on your face when you saw the Omega nebula for the first time," he confessed.

"Yeah?"

Rhett nodded. "It made me think there was more to you than…well, than what I first saw."

Brae knew exactly what he meant. She was about to respond when the slightest movement just over Rhett's shoulder caught her eye. She lifted up on her good leg while using Rhett's shoulder to balance. The sight sent a wave of chills up and down her body. Her face was now just a couple of inches away from Rhett's. He seemed a little flustered by her movement.

"It's behind you!" she whispered.

Rhett's countenance transformed to alarm. At Brae's warning, he slowly turned his head and shifted his body to gain a visual. As he did so, he laid eyes on a terrifying, massive albino zefflyn. Rhett started to reach for his blaster then stopped.

The zefflyn was barely twenty feet away, glaring at them, eye to eye. Brae could hardly breathe. Adrenaline flooded her bloodstream, begging her to run. Then she realized something odd about the creature. It was not poised to pounce. It stood straight and tall, gazing at them as if curious. Although the pearl-white razor-sharp teeth were absolutely frightening to behold, it was the creature's eyes that melted Brae's heart. They appeared as sparkling diamonds—mesmerizing yet nearly too fierce to look into.

"Slowly," Rhett whispered, backing them up one step toward the shuttle. Although they were only ten feet away from the shuttle, they wouldn't make it in time if the zefflyn decided to attack.

They took one more step, but this time the zefflyn advanced. It took three steps toward them then stopped. Rhett reached for his blaster, but as his hand fell on the grip, the zefflyn slowly sank to a crouching position, baring its teeth.

"Don't," Brae whispered.

Rhett removed his hand, lifting it into the air for the zefflyn to see. Slowly the creature lifted itself back to a standing position. They took one more step toward the shuttle, and the zefflyn advanced three more steps, closing the distance between them to just ten feet. As the creature came closer, its visage became even more terrifying. They didn't dare take another step for fear the momentary and precarious reprieve from certain death would abruptly end.

"What do we do?" Brae dared whisper to Rhett.

"You get to the shuttle. I'll draw it away and try to get a shot off," Rhett returned.

Brae clung to his arm and shoulder. "No! I will not!"

Just then, the zefflyn walked slowly toward them until it was inches away from Brae's face. She could feel the creature's hot breath on her face and neck, its bright diamond eyes glaring hard at her. Rhett slowly tried to place himself between the zefflyn and Brae, but the creature nudged Rhett back to the side, briefly opening its mouth to show the frightening glory of its mouth full of over-sized incisors as if to say, "Stay put." The zefflyn then sniffed Brae from head to foot, stopping briefly at her injured thigh. *Would the smell of blood trigger some vicious response?* Brae wondered.

After the zefflyn was satisfied with its inspection, it looked once more into Brae's eyes, then silently turned and left. Rhett didn't hesitate in getting Brae back into the shuttle and closing the door. He set her down in one of the passenger seats then took one of other passenger seats himself. They both sat in silence for a time. After a couple of minutes, Brae was able to calm down enough to take a few deep breaths. Rhett still looked utterly distraught.

"I'm so sorry, Thornton. I should never have agreed to go out there."

"I'm okay," Brae encouraged. "That was spectacularly frightening, but I'm okay."

Rhett just shook his head. "I'll never do that to you again."

Brae leaned toward him, placing a hand on his arm. "Hey…I'm the one that asked to go out there. This isn't all on you. We're alive and have a story to tell…okay?"

Rhett seemed hesitant to accept her offer, but he looked up and returned a single nod, his eyes narrowing to slits as he gazed at her.

"Why are you looking at me like that?" Brae asked, leaning back into her chair.

"I'm pretty sure no one has ever been that close to a zefflyn and survived," Rhett said. "And it definitely singled you out."

"Is that supposed to mean something?" she asked.

Rhett shrugged, relaxing his examining gaze. "I don't know. It's just strange…very strange."

Brae wasn't sure what to make of Rhett's comment, so she changed the subject.

"How long do we need to wait here?" she asked.

"Hard to say, but to be safe we should wait a few hours. How's your leg doing?"

Brae gently rubbed her thigh on each side of the wound. The release of adrenaline was causing it to ache more than usual. "It's fine. If you're okay, I think I'd like to rest for a bit."

"You got it," Rhett said, standing to move back to the cockpit.

"Hey, Stryker," Brae called.

Rhett turned back to look at her.

"Thanks."

Rhett nodded, then turned away to take the pilot's seat.

Brae reclined the passenger seat and closed her eyes. The last forty-five minutes had been intense, taking a toll on her weakened body. After replaying recent events of evading the missiles and then escaping the jaws of the zefflyn, she opened her eyes just enough to take a glimpse at the back of Rhett. He had saved her life again, and she was humbled by his courage and loyalty once more. How wrong she had been about him. As she thought about Rhett, she recognized a warmth in her heart that hadn't been there before. Their growing friendship was something that delighted her. Where there was once annoyance and derision, fondness and peace now resided. It was odd to anticipate spending time with a person she had previously wanted so badly to avoid.

Rhett's head turned toward her, and she quickly closed her eyes, feigning sleep. Within just a couple of minutes, she yielded to slumber.

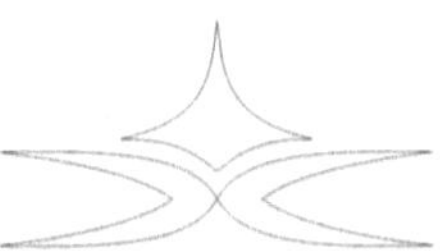

CHAPTER

3

Finding Home

Rhett waited until late in the afternoon before deciding to launch. Brae was still sleeping, so he carefully strapped her into the passenger seat without waking her. He spooled up the engines and lifted off as gently as possible. Easing his way out of the cavern, the rushing water on the fuselage of the *Aviel* didn't even wake Brae. He constantly checked his radar warning system as he carefully navigated the Crystal Woods canyon. Keeping his velocity slow, he was sure to give a wide berth around any remaining rocky columns.

Over the course of a few miles, the canyon floor gently rose to meet the normal elevation of the rest of the forest. Once clear of the canyon, Rhett chose to continue a low-level flight path for another two hundred miles. After convincing himself that they were clear of any Raylean Guard patrols, Rhett climbed to 5,000 feet and set a course for Brohn on the southern continent of Rayl. The safest place for Brae would be off world, but making such a trek could prove to be problematic since the Morian space patrols would likely intercept them. Being quite sure that Prefect Terrok and his regime still believed Rhett to be dead, his next best choice was to take Brae to his home near the city of Brohn. He had reconnected with his family there and knew that they would welcome Brae with open arms.

"Please keep her and my family safe, Sovereign Ell Yon," he whispered. Rhett huffed, smiling inwardly. *She even has me talking to him now*, he mused.

Rhett made the city of Brohn at twilight. Since his home was on the edge of the city and he didn't want to risk landing at the Brohn spaceport, Rhett decided to fly directly to his parents' estate. Getting the *Aviel* refueled or having any maintenance done here would be challenging, but the risk of exposure wasn't worth going elsewhere. The *Aviel* was a small enough craft that it wouldn't draw much attention from neighboring estates.

Rhett's parents owned a large, well-kept six-bedroom home on 15 acres of partially wooded land located on the outskirts of the city. Although more affluent than the average citizen of Brohn, Rhett's parents, Wescott and Kara Stryker, demonstrated no air about them that attested to such. Wescott was the Chief Master of the Phystech Order at the Brohn Institute and Kara had just resigned as the lead tech of the engine design team at the aerotech facility in the nearby city of Kaysic.

Although there was a landing pad closer to the back side of the home capable of receiving small transport craft, Rhett chose a secluded section of their property further away, with just enough of a clearing to set the *Aviel* down. As the struts of the shuttle compressed to support the full weight of the craft, Brae stirred. Rhett shut down the engines and did a quick check before turning his attention to Brae. She was stretching and yawning.

"Hey, sleepyhead," he said with a smile, taking up the seat he had vacated hours earlier.

"Are we ready to leave?" Brae asked, squinting to see out the front canopy.

"We're already here," Rhett replied.

"What? You're kidding," Brae said, wiping sleep from her eyes. "Where is here?"

Rhett turned and entered the code to open the shuttle door. A second later the door split in the middle, the top half opening upward and the lower half opening downward to the ground. The fresh smell of evergreen and fragrant flowers immediately filled the shuttle, replacing its sterile reconditioned air. Brae turned, a subtle smile landing on her lips.

"Welcome to Brohn, my home."

Brae's brows furrowed. "Really? Like...your family home?"

Rhett nodded, holding out his hand for her to grab on to. Brae hesitated.

"I'm not so sure I should be here, Stryker."

Rhett smirked. "Where should you be, Thornton?"

"I...I guess I don't know," Brae replied, looking lost.

"Well, until you figure that out, this is home. Come on," he said, grabbing her arm and lifting her out of the chair.

Rhett supported Brae as she navigated the stairs and then moved on toward the estate. The warm glow of the Stryker home lights, both interior and exterior, was a welcoming sight. Yet Rhett could tell that Brae was apprehensive.

"Hey, it's okay. My parents are great, and they know we're coming."

"You should have warned me," Brae said coldly.

"Yeah...probably, but I didn't want to argue with you," Rhett returned. "This is the best place for you, Thornton. You said you would trust me, so here we are."

Brae flashed him a scowl just as they reached the back patio.

"Welcome!" came the call from the door of the estate.

Rhett looked up to see his mother and his father coming their way. He glanced over at Brae, noticing that she quickly exchanged a scowl for a more pleasant facial expression. He chuckled.

Brae smiled at Rhett's parents as they approached, but inwardly she was embarrassed and angry...angry at Stryker. She imagined that she looked a complete mess. Rhett should have warned her. *Trust? Huh!* she thought.

Brae was feeling completely out of her element. Although not opulent, the Stryker home was beautiful and much grander than anything Brae had expected.

"We're so glad you're here," Rhett's mother said, holding out her arms to Brae.

Brae wasn't sure what to do. Was this a hug? Were these touchy-feely people? She tried to retreat, but the woman instead took over the support that Rhett was offering and continued to guide her into their home. She was strong and warm.

"I'm Kara, and this is Wescott," the woman said, nodding to Rhett's father who was walking on Brae's left as if to be ready to offer additional help just in case. Rhett seemed to be left behind.

"I'm Brae."

"Yes...Rhett has told us all about you," Kara said, softening her enthusiasm to one of gentle consolation.

"I really don't want to impose on you," Brae said, as Kara directed her to a large, soft chair inside the living space of the home.

Kara took Brae's hand in hers as she bent down and looked her straight in the eye. Brae had no choice but to gaze into Kara's warm eyes. Brae instantly felt an unconditional love from this kindhearted woman like she had never felt before. Something deep inside her soul began to ache, threatening her emotional fortress.

"Brae...our home is your home. We're here to help you, and we want you here...with us."

Kara continued to pour her tender, loving gaze into Brae's soul. Brae bit her lip, wishing that whatever it was that was unraveling her so quickly would go away.

"Thank you, ma'am," Brae said, turning her eyes toward Rhett's father. "And thank you, sir."

The man came to stand beside his bonded. "It's our pleasure, Brae. As Kara said, this home is yours for as long as you need to be here. And please call us Wescott and Kara," he said, placing a hand on Kara's shoulder.

Brae took a deep breath and looked beyond them to Rhett. He smiled and nodded.

"You are incredibly gracious. I hope my presence here won't put you in harm's way."

"Nonsense," Kara replied. "Terrok hardly knows we exist down here. You're safe here, and so are we. Now, you must be starving. I've just finished preparing the evening meal, so when you're ready, we'll eat."

The thought of food helped Brae finish quenching any emotional response to the kindness Rhett's parents were offering. She took a deep breath. "That sounds wonderful," she said with a genuine smile.

After the meal, Wescott produced an antigrav hover chair that just happened to be found in one of their storage ports. Brae was again humbled by their thoughtfulness. Kara then took Brae on a tour of their home, ending at the door of a spacious and perfectly prepared bedroom. There was the touch of a woman here.

"This is your room, Brae," Kara said, leading the way into the room. "Please make yourself comfortable. Rhett said you didn't have much with you in the way of clothing, so I took it upon myself to outfit your closet with a few things." Kara pressed a recessed button in the side of the wall, and a section split open to reveal a large walk-in wardrobe, both sides hosting a dozen outfits. "I'd say that Rhett guessed your size pretty closely, so I hope you find them suitable."

Brae gawked at the clothes, unable to craft an adequate response. In just seconds, that same overwhelming ache inside her soul rushed to take control of her emotions, and this time it was unstoppable. She turned her head away from Kara as tears formed in her eyes. She wiped them away as quickly as she could.

"Thank you," she finally muttered through sniffles. She felt Kara's gentle hand on her shoulder.

"You've been through a lot. I can't imagine. Don't mind the clothes...I couldn't help myself."

Brae wiped away a few more tears, managing a smile. "Thank you so much. Your kindness is overwhelming."

Kara squeezed Brae's shoulder. "Do you need help getting ready for bed?"

"No, thank you. I can manage just fine," Brae replied.

"If you change your mind, just give me a call. I'll leave you then to get comfortable with your room, but please feel free to go anywhere you like."

Brae watched Kara leave then pressed the button to close the wardrobe doors. As the walls closed, they transformed into a mirror. Brae glared at the young woman staring back at her. She looked so weak and broken. Growing up, Brae would have been considered stoic compared to other girls her age, but right now she felt like an emotional mess. She missed her dad. She missed Shayde. She missed Rivet. And she missed the mother she never had. Brae had often wondered how different her life would have been with a mother but had no real point of reference. When her dad died, the grief she felt—and was still feeling— seemed a double measure, even more noticeable as Kara appeared to dote on her in the way she imagined a mother might.

She wiped away the remaining tears on her cheeks, took a deep breath, then directed the hover chair to the large viewing port doors on the opposite side of the room. She touched the silent transparent energy field, and it dissolved away. She moved through and onto a third-floor deck. The home had multiple decks at different levels, the lower deck wrapping all the way around the entire home. There was a simple elegance to the home both inside and out that seemed to mimic the character of its owners. Brae went to the railing, allowing the evening sounds and the cool, fragrant air of encroaching night to sooth the lonely ache in her heart. The lofty elevation of this deck and its low railing allowed her to gaze out into the charming country of the region. It wasn't unlike the country she had grown up in. She wondered if Rhett enjoyed the outdoors as much as she did.

"Hey there," came a calm voice from her right.

Brae glanced over to see Rhett exiting from his own room two doors down.

"Oh...hi," Brae offered. She flashed a quick smile. "Your home is amazing. And your parents even more so."

Rhett joined Brae at the railing. He leaned one elbow on the top rail while setting his right foot on the lower rail. "Yeah...I was pretty spoiled growing up in a place like this." He pointed out toward a distant set of rolling hills just off to Brae's left. "That grove and set of hills offers some of the best hunting on the continent. It was the favorite place for my brothers and me to hunt."

Brae looked that direction, just able to make out the destination on the murky horizon. She let her gaze linger there, wondering what it would be like to have siblings.

"You okay?" Rhett asked.

Brae took a deep, cleansing breath. "Yeah. I do wish you would have told me before coming here," she said, turning her eyes up toward him.

Rhett opened his mouth, apparently to begin a defense, but Brae cut him off.

"But I also understand why you didn't," she finished. "Thank you."

Rhett seemed a little surprised. "This place...and my parents...I think will really do you good, Thornton."

"They're too kind. I'm not used to having to need so much help," Brae said with a shoulder shrug.

"Well, don't get too comfortable. Tomorrow we start working on that leg." Rhett offered a crooked smile.

"Can't wait," Brae responded.

Rhett looked at her in a way she had never seen before. How different he seemed now. He stood straight.

"Good night, Thornton."

"Good night, Stryker."

It took Brae a while to ready herself for bed, nearly taking Kara up on her offer. When she finally laid down, the soft bedding enveloped her in comfort. It was a glorious night's sleep.

When Brae showed up for breakfast the next morning, there was an entirely new level of energy in the home. Two young men with features resembling the Stryker family were present, smiling and laughing while conversing with and teasing Rhett. They looked to be about 20 and 25 respectively. As Brae entered the dining room, the younger glanced her way, broadening his smile.

"There's the mystery girl. We were beginning to wonder if Rhett had made up this whole crazy story he's been telling."

Rhett smirked at the guy, and the other young man shoved him out of the way so he could approach Brae.

"Don't mind our little brother. He's made a habit out of embarrassing himself...and us when he has a chance. I'm Bridger, Rhett's older brother."

Brae smiled at him. "Pleased to meet you. I'm Brae." She offered a hand, and Bridger took it, offering a gentle shake.

"And I'm Kase—shy but the most likable of the three of us," the younger brother said with a charming smile and a wink at Brae.

Brae couldn't help the big smile that spread across her face. "I'm sure," she replied, offering her hand to him as well.

Kase kissed the back of her hand while bowing.

"Good grief, Kase. Go sit down," Rhett said, looking at Brae. "I should have warned you about him."

Brae laughed.

With the addition of Bridger and Kase, Kara arranged the meal in their larger dining room, hosting a table that could seat up to ten people. Wescott and Kara sat on each end of the table with Bridger and Kase on one side and Brae and Rhett on the other. Breakfast was delicious and diverting. Brae noticed that everyone carefully avoided any conversation regarding the events at Jalem and her involvement there. She deduced that it was their way of leaving the time to share such things up to her, and she was grateful, for the pain of those memories was too raw to share with anyone just yet.

As the meal came to an end, Kase, who was sitting directly across from Brae, glanced over at Rhett and then back to her. "You know, big brother, she isn't nearly as intolerable as you said she was."

"Kase!" Kara scolded.

Kase shrugged when Rhett glared hard at him. Rhett then looked toward Brae, his cheeks flushing slightly as the room fell silent in the awkward moment.

"I...I didn't—" Rhett began.

"Actually," Brae interrupted, saving the poor man. "Rhett was right...I was indeed quite intolerable." She looked Rhett in the eye, her countenance stern and sober. "It was a long three years for him."

Rhett looked painfully embarrassed, but Brae winked her right eye at him so Kase couldn't see it. She then turned a fierce gaze toward Kase.

"And would you like to know what the most intolerable thing about me was?"

Kase lifted an eyebrow, curiosity ebbing across his face.

"It was saying things that I ought not to have said."

Brae let the moment hang then slowly began to smile at Kase until illumination flashed across his face. Suddenly Wescott, Kara, Rhett, and Bridger all burst into laughter. Bridger put Kase into a brief headlock then let him loose to endure more of the ridicule that everyone was enjoying at his expense. Kase finally smiled and nodded, accepting his due humiliation.

After breakfast, Bridger and Kase left, and Rhett was true to his word. In short order, he had Brae out of her hover chair and onto a standing anti-grav walker support. He escorted her to a two-acre garden located just off the rear patio of the estate. It was a beautiful addition to the Stryker property that Brae instantly fell in love with.

"Okay, Thornton, time for training to begin," Rhett said, motioning toward the outer walkway of the garden.

The anti-grav support proved to be a challenge for Brae to manage, but she fought it and the pain in her leg regardless. Rhett stayed close as she hobbled, bobbed, and stumbled her way halfway down the first walkway. It took twenty minutes to make it just a hundred yards. In frustration, Brae sat down on a nearby bench, pushing the anti-grav support away from her.

"Can't give up so quickly, Thornton. Come on," Rhett said, reaching to recover her hovering support.

"No...that thing is too frustrating to use. I feel so unstable, like I'm going to fall over any second."

Rhett smirked. She waited for a snide comeback, but it didn't come.

"Here," he said, sitting beside her. "Put your arm over my shoulder, and I'll get you started."

Brae reached up and held on to his shoulder. He grabbed her wrist to strengthen her hold and then wrapped his other arm around her waist. The awkwardness of their closeness lasted but a second as he lifted her to a standing position. She was a bit surprised by how easily he seemed to bear her extra weight.

"How's this?" he said with a quick glance her way. "Can you walk now?"

Brae nodded.

"Okay...here we go. Use me as much or as little as you need."

With Rhett as her live crutch, she was able to walk with a more normal gait, adding weight to the leg as she dared. It was comforting to know that even if her leg completely gave out, Rhett wouldn't let her fall.

"This is good...thanks," she said.

"Mm-hm," he replied.

After a few minutes of Rhett's help, Brae felt like she was actually making some progress. They made a couple of circuits through the beautiful garden. Although she was tiring, she was encouraged by how her leg felt. At one point Brae glanced over at Rhett, once again humbled by his loyalty.

"Your family is amazing, Stryker. You have everything I wish I'd had growing up—siblings and...a mother." This confession slipped out from somewhere deep inside her in an unexpected emotional way. Her voice even trembled as she said it, and she immediately regretted it.

Rhett didn't respond right away, seeming to understand she had just exposed a deeply held vulnerability.

"Well, they all seem pretty taken with you. I'm sure the lot of them would adopt you if you'd let them. My mother would never admit it, but I know she's thankful for another female in the home, if even for a short time."

Brae turned her head away from Rhett just far enough so he couldn't read the pain in her eyes.

"So…you said you had a few things you were going to be honest with me about," Rhett said, offering Brae an alternate conversation. "Is this a good time to start?"

Brae took a deep breath. "As good a time as any," she said, pointing to a bench just a few paces ahead.

Rhett gently sat her down and took a seat beside her. He tapped a sequence on his wrist control, and a service bot appeared with two cool drinks. He opened one, handing it to Brae. She received it with a smile. "Honestly, I'm still not used to having a normal conversation with you. Forgive me if I don't respond as I should right away. I'm trying to…to…"

"I get it," Rhett interrupted. "We have a long history of getting each other's ire up. And I'm sure I was intolerable to you at times too."

Brae appreciated his comment.

"But I'm willing to start fresh," Rhett added. "All along, I think in some odd way I was hoping we could have a friendship. We've been through a lot together."

Brae's shoulders relaxed. "Me too." Rhett flashed a quick smile her way. She lowered her head as she thought about where to begin. She looked back up into his eyes.

"Are you sure you're ready for this?" she asked.

"I've been waiting for three years…shoot."

"My name isn't Brae Thornton."

Rhett's eyes widened. Surprise, anger, and frustration flashed across his face. Brae wondered if their promise to start fresh with each other had already been undone.

"You…I…what?" he finally asked. "Seriously?"

Brae saw that old fire of exasperation in his eyes. She quenched her own reaction and instead reached over and touched his arm. It seemed to calm him. Rhett's eyes softened.

"Okay," he said, glancing down at her hand. He took a deep breath. "What's your *real* name?"

"Telling you my real name is going to be the first step in a very long and difficult-to-believe story. But I hope that by now, with what you've seen at the Magnifical Festival, that you can at least hear me out. I trusted you, Stryker. Will you trust me?"

Rhett looked deeply into Brae's eyes. "Even if I don't know your real name, I've been with you long enough to know what you're made of. I can trust in that."

Brae nodded. "Very well...then here it goes."

When Brae began to regale Rhett with her bizarre and fanciful story, he resolved in his mind not to interrupt her, allowing Brae the opportunity to reveal all she had to say in her own way and in her own time. The questions he had for her would come later. As Rhett listened to Brae, he also watched her very closely. He watched her eyes, her lips, her hand motions, and even the positioning of her body in an attempt to build a supposition as to the truth of her words. And as he did so, he began to see a different woman than the one he had come to dislike intensely over the past three years. Something about her had indeed changed, and Rhett couldn't help but begin to change his attitude toward her and his understanding of her.

"To know who I really am, you must first understand who my father truly was," Brae began. "Clearly, he was much more than simply a geomapper. As the world saw, he was a Navi." Brae looked carefully at Rhett, then down at her hands folded in her lap. He waited. She seemed to struggle with her next words. "He wasn't just a Navi, Stryker, he was—" She swallowed hard. "He was Daeson Starlore, the Navi of most of the great stories of our past."

She slowly looked up at Rhett, seeming to anticipate a response. This was indeed a stunning revelation he certainly didn't expect. He momentarily considered the possibility that she was delusional, but he refused to admit his thoughts or display a response yet.

"Did you hear what I said?" Brae asked.

Rhett offered a single nod of his head. "I'm waiting for an explanation before I offer an opinion," he said quietly.

Brae tilted her head, her eyes narrowing ever so slightly. She looked both perplexed and pleased. "Huh...you're right...thank you."

Rhett nodded once more...curious to hear how this story, fact or fiction, could possibly sound reasonable to a person possessing any measure of analytical thinking.

Brae carefully explained in exquisite detail how Daeson and Raviel Starlore had journeyed through time, intersecting the history of the Raylean people at key moments to provide the guidance and leadership they needed. Rhett listened intently, reflecting on each word Brae spoke, all the while looking for a flaw in this fantastic story of hers. He already knew the legends, but he had never heard them from the perspective of Daeson Starlore as the author of nearly all the Navi stories that Brae had told when teaching Jeshu. Rhett couldn't deny the fact that he had been drawn to her stories, even when he disliked her so severely. But now there seemed to be an element of her telling that drew his soul like he'd never experienced before.

After nearly two hours, Brae finished. Many of Rhett's questions seemed immaterial once he'd heard her entire oration. Brae sat quietly next to Rhett, waiting, her eyes eager for his response. There was too much to process immediately, but he realized she deserved something.

Rhett chose his words carefully. "I am by nature a bit of a skeptic. I suppose being a pilot for the Raylean Guard fostered that in me. Therefore, I can see why you would have struggled to tell me any of this before."

Brae looked relieved. "There were so many times I wanted to, but I just didn't know how to even start."

Rhett nodded. "It's pretty crazy."

Brae turned slightly, her gaze drifting out past the garden to some unknown time and place. "I know...it really is, and it took me a couple of years to accept it as truth myself." She turned back to look at Rhett. "I don't blame you if you don't believe it...at least not yet. But I do hope that someday you will. I think I need you to, Rhett. No one else on the planet even knows this story except me and now you."

Rhett didn't dare respond. How could he possibly commit to such a thing?

"I'm glad you told me. One thing for sure...the day I met you, my life went from boring to crazy." Rhett was doing his best to absorb all she had said as quickly as possible. "So...your real name is Brae Starlore?"

Brae's eyebrows lifted as she sheepishly nodded.

"Is that what I should call you?" Rhett asked.

Brae shrugged her shoulders.

"After three years of calling you Thornton, it might take me a while to adjust," Rhett said.

"That's okay," Brae offered. "I don't want to have to explain it every time you do, so let's just keep it our secret for a while. Agreed?"

"Sounds good to me," Rhett replied. "By the way, I have an inkling that we aren't the only ones on the planet that know this story."

Brae's brows furrowed in confusion.

"A lot of the mystical comments Jeshu made make sense now," he offered.

"Yes, I think you're right," Brae acknowledged, then became very quiet.

"What's wrong?" Rhett asked.

Brae took a deep breath as if trying to subdue rising emotions. "If only he'd been there."

Rhett wasn't sure how to respond. They both sat in silence for a minute.

"Do you think of him often?" Rhett finally asked.

"All the time," Brae returned.

Rhett nodded. "Me too. I hope he's okay. I wonder what he's going to do and when."

"Whatever he's going to do, I've come to believe no man can expect it. His ways are not our ways. They're higher, much higher," Brae said with a distant gaze.

Rhett looked over at her, thinking about what she'd just said. "You speak like a Navi. Have you so quickly assumed the role that your father placed before you?"

Brae broke from her apparent distant trance and huffed. "I can't imagine Jeshu needing the likes of me for anything important. No...I think my role is complete."

Rhett's thoughts turned to that moment when the white zefflyn had responded so unusually toward her. *I don't believe that for one minute,* he thought. "Should we get you back to the home?" he asked.

Brae nodded while making an effort to stand. Rhett steadied her, resuming their previous arm-over-shoulder position. Once they began, Brae looked over at Rhett.

"Stryker?"

"Yeah?"

"Thank you for hearing me out."

"Sure thing, Thornton...er...Starlore. But you didn't really give me much of a choice, now did you?"

Brae huffed and nudged her shoulder into him. He snickered.

"Friends?" Brae asked.

Rhett couldn't help but still be cautious. In previous times, Brae could feign kindness to get what she wanted but quickly resort back to her ornery self once it was over. *Would this be the same?* he wondered, but his gut told him this was different.

"Friends."

CHAPTER

4

Friend or Foe

Brae was determined to recover the use of her leg as quickly as possible. She understood that the nine days she wallowed in self-pity, wishing she had not survived that tragic day at the Magnifical, had significantly delayed her healing. Because of this, she felt as though she needed to make up for lost time with self-discipline and resolve.

Wescott and Kara truly did open their home and their hearts to her. Kara demonstrated a tenderness toward Brae that awakened a longing she had learned to repress ever since she was a little girl...the desire for a mother. Moments that threatened her emotional stability had come unexpectedly and surprised her. There was such a strange conflicting notion inside her to both reject and accept those powerful feelings.

Early one evening after a particularly difficult workout, Brae showered and was struggling to finish dressing herself because of exhaustion and how painfully sore her leg was. As she sat on the side of her bed wondering if she had the energy to finish the job, a knock came on her door.

"Brae…it's Kara," she heard through the door.

"Yes?" Brae called.

"May I come in?" Kara replied.

Brae was a bit annoyed but covered her exposed legs with her bath towel. "Open," she commanded, and the door slid away.

Kara stepped through the door, allowing it to close quickly behind her.

"I'm sorry for the intrusion," Kara said, as she came closer to Brae. "I noticed that you seemed quite spent and wondered if I could help you in any way."

"No thank you," Brae said hastily. "I'll manage."

Kara produced a vessel that she opened, immediately filling the room with a medicinal fragrance that was soothing and pleasant.

"My medtech master, whom I trust implicitly, said that this cocos nucifera cream would help heal and relieve muscle pain." Kara reached for a chair nearby, setting it so she could sit and face Brae. "May I see your leg?"

Brae hesitated but only for a moment. Kara seemed to possess the ability to instantly disarm her like no one she had ever met before. Brae carefully moved the towel off her right leg to reveal an angry but healing wound on the outside of her thigh. After a quick inspection, Kara looked up at Brae.

"You're pushing awfully hard, Brae. I understand, but please be careful. You must allow enough recovery time in between your workouts."

"I'm eager to recover my strength," Brae replied.

"Rhett told me that about you," Kara said, as she dabbed her fingers into the ointment she had brought.

"That I was difficult and harsh?" Brae asked.

"Hardly. That you are a tough and determined young woman." Kara moved her hand to Brae's healing wound. "May I?"

Brae wanted to refuse but acquiesced, nodding her approval. Kara gently began applying the ointment to the outer regions of the wound, slowly working inward. In just a few seconds, Brae could feel the warmth of the ointment working magic on her leg.

"The medtech told me there was some nerve damage she couldn't repair and that my recovery would take longer because of it," Brae offered.

"I'm sure," Kara replied.

Kara's touch softened as she approached the spot where the shard of metal had penetrated Brae's leg. When Brae winced, Kara eased off further. She placed her other hand on Brae's hand, and oddly it helped. When she was done, she wiped her hand on the towel. Brae took a deep breath, feeling remarkably better.

"Thank you," Brae said. "That really helps."

Kara nodded, offering a kind smile. "With three boys and lots of activity, I was constantly bandaging up wounds and helping heal injuries."

"I can only imagine," Brae replied.

"How about your mother? You strike me as having been a pretty active girl growing up. I imagine she did her share of bandaging as well."

Brae forced a weak smile. "I *was* active...and had my share of injuries. I'm a country girl and love being outdoors. My dad took care of all my cuts and scrapes though." Brae lost her smile. "I never knew my mother. She died just after I was born."

Kara put a hand on Brae's knee, not saying a word but conveying all the sympathy that no one else had ever dared. Brae knew she should just sit quietly, but rarely did anyone ever ask about her mother.

"Her name was Raviel. My dad told me stories about her nearly every night." Brae's voice quavered ever so slightly. "The way he told them, you would think she was the most amazing woman that ever lived." Brae's eyes began to brim with tears, feeling the full measure of the ache of her neglected childhood rush in on her.

Kara abandoned the chair to sit next to Brae on the bed. "I'm certain she was. Her daughter is sure amazing."

Brae wiped a few tears. "I'm sorry. This just isn't me."

Kara wrapped an arm around Brae's shoulder. "It's okay, Brae. You've been through so much in the last few weeks. We all know how tough you are, but everyone needs time and a way to grieve loss."

Kara's permission for Brae to hurt opened the door to her raw emotions. She began to weep. "I miss my dad so much," Brae said, leaning into Kara.

Kara wrapped her other arm around Brae and held her. "I'm so sorry. We'll help you through this. I'm here for anything you need, okay?"

Brae nodded, trying to recover herself. "You, Wescott, and Rhett have been so kind to me. I don't know what I would have done without you. Thank you."

After holding her for a few minutes, Kara loosened her embrace and leaned out, feeling Brae's wet hair. She stood and found some tissues and a hairbrush. Returning to Brae, she sat down. "You know, I never had a daughter to dote on. Perhaps you'd allow me the selfish pleasure of doing so with you?"

Brae smiled, guessing that Kara didn't have a selfish bone in her body.

Over the next couple of weeks, Brae slowly became part of the Stryker family. Her bond with Kara grew each day in such a way that a small measure of her ignored sorrow began to heal. She especially came to enjoy and anticipate mealtimes. Their conversations were deep and joyful. She had no idea that eating food could be such a celebration of life. Bridger and Kase frequently participated in the evening meal, affording Brae the opportunity to grow fond of them—Bridger for his kind and thoughtful heart and Kase for his enchanting and quirky view of life, although his teasing became tiresome at times. She even dared briefly allow herself to imagine being a sister and a daughter, but then she would come to her senses and scold herself for such foolish notions.

Rhett worked with Brae every day to strengthen and recover mobility in her leg. When she was strong enough to complete an entire session without relying on Rhett to help her, she insisted on two workouts a day. The first workout was early in the morning and was comprised of extensive stretching and strengthening exercises followed by a brisk walk about the garden. The brilliant sun of the Kayn System rose each morning over the eastern horizon, inviting birds to fill the air with their delightful songs. Rhett looked forward to each day, discovering a new and different Brae than what he had formerly thought her to be.

"Your leg is certainly getting stronger, Thornton," Rhett noted as they began their morning workout on one particularly splendid day. "Pretty soon you won't need me at all."

Brae looked up from a leg stretching exercise.

"You seem almost sad to say it," she said, then her eyebrows lifted with understanding. "Ah...you think that when I am well, I'll return to my former self, forgetting the kindness you've shown me."

Rhett was more than surprised at her keen discernment. Though he wouldn't admit it, she was spot on. When he didn't respond, Brae stood and came to him, making a point to look him straight in the eye.

"I assure you, Stryker, I'll not forget what you've done for me nor abandon our attempt at friendship."

Rhett instantly felt awkward. "I have no idea what you're talking about."

Brae held his gaze for a few seconds, her eyes narrowing. Then a subtle smile spread across her lips. "Oh, really?"

"Really. Are we going to work out or chat all morning?" he asked with a gleam in his eye.

Brae punched his shoulder.

"Jerk...let's go."

After they made their fourth circuit through the garden, they took a short break.

"We're all pretty amazed at the speed of your recovery," Rhett said.

"Before the festival, my father was training me in the ways of the Navi," Brae said. "I think the physical training he gave me has really helped."

Of course, Rhett thought. He had noticed that her athleticism had improved, now even more evident than in their previous time together.

"Well, it's impressive." Rhett glanced her way. "I'm not looking forward to when you want to start running. I probably won't be able to keep up with you."

Brae laughed. "That'll be the day. Speaking of which, I thought we could start jogging a bit for this afternoon's workout."

"Seriously? Already?"

"Mm-huh."

Rhett nodded. "You got it."

Just then, the communication band on Rhett's left forearm alerted him to an incoming encrypted message. He diverted to an alcove beneath an arched gate that hosted a lush thick vine abundant with brilliant small flowers of three different shades of blue.

"I need to take this," he said to Brae. He turned to face her so that whoever was on the other end of the message couldn't see her.

Brae nodded, stepping back. "I can leave."

"No, just hang tight and stay out of sight," Rhett said.

Rhett pressed the "ACCEPT" icon, and a pixelated image appeared above the com band. Two seconds later it cleared to display the crisp image of Major Kamp. Rhett didn't recognize the background, but he knew the major wasn't in the squadron.

"Hello, Stryker," Kamp said with his usual dour look. "It's good to see you're alive."

"Hey, Major. Likewise. How are you doing?"

Major Kamp's face sobered further. "As well as can be expected considering the aftermath of the Magnifical Festival. Terrok has had the entire Raylean Guard on alert ever since that debacle."

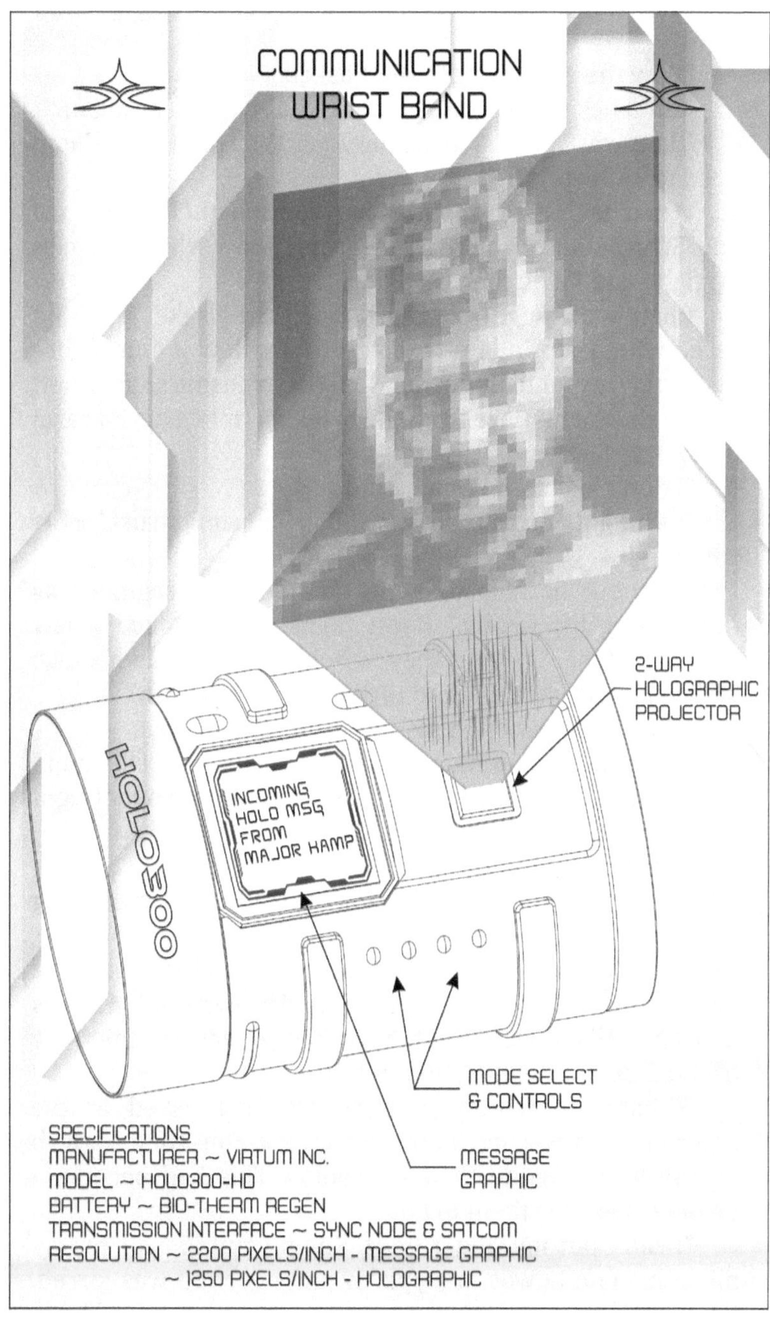
COMMUNICATION
WRIST BAND

2-WAY
HOLOGRAPHIC
PROJECTOR

HOLO300

INCOMING
HOLO MSG
FROM
MAJOR HAMP

MODE SELECT
& CONTROLS

MESSAGE
GRAPHIC

SPECIFICATIONS
MANUFACTURER ~ VIRTUM INC.
MODEL ~ HOLO300-HD
BATTERY ~ BIO-THERM REGEN
TRANSMISSION INTERFACE ~ SYNC NODE & SATCOM
RESOLUTION ~ 2200 PIXELS/INCH - MESSAGE GRAPHIC
~ 1250 PIXELS/INCH - HOLOGRAPHIC

Rhett quickly glanced up at Brae to see the angst on her face.

"Why the call, Major?" Rhett asked.

Kamp hesitated. "I'm assuming you're not near Jalem?"

Rhett was starting to get nervous. Why did Major Kamp need to know this?

When he didn't respond, Kamp continued. "I need to see you, Stryker. Since you're not nearby, I know where you are. Sit tight, and I'll be there in a few hours."

Rhett was caught off guard. For Brae's sake, his mind raced with a dozen lame excuses to disallow it, but before he could respond, Kamp ended the transmission. Rhett slowly shifted his gaze from the blank air above his forearm up to Brae face.

"I don't like it," he finally said.

"I thought you said he was a man you could trust," Brae countered.

"Yes, but he also told me that Terrok's regime was threatening his family." Rhett turned and walked a few steps, thinking. "What if they're holding his family hostage and he had no choice but to turn us in...turn *you* in?"

"Does he know I'm here with you?" Brae asked.

"I'm not sure, but Kamp is a smart and resourceful man." Rhett walked back to Brae. "We need to keep you out of sight when he arrives. Got it?"

Brae nodded.

The rest of the day seemed wrought with escalating tension. Rhett found it difficult to be out of sight of Brae, even for a few minutes. It was a strange compulsion he could only attribute to the notion that he had grown fond of her as a friend. His loyalty to her was now accompanied by friendship. Brae seemed to notice too.

"What's up with you, Stryker?" Brae asked as the afternoon sun reached for the distant horizon. They were up on the deck outside their bedrooms. This had become a favorite place for them to talk.

"I can't put my finger on it. Kamp would never betray me. If his family was in jeopardy and his hand was forced, he would at least give a signal of some sort. I keep replaying his message in my mind, but there was nothing there."

"And yet?" Brae prodded.

Rhett looked over at her, his eyes narrow. "And yet there was something unusual... something off."

"Now you've got me nervous," Brae replied.

"I think we'd better do more than keep you out of sight. I'm going to have Dad take you to a safe place in the city."

Brae looked up over Rhett's shoulder. "Too late," she said, nodding upward.

Rhett turned to see a small craft approaching from the north. He grabbed Brae's arm, whisking her back into her bedroom.

"I'll be right back."

Rhett went to his room and grabbed his ATP-3 short-barreled plasma rifle. When he returned to Brae's room, he held it out for her to take. She looked at him, raising her left eyebrow. Rhett shook his head.

"Just in case," Rhett said. "I assume you know how to use this?"

Brae grabbed the rifle, slapped the power module up and into place, set the mode switch to rapid fire, and disengaged the safety. "Yup."

Rhett couldn't help but smile. "There's more to like about you every day, Starlore." He walked to the viewing port door leading to the deck and swiped it so that the transparent energy field became a one-way view looking out. He then walked to the door leading to the hallway.

"You okay?" he asked.

"Yeah...you?" Brae returned.

Rhett tilted his head. "I'm about to find out."

Rhett exited the room and hurried down to the back of the home where a six-passenger transport was just setting down on the landing pad. Rhett took a deep breath and started walking toward the craft. When he was fifty or so feet away, Rhett could see that Major Kamp was not alone. He stopped. *What did this mean?* he wondered.

The pilot side of the canopy opened, allowing Major Kamp to exit. He lifted an arm, offering a friendly wave to

Rhett. It was enough to encourage Rhett to continue his walk toward the major. Kamp closed the distance, leaving his passenger inside the transport. To Rhett's surprise, the major looked extremely at ease, not at all giving the appearance of someone who was about to betray a friend.

"It's been a long time, Stryker...it's good to see you," Kamp said, holding out his arm for Rhett to take.

Rhett took it. "And you, Major. You didn't say anything about bringing someone with you." Though Rhett couldn't make out who it was that was in the transport, Rhett kept his eyes glued to the cockpit.

"Yes, well, that's going to take a little explaining," Major Kamp said.

Brae couldn't deny that the growing friendship between Rhett and her was better than she'd hoped it would be. She actually enjoyed and looked forward to his company each and every day. But today Brae's response to seeing Rhett overly concerned for her safety evoked the strangest of emotions within her. At first she was offended, but then she felt something quite different...protected. She wasn't sure what to make of it, but she had to admit that part of her heart enjoyed the attention. *I guess he really is becoming a true friend*, she thought.

Brae held the plasma rifle while peering out the one-way glass of the deck door portal as best she could. It felt odd.

"I don't think so," she said, flipping the safety on and retracting the power module. She tossed the rifle onto her bed then returned to gaze out the window.

"Zoom here," she said, touching the place on the viewing port doors where she could see the transport just setting down. That portion of the silent energy field zoomed the optical view so that it was twice normal size. When Rhett approached and the major stepped out, Brae still couldn't see the major's face very well. "Zoom again," she commanded. The size of the image doubled again.

"Maximum zoom reached," a soft female voice replied.

Brae watched intently as Rhett greeted Major Kamp. What she saw next nearly caused her heart to stop. The passenger canopy opened, and a woman stepped out.

"No...impossible!" Brae gasped as chills covered her whole body. She watched in stunned silence as the woman approached Rhett. When she saw Rhett hug the woman, she couldn't stand still any longer. As much as her leg allowed, she ran out of her room and bounded down the stairs. Brae's thoughts were a jumble of wild speculation as she exited the house and hurried toward the three people near the transport. When she was within fifteen feet, she stopped, hoping that what she had seen through the zoomed portal hadn't been a cruel optical trick.

"Shayde?" she said, almost too quiet to be heard, hoping that her words wouldn't shatter this dream she was having. Standing before her was the dear friend she thought had been killed in the attack by the Raylean Guard destroyers at the Omega Nebula. Shayde was one of the few people at the Raylean Astrotech Institute that had supported and believed in Brae and her master program mission to the nebula.

Shayde came quickly to her, eyes spilling tears upon tears.

"Brae! Oh, Brae!" Shayde exclaimed. The two women wrapped their arms tightly around each other.

Brae squeezed Shayde with nearly all her might, feeling a portion of her soul mend with each passing second. They swayed back and forth, unable to let loose. Finally, Brae released Shayde, pulling back just enough to see her face. She placed a hand on each side of Shayde's neck, feeling giddy with glee.

"How is this possible?" she asked, fixating her eyes on every detail of Shayde's face to make sure this wasn't some cruel ruse.

Shayde's eyes were older...more careful than before. She turned to look at Major Kamp. "He did it...he saved me."

Brae went to Major Kamp and hugged him. His stiff composure eased slightly.

"I don't know what miracle you performed to make this happen, but I am so grateful…thank you, Major!"

"I am equally pleased to see that you are well too, Miss Thornton," Major Kamp replied.

Brae returned to Shayde, pulling her into her arms once more. "I can't believe it…I just can't believe it. Thank Ell Yon!"

After another minute of convincing herself that this wasn't a dream, Rhett stepped up beside them. "Come…let's go inside and hear the story."

Brae nodded. She and Shayde led the way, walking arm-in-arm back toward the house. Once inside, Kara greeted them with drinks, offering the reception parlor as a place to talk. Once settled, Rhett looked toward Major Kamp.

"How, Major…how is this possible? We saw the *Stalwart* explode."

Major Kamp finished a long drink from the glass Kara had handed him. He set it on the end table beside him then briefly looked toward Brae and Shayde. Shayde was smiling ear to ear, apparently eager for the major to share the story. Kamp looked at Rhett.

"The official story that came down from Command was that the *Stalwart* was destroyed by a massive plasma discharge from the Omega Nebula. They told us that all souls on board were lost, along with many other ships in the region." Major Kamp hesitated. "We had no reason not to believe them especially when some very incredible distant images of the discharge were published. When you called me and we arranged to visit a few days later, I tried to launch a rescue mission and was shut down. The more I checked into things, the more they didn't add up. I quickly discovered a cover-up on a grand scale. The intensity of threats levied against me and my family by Terrok's Royal Guard was intimidating to say the least. Then after talking with you, I knew we were being lied to, and I had to find out why."

Major Kamp glanced once more toward Shayde and back to Rhett. "I have a retired buddy who buys, restores, and rents discontinued military craft, so I made a clandestine flight to the nebula to see for myself." Kamp's face sobered with the truth of that fateful day. "Thousands were killed, and not by the nebula. I ran scans and found plasma residue signatures that matched the weapons of the Royal Guard. It confirmed everything you had told me," Kamp said, nodding Rhett's direction. "I've never seen such carnage outside of battle. But as I was scanning, I got the faintest of life signals. It was coming from inside the remains of the *Stalwart*." Kamp looked toward Shayde, offering her a chance to speak her part.

Shayde took a deep breath before starting. "It was terrifying. Ensign Cuttler had called me to the cockpit command center to help communicate our findings to the approaching Royal Guard destroyers. When I arrived, they began firing at us. The first shot obliterated the research lab and observation deck. That's when we lost Verlin, Anthros, and Korak. The next round breached the hull near the sleeping quarters. Quinn died there." Shayde began choking up as she remembered the horror of those few moments. "Cuttler told me to get to an escape pod. I tried to get him to come with me, but he wouldn't leave the cockpit. I finally left and ran as fast as I could. I made it to one of the escape pods just as the last round hit the command center." Shayde shook her head, the frightful memory evident on her face. "The fire, the heat, the chaos...it was all so horrible! I was barely able to get the door closed before everything exploded. I tried to launch, but it wouldn't. The ship was destroyed." Shayde looked over at Brae sitting next to her. "I thought I would be dead in seconds, but the pod protected me, and its life-support system continued to work in spite of being trapped in the mangled mess of the destroyed *Stalwart*." Shayde stopped, closed her eyes, and bit her lower lip. "Five days later, Major Kamp found me."

"Getting her out of the mangled mess of the *Stalwart* was a challenge," Kamp added. "Starving and dehydrated, she was barely alive. I took her to a secret location near Kirak and hired a retired medtech to nurse her back to life."

Shayde held tightly to Brae's hand. "I owe Major Kamp my life. He put himself and his family at grave risk to save me."

Major Kamp looked over at Rhett, stoic as ever. "I didn't dare tell you anything, just as you and I kept our exchange of information to a minimum. When secrecy is paramount and lives are at stake, separation and isolation are the only safe actions to take."

Rhett nodded in agreement, knowing full well that the less you know, the less you can divulge when extreme measures to extract information are used.

"I thought you had perished too," Shayde said, glancing toward Rhett and then Brae.

Major Kamp grimaced slightly. "That may have seemed cruel, Shayde, but I truly didn't know if Brae had survived, and I had to keep Stryker's survival completely secret for his own life. It wasn't until the broadcasting of the Magnifical Festival and the remarkable events initiated by Elias Thornton that we knew you had survived," Kamp said, nodding toward Brae.

"I couldn't bear the thought that you had survived the attack on the *Stalwart* only to learn that they had perhaps succeeded in killing you at the festival," Shayde quickly offered. "That's when I began relentlessly pressing Major Kamp to bring me to you."

Major Kamp looked disappointed. "This goes against my better judgment, but it's time." He took a deep breath, looking a bit relieved at the transfer of such a weighty burden. He stood, and the others stood with him. "So, I leave her with you." He looked at Shayde. "Be careful."

Shayde went to Major Kamp and wrapped her arms around his neck, hugging him tightly for a long while. The major gently hugged her back.

"How can I ever repay you?" Brae heard Shayde whisper.

"No such thing will ever be needed," Kamp said.

When Shayde released him, Kamp stood straight, looking at Rhett.

"This place may be safe for a while, Stryker. I haven't come across any communication that implicates you in any way, probably because nearly everyone still thinks you're dead. However, you should all consider getting off world. It's the only truly safe play."

Rhett and Brae exchanged looks.

"We did that, Major. I'm not leaving again," Brae said.

Kamp frowned.

Brae felt something powerful and deep inside her awaken.

"What you saw at the Magnifical Festival…it's just the beginning," she finished.

Kamp's eyes widened. He thought for a moment. "Then all the more reason for me to leave you. I must attend to my family now."

Rhett reached out his arm toward Kamp. "We are forever in your debt, Major…thank you."

Major Kamp took Rhett's arm, and with one firm nod, he turned and exited the home.

CHAPTER

5

Fractured Friendship

Wescott and Kara offered Shayde a room next to Brae. The reunited friends talked for hours on end catching each other up on the past three years of their lives. Brae woke up more than once in the middle of the night wondering if she had dreamed of Shayde's survival and subsequent rescue.

One evening a few days after Shayde arrived, Brae woke from a nightmare where her mind had tortured her with vivid details replaying the explosion of the *Stalwart*. The final dramatic visual was that of a dead and frosty-white Shayde floating through space. Unable to recover her sleep, Brae stepped out onto the balcony to catch some fresh air, but it wasn't enough. She knocked on Shayde's balcony portal door until it opened. She grabbed Shayde and hugged her. Shayde embraced Brae then pulled her into her room.

"Come sit with me, girl," Shayde offered.

Brae welcomed the invitation.

"I used to think I was pretty tough, but losing my dad shattered a lot of that perceived strength," Brae confided as she sat next to Shayde in the middle of the night.

Shayde wrapped an arm around Brae.

"I know you, Brae…you'll bounce back and be the same Brae Thornton…tough as ever."

Brae feigned a smile. "I'm hoping not all of the old Brae returns. Some of her I've learned wasn't so good."

Shayde gave Brae a squeeze. "The Strykers have really taken you in," Shayde said. "They seem like pretty amazing people."

"They are," Brae replied. "I'm so grateful."

"They're doing for you what Major Kamp did for me."

"Yeah…I guess so," Brae nodded.

"So you spent three years with Lieutenant Stryker on Jypton?"

Shayde's tone caused Brae to sit up and face her. "Yeah?"

"Anything happen between you two?" Shayde asked, a sly look on her face.

"Happen? Are you serious?" Brae became incredulous. "We couldn't stand each other." Brae shook her head, remembering those long years and her frustrations with Rhett. "Believe me, Shayde, it was not by his or my choice…at all."

Brae's emphatic denial of the insinuation alarmed her, and she quickly began to feel bad because of how far their relationship had swung around.

"I find it hard to believe he was such an ogre to you," Shayde said, a look of disbelief in her eyes. "Was it really that bad?"

"It was really that bad…but I was just as—"

"And now you're *close* friends?" Shayde teased, interrupting Brae's thoughts.

"We're just friends, Shayde…and hardly even that," Brae defended, finding herself annoyed and defensive.

"Uh-huh," Shayde sarcastically agreed.

Brae's annoyance slipped into anger. "He's helping me get my leg in shape…that's it. Once I'm good, I'm leaving, and we'll probably never see each other again—I'm fine with that."

"The harder you protest, the less I am convinced," Shayde said with a sweet smile.

Brae shook her head, moving to slip off of Shayde's bed to leave. Shayde grabbed her arm.

"Okay...I'm sorry. I don't mean to tease. It's just that he seems like quite a catch."

Brae stopped and looked at Shayde. "You catch him then," she blurted. "I've more important things to do than become infatuated and silly." Brae hoped Shayde wouldn't call her out on this because the truth was that she had nowhere to go and nothing else to do.

Shayde scooted up next to Brae. "I get it. I won't ever tease you again. I can see you're still the same matter-of-fact Brae Thornton I always knew."

Brae smirked. "Got that right!" she said, pushing Shayde's shoulder.

"So...if another girl catches Rhett's eye, you're good with that?"

"Absolutely...wait," Brae said, her eyes opening wide. "Is that what this is all about?"

Shayde held up her hands. "Of course not...I'm just making sure I know the rules around here."

Brae laughed out loud. "You haven't changed either. As far as I'm concerned, Rhett and I are what I said we were...just friends."

As Brae spoke words she had convinced herself were true, deep down in the middle of her chest something began to hurt, and she wished she could redo this entire conversation with Shayde. *Perhaps in the morning I'll feel better*, she thought.

Rhett awoke and heard footsteps on the balcony, so he went to his door portal intending to investigate. He motioned for the portal to dissolve away, and as he did so, he caught a glimpse of Brae giving Shayde a hug. Now that Shayde was here, his one-on-one time with Brae had diminished significantly. He was genuinely overjoyed for Shayde's survival and reunion with Brae, but he couldn't help feeling a bit neglected. He made every effort to dismiss the notion of such feelings for it felt childish—and yet it lingered. He knew he should immediately retreat to his room, but their conversation tempted him to listen for just a minute. Because the night was still and warm, Shayde had not reactivated her door portal, allowing their words to easily carry to Rhett's ears…

"We're just friends, Shayde…and hardly even that."

Brae's words stung. Rhett started to retreat to his room but one more sentence landed on his ears.

"He's helping me get my leg in shape…that's it. Once I'm good, I'm leaving, and we'll probably never see each other again—I'm fine with that."

Back in his room, he fully intended to lie back in his bed and return to sleep, but that isn't what happened. The emphatic tone of Brae's words that diminished their friendship to little more than an acquaintance was impossible to dismiss.

What did you expect, Stryker? he thought. *And why are you upset? She'll use you to get better and move on…she said so. Don't expect anything more than that.*

Rhett closed off that corner of his heart and tried for sleep once more. He rolled over to try a new position and saw the soft glow of his com band on the nightstand signaling an encoded message had arrived. He reached for it.

The next morning, Brae met Shayde in the hall and descended the stairs together to the breakfast table. Bridger and Kase were there, and introductions were made. Later than usual, Rhett showed up. Brae smiled his way, but he didn't seem to notice.

The Stryker table was filling quickly, seating seven people with only three empty seats. A few minutes into the meal, Brae could tell that Rhett was off. Bridger and Kase filled the gap with stories and exaggerations. Toward the end of the meal, Rhett looked over at Brae.

"I can't work out with you this morning," he said flatly.

Brae stared back at him, waiting.

"Major Kamp contacted me and has asked for me to meet him in Zareth."

"Zareth," Brae said. "Why Zareth?"

Rhett glared at Brae, a twinge of his old annoyance evident in his eyes, which upset Brae and by no small amount. She tried to guard herself, but this brief exchange with him was igniting old feelings.

"He wouldn't say…just that there was something important for me to see there," Rhett said, looking away from her before she could respond.

"I should be back by nightfall," he said to Wescott and Kara.

"I'm coming with you," Brae blurted out.

"No!" Rhett countered.

Everyone at the table instantly fell silent at the tension between the two.

Brae and Rhett exchanged ice-cold looks. Then for one brief moment, Rhett's eyes softened.

"It's not safe for you there yet," he finally explained.

"I'm not going to hide here forever," Brae countered. "Besides…I have a feeling that whatever Major Kamp has for you is directly connected to me."

Rhett shook his head. "No…it's too risky."

Brae glared hard at Rhett, failing to suppress old feelings of resentment. "You don't get to tell me what I can and can't do, Stryker!"

Rhett's face flashed full of fury, but before he could speak, Bridger put a hand on his shoulder.

"How about the five of us go? I've been wanting to get away for a day anyway," Bridger said, clearly trying to lighten the mood. "There's an extra measure of safety in numbers."

Rhett looked as if he was about to protest again, but then Shayde added her support for Bridger.

"I think that's a great idea. I've never been to Zareth and would love to see it."

Before long, Rhett was beaten into submission, but Brae could tell that he would be sore about it for a long time.

Whatever had happened this morning seemed to have sabotaged every inch of gain they had been making toward a friendship. Though Brae was angry, she was also incredibly sad. To have tasted such sweet companionship and have it snatched away in a moment hurt. Why had he responded so?

As they finished the meal and prepared to leave, Brae tried to speak to Rhett and possibly make amends, but the man found every opportunity to avoid her. If there hadn't been anything wrong before breakfast, their exchange during the meal had certainly caused a fissure that Brae wasn't sure could be fixed.

Before long, Brae, Rhett, Shayde, Bridger, and Kase were strapped into the *Aviel* and lifting off from the Stryker estate. Rhett set a course for Zareth, a near scowl on his face. Brae sat in the copilot seat, staring at him. She didn't dare say much for fear of the others listening in on them. The 45-minute flight was long and painfully silent.

Rhett navigated to a small private spaceport on the western fringe of Zareth called Blue Star. Once they touched down, Brae remotely activated the door-open code so Shayde, Bridger, and Kase could exit. Rhett unstrapped and made haste to join them, but before he could stand, Brae reached over and grabbed his arm. He froze, halfway out of his seat.

"What's wrong?" she asked gently.

Frowning, he looked at her hand and then up at Brae. "I wish you wouldn't do that."

Rhett sat sideways in the pilot seat, still poised to rise and exit if need be, but this position also put him closer to Brae. She began to pull her hand off his arm, but as she did so, he grabbed her hand, startling her. Slowly he leaned toward her, his eyes searching hers. Brae's heart began to race, unsure what this meant. His countenance was unreadable. She froze as he continued to close in on her. Just inches away he stopped, a look of desperate hope in his gaze. Then the corners of his eyes fell ever so slightly.

"I thought you had changed," he said quietly. "I almost believed it."

The moment hung for another two seconds. Brae didn't dare move, taking in every detail of Rhett's face as the words he'd spoken began to fracture her heart.

"I have, Rhett. Why would you say that?" Brae asked, realizing that he was still holding on to her hand. He let go as he backed away from her, a look of mild disappointment in his eyes.

"Are you the Thornton of the past or the Starlore of today...it's hard for me to tell from where I'm standing." He turned. "They're waiting for us. Let's go," he said, as he walked toward the door.

Brae sat still in her seat, somewhat stunned by Rhett's words and actions in two completely different ways. It was very confusing. As she absorbed his words of rebuke, her mind returned to the words she'd spoken to Shayde about Rhett and their friendship the night before. She cringed. *Is it possible that he heard us?* she wondered.

She finally unstrapped, wondering how to fix that which she had unwittingly broken yet come to cherish so much. Outside the shuttle, the group was already making plans.

"Let's not be foolish," Rhett scolded. "Royal Guard patrols could show up anywhere and at any time. Even though reports claim that Terrok's search for the Partisans is over, we must be vigilant."

Kase saluted. "Aye, aye, sir."

"I'm serious," Rhett said, scolding his younger brother. "It won't be funny when you've been arrested and are facing an execution."

Kase instantly lost his smile and nodded. The tyranny of Terrok was all too real for any such levity.

Rhett turned to look at Brae. "You should stay here since you are most at risk."

Brae shook her head. "I didn't fly all the way to Zareth to sit in the shuttle. I want to go to the sanctum," she said, lifting her chin in defiance.

Rhett looked frustrated.

"It's okay," Bridger said. "Kase and I will go with her. You take Shayde so we all have at least one look-out."

Shayde seemed delighted by the suggestion. "That's a great idea," she said. "I'd like to see Major Kamp again anyway."

Rhett glanced toward Bridger, begrudgingly offering a quick nod. "We can rent a couple of surface speeders just over there," Rhett said, pointing to a building just a short walk away.

Soon the two groups were getting ready to part ways, their speeders sitting side by side. Everyone seemed upbeat and excited for a small adventure...everyone except for Rhett and Brae.

"Hey, big brother," Kase said with sly grin. "It's okay to have a little fun from time to time too."

Shayde nudged Rhett with her shoulder in agreement with Kase. Brae smirked, recognizing Shayde's signature flirtation move. Such subtleties seemed so natural for some girls, but for Brae these things completely eluded her. Shayde winked at Brae, but Brae just rolled her eyes, turning to enter the speeder. Once strapped in, she looked toward Rhett who had just finished strapping into his own speeder. They exchanged glances that lingered for a couple of seconds. She offered a sheepish smile. He didn't. A minute later both parties had entered the city of Zareth, setting their courses in opposite directions.

As Brae, Bridger, and Kase approached Zareth's sanctum, it was clear that something out of the ordinary was happening. Brae and Jeshu had frequented the sanctum often during their time in Zareth, and she had never seen more than a few hundred or so people on its campus or inside the sanctum itself. As they drove past the sanctum, Brae estimated nearly 2,000 people were present.

"Wow," Kase exclaimed. "Is there some sort of festival happening we don't know about?"

Bridger seemed as surprised as Brae and Kase. "I don't think so, and I don't see any patrols or Morian Commandos either. Something else is happening."

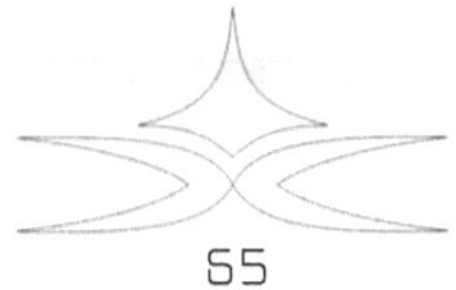

CHAPTER

5

The Return

"The Protector of Ell Yon is with me for He has given to me the mission to offer hope and truth to the poor. He has sent me to heal the brokenhearted, to deliver the captives, and to cause the blind to see. To bring freedom to those that suffer, and to speak truth in this the year of Ell Yon." ~ Eziam, Oracle of Ell Yon

Jeshu stood on a hill overlooking Zareth. The Protector on his arm was indelibly merged with his neuro pathways. The very real and present mind of his father, Sovereign Ell Yon, was now a constant companion to his thoughts, strengthening his heart for the grand mission before him. With the trial of Dracus behind him, Jeshu stood in the full power of Ell Yon, eager to begin intersecting humanity with his kingdom of the Ruah. As Jeshu stepped forward toward Zareth, so did the reclamation cross over the threshold of the galaxy and move nearer to the trillions of souls that needed it.

Jeshu approached the sanctum of Zareth, his heart glad to be near that which testified of Ell Yon's historical commitment to the Raylean people. Jeshu had been here many times before with Brae. Today the activity at the sanctum was greater than usual because, in addition to the usual managing staff of three Keepers and their associates, a delegation of five Keepers and three Builders had arrived from Jalem to conduct their annual visit and inspection of the Zareth sanctum. Due to the recent events in Jalem surrounding the advent of Navi Elias Thornton, an entirely new level of interest had stirred the hearts of the Raylean people. The campus courtyard was filled with thousands of zealous Zareth citizens.

Jeshu walked across the sanctum's beautiful granite courtyard framed with high arching gateways. The walkways were trimmed with fragrant flowering plants, including large plots of the Wild Crimson Rose flower. Jeshu knelt down, gently holding one of the bright red flowers in his hand.

"I've come to take your place," he said quietly while stroking the velvet leaves of the delicate flower.

"Don't touch those," came a firm voice from an associate Keeper who was policing the courtyard. "You are certainly unworthy to touch such a treasure. Those are reserved for the Keepers only."

Jeshu stood to look at the man. Though the visual exchange was brief, the associate chose to say nothing more and move on. At the entrance to the sanctum, another associate Keeper was scanning those who chose to enter, ensuring that they met the minimum genetic requirement of being at least 20 percent Raylean. Jeshu allowed the scan. The associate Keeper nodded his approval after reading Jeshu's 100 percent status.

One section inside the sanctum building was dedicated to housing a vast library of ancient oracle writings and a database of the history of the Raylean people in various media formats. This was a favorite place for Jeshu to be when he was a youth, spending hours absorbing every word of the oracles and all the historical documents. The sanctum in the capital city of Jalem had an elaborate replication facility below ground that the Builders managed in order to create the next Protector when enough omeganite was gathered from the collector array at the Omega Nebula, but here in Zareth no such facility existed. Additionally, there were chambers where Keepers offered counseling, as well as meditation rooms and a large open stadium oration chamber where the Master Keeper of the sanctum would often teach the people the ways of Ell Yon or offer a dissertation on the history of their people.

Jeshu entered the oration chamber, sitting down near the front as Master Keeper Vice Maltor from Jalem, second only to Preeminent Keeper Fasa Kylos, began to teach an audience of nearly 800 people about the demands of Ell Yon upon their people. The other Keepers and Builders were positioned behind him in elevated and esteemed seats. One sanctum guard stood as a stoic sentry on the left of the Keeper platform. His presence was more for adding a sense of respect to the chamber. Rarely if ever were sanctum guards required to perform any of their historically assigned security duties for the Rayleans as a whole honored the sanctum's legacy even if they themselves were not dedicated to the service of Ell Yon.

"We the Rayleans are Ell Yon's chosen people to show the world how Deitum Prime must be abstained from in order to recover our right to immortality. The only way to ensure you are properly abstaining is to allow a purified Keeper to scan your Deitum Prime body contamination level on a regular basis. What price can you put on your commitment to the Sovereign?" The Master Keeper pulled back his sleeve to reveal one of the six precious Protectors the Rayleans had built over the centuries. "Given to us by the hand of Sovereign Ell Yon himself, the Protectors have been passed down through the centuries from Navi to Navi and now to the esteemed order of the Keepers. We are the keepers of the ways of Ell Yon and the protectors of your futures," Master Keeper Maltor said with chin raised and pride upon his face. "We are of Ell Yon!"

Immortal anger lit within the heart of Jeshu as the arrogance of the Keeper and his sect saturated the oration chamber. As a child, Jeshu had restrained himself, but now, under the anointing of his father Ell Yon, his time had come, and so had the manifestation of the hypocrisy of the Keepers and the Builders.

Jeshu slowly stood, causing every eye in the oration chamber to turn upon him, including those of the Keepers and Builders. The Master Keeper's countenance transformed to one of deep disdain for a lowly Raylean so brazenly interrupting his oration. The silence in the chamber lingered, effortlessly escalating the tension.

"And what of Navi Elias Thornton?" Jeshu finally said, piercing the silence with a voice of authority. "Was he of Ell Yon?"

The question instantly shattered the Keeper's poise, for Elias Thornton, aka Daeson Starlore, had won the hearts of millions by his performance at the Magnifical Festival and by his public rebuke of Prefect Terrok and his pernicious ways. None of the Keepers or the Builders dared deride the man that had garnered such awe and respect of the people in such a short time—one who had demonstrated true Protector power.

"We...cannot tell," the Keeper said guardedly. "Who are you?"

The Zareth Master Keeper stood from his seat behind Maltor and came forward. "I know him. He's nothing but a local citizen of Zareth, unlearned in the ways of the Keepers—no one to be regarded," the man said with a scowl.

"Be seated, or you will be removed from the oration chamber for contempt of Ell Yon's sanctum." Maltor glared at Jeshu, but Jeshu did not sit, nor did he move.

The Zareth Master Keeper came to Maltor and whispered in his ear.

Maltor scoffed as if given some deep understanding about Jeshu. He glowered down at him.

"What do you want?" he asked.

Jeshu walked to the front of the oration chamber as if to address Maltor but instead turned his back to the man, facing the people directly.

"In the thirty-fifth year of Eziam, Oracle of Sovereign Ell Yon, he wrote, 'The Protector of Ell Yon is with me for He has given to me the mission to offer hope and truth to the poor. He has sent me to heal the brokenhearted, to deliver the captives, and to cause the blind to see. To bring freedom to those that suffer, and to speak truth in this the year of Ell Yon.'"

Jeshu scanned every person in the oration chamber from left to right, taking in the gaze of nearly 800 Rayleans. "By the authority of Sovereign Ell Yon and in the power of His Protector, Navi Elias Thornton was sent before me to prepare my way. Today in your presence, this oracle of Eziam is fulfilled."

Every soul in the chamber immediately understood what Jeshu was claiming, and it ignited an uproar, beginning with the Keepers.

"Silence!" Maltor screamed. "You disgrace this chamber and the sanctum itself by your profane words. Sanctum guard…cast this man to the street!"

The guard descended quickly from off the Keeper platform to make his way toward Jeshu, but as he approached, Jeshu captured the guard's gaze. In an instant, Jeshu, through eyes that foretold of his Immortal power, poured the eternal fire of Ell Yon into the unsuspecting man's soul. The guard froze, unwilling to take one step closer.

"Cast him out, I said," Maltor ordered, but the guard would not move, his eyes fixed upon Jeshu.

"It is you who should be cast out of Ell Yon's sanctum," Jeshu decreed, turning his eyes on the Master Keeper. "You and every Keeper who has exalted himself or herself above the people, claiming purity from Deitum Prime, yet lording your power over them through extortion and shaming the purpose of the Protector."

Maltor's face reddened with anger as he pulled back the sleeve from off his right arm to reveal the Protector.

"You have earned the humiliation of public contamination exposure," he said, as he brought his forefinger and thumb together. Quickly separating them, an amber beam illuminated the space in between. "Let the people of Rayl see how this man has been thoroughly absorbed and corrupted by Deitum Prime. You will be cast out of all sanctums forever!"

Maltor scanned Jeshu from head to foot, but upon the scan's completion, the man's face contorted into a look of utter confusion. Before Maltor could reveal the results to the other Keepers or to the stunned onlookers in the chamber, Jeshu stepped onto the platform. He spread his right hand wide, and every person present witnessed the revelation of Jeshu's Protector…a Protector he had borne from before his entrance into this realm. Powerful blue arcing flames spewed forth in a frightening display of justice. He swept his hand across the entire platform, bathing every Keeper and Builder in a piercing barrage of Protector energy. Instantly, Maltor's amber display of Jeshu's scanning results dissolved away. Instead, in lingering and humiliating fashion, the Deitum Prime levels of every Keeper and Builder appeared in glowing numerals above their heads.

Maltor looked up to see his number, revealing nearly total absorption, brilliantly displayed for every eye in the chamber to see. Jeshu closed his hand, and the brief but humiliating reveal disappeared.

"Beware, people of Rayl…the Keepers and Builders are servants of Dracus and the Scourge."

The contempt from the disgraced Keepers and Builders was palpable, but Jeshu did not remain to contest them any longer. He stepped away from the platform and walked through the crowd and out of the chamber. The clamor and stir left behind was the oddest mix of excitement and rage.

"Another Navi has come!" one man declared.

"He's disgraced the Keepers…he will surely die!" said a woman.

Within just a few minutes, the sanctum of Zareth was in mild chaos as people debated and discussed what had just happened. Outside, people were gathering as the stir of the chamber rippled outward, but they did not recognize the one who had caused it all. Jeshu became lost in the throng of people until no one knew where he had gone.

"There's quite a ruckus happening over there," Bridger said, as they exited the speeder.

Brae was craning her neck to see toward the outer courtyard of the sanctum. They were over a hundred yards away.

"Let's go," Brae said, but Bridger grabbed her arm.

"I see some patrols of some sort there...could be Royal Guards, Brae. Rhett would never forgive me if I got you mixed up in that."

Brae frowned. The throng of people gathering reminded her of the crowds at the Magnifical Festival. She had a quick flashback of plasma rifle fire and Royal Guards shooting at anyone that remotely looked like a threat.

"Then you and Kase go and find out what's happening. It's killing me not knowing."

"You sure?" Kase asked, his eyes glued to the activity near the sanctum.

"Yes! Go...I want to know," Brae urged. "And keep me updated on our com link."

Kase started off. Bridger hesitated then followed behind, running to catch up. After a few minutes passed, Brae felt like she had waited longer than she should have. Pacing next to the speeder, she tried to activate the com link with Bridger and Kase but was unsuccessful. After twenty minutes, she was about to disregard caution and go see the cause of the ruckus herself. She decided to try the com link once more, but she never made the connection.

"On the ground!" came a yell from behind her. Brae heard two class-one plasma rifles powering up. She tried to turn around but instead felt the heavy hand of a burly Royal Guard shove her to the ground with a jolt of pain to her leg, keeping a tight hold on the back of her neck with his free hand.

"On the ground, I said," the man screamed.

The force on her neck pushed her face hard into the pavement. She hardly felt the removal of a layer of skin from her right cheek as adrenaline coursed through her body. The action of the guards began to draw attention from bystanders, and a crowd gathered around them. Brae got a glimpse of her captors. One brute had a firm grip on her neck while another was providing cover with his plasma rifle. A third, their commanding officer, was a few paces away directing their actions.

"Everyone stay back," the officer ordered. "We are Prefect Terrok's Royal Guard. Keep clear!"

"She's the one Prefect Terrok is looking for!" shouted the brute on her neck. His knee was now planted firmly in the middle of her back, making it hard to breathe.

"Do a dermal scan to make sure," the commanding officer ordered.

The guard handling Brae pulled her hands behind her back, locked electromagnetic coded fetters on her wrists, then brutishly lifted her up and shoved her against the speeder. Brae glanced toward the crowd just in time to see Rhett arrive. His countenance was full of fear and fury. When he dropped a package he was carrying, Brae could tell he was going to make a move on one of the Royal Guards. She shook her head enough to try to stop him, but Rhett clearly intended to ignore her refusal of help.

The guard holding her produced a small device, which he subsequently pushed up against her neck. After three seconds, his armband alerted as to her identity. He looked at his commanding officer. "We got her!"

"You are under arrest for high crimes against Prefect Terrok and the Raylean government," the officer declared. "Your treasonous acts have been judged. You will be returned to Jalem to serve your sentence of public execution."

Brae felt the blood leave her face as she realized there was nothing to stop the terror of Terrok.

"That's not going to happen," a strong voice called out from behind Rhett.

Everyone turned to see a man step forward. He walked straight toward the two guards, which immediately escalated the situation.

"Stay back!" ordered the commanding officer, but the man continued straight toward Brae. He moved so quickly that Brae couldn't get a clear look at him, but there was something very familiar about him.

The commanding officer and the guard lifted their plasma rifles to a ready position while the other guard continued to hold Brae up against the speeder, trying to ready his own rifle at the same time. All weapons were charged and leveled at the chest of the approaching man, but the stranger kept coming.

"Release her," the man ordered as he came to stand but a few feet from the officer.

Brae craned her neck to see who would dare oppose three Royal Guards on the hunt for a fugitive. She caught a glimpse of Rhett's face as she turned. He looked paralyzed by awestruck wonder. The guard holding Brae loosened his grip just enough for her to turn and see the entire scene unfolding around her. She now understood Rhett's visage for before her stood the frightfully powerful form of none other than Jeshu.

"Back away or you will be arrested for obstruction of the law of Terrok," the officer ordered, his finger pressing tightly on the trigger of his blaster.

Jeshu lifted his right hand toward the man. Then with two fingers extended, he made one quick flick of his wrist, and all three plasma rifles immediately powered down. The commanding officer pulled the trigger, but the weapon was dead. He tried to power it back up, but there was no response at all.

"Release her," he commanded again.

The officer became fierce and indignant, reaching for a second weapon from his belt. Brae felt the grip of her captor loosen slightly.

"It's a Navi, Commander. I would listen to him," Brae heard the other guard say.

The commanding officer snarled. "I don't care who he is. We have orders to bring her in for execution, and no pretend Navi is going to stop us. We killed the last one, didn't we?"

He quickly drew a blaster, but before he could aim it, Jeshu stepped forward and grabbed the weapon and the hand that held it with his left hand. Though the man struggled to be free from his grip, the force that held him was immovable. The officer then reached for a knife with his left hand, but before he could thrust it forward, Jeshu opened his right hand—one single burst of power exploded from the Protector and into the chest of the man. He flew backward five feet, falling unconscious to the ground. Jeshu's back was now toward Brae and her captor. The guard abandoned Brae, lunging toward Jeshu.

"Jeshu!" Brae yelled.

In one swift move, Jeshu deftly ducked, using his torso to flip the man completely over his head to land with a thump on the ground. The other guard seemed too stunned to take action or perhaps too wise to do so. The brutish guard on the ground quickly recovered his feet while drawing a Talon-style blade. He attacked again. This time Jeshu deflected the man's knife-arm while grabbing his wrist with his left hand. In a fraction of a second, Jeshu had locked the man's wrist in such a painful position that the knife fell harmlessly to the ground. The man snarled curses until Jeshu grabbed the man by the back of his neck with his right hand. The Protector surged in power, unleashing a glimpse of Ell Yon's condemning judgment into the mind of the brute. The man's eyes opened wide with fear, then his eyes rolled back in unconsciousness. Jeshu gently laid him on the ground. He then turned to look at the remaining guard, but there was no fight there. The man held up his hands while backing away from both Jeshu and Brae.

"Tell Terrok the one he fears has come."

The man's eyes filled with alarm. He swallowed hard while carefully moving toward his prone and unconscious commanding officer. Jeshu turned to Brae, reaching for the fetters that held her. With the touch of his hand, they opened, and she was free. She turned to look at Jeshu, having to confirm in her mind that he was the child she had raised, for his countenance was full of maturity, wisdom, and power.

"Jeshu…is it really you?" she said, gazing into his eyes. As she did so, she glimpsed the eternal flame of Ell Yon reflecting like diamonds.

"It is I," he said calmly.

Brae wrapped her arms around him, and he allowed it, gently hugging her back. When she released him, something wholly and significantly different resonated between them, vastly different than when they had parted months earlier. Jeshu had transcended far beyond the status of his upbringing. She instantly felt small and unworthy. This was no longer her adopted son...this was the Commander of the Malakians...King of the Ruah! She slowly began to fall to one knee, but Jeshu caught her, lifting her up.

"Stand up, Brae Starlore. It's okay."

Hearing him speak her name filled her body with strength.

"Jeshu," Rhett said, carefully approaching from behind them.

Jeshu turned. "Rhett Stryker," came the voice of the leader of worlds. *How different than the voice of the child who had uttered that name just a few short years ago*, Brae thought.

Rhett, his eyes full of wonder and yet sorrow, came forward to stand before Jeshu. Rhett began to shake his head. "I've been a fool...forgive me."

Jeshu placed a hand on Rhett's shoulder just as a father would a son.

"Not a fool, Rhett," Jeshu said with compassion. "A loyal servant of the Sovereign."

Jeshu's offer of grace seemed to humble Rhett significantly.

"Come," Jeshu said, as thousands of people began gathering and sharing stories. Many began to press Jeshu with questions. "We must leave while we still can."

Sirens drew close as city sentries began to arrive in an attempt to bring order to the chaos that had started at the sanctum and spilled over into the surrounding areas and buildings. By now, Bridger and Kase had also arrived. Rhett went to Brae. She favored her aching leg as he helped her get into one of the speeders.

"Are you okay?" he asked. She could tell he was still put out with her, but his concern for her safety was just as evident as before.

"I'm fine."

Rhett didn't look convinced. He was about to back away when she looked up into his face from the seat of the speeder.

"Now it begins."

"What begins?" Rhett asked.

"Everything!" Brae responded.

Rhett hesitated. "I don't know what that means, but I suppose you're right."

"Hey...where's Shayde?" Brae asked.

"She's with Major Kamp. We'll meet up with them shortly," Rhett said, as Jeshu jumped into the pilot seat next to Brae.

"Our shuttle is at the Blue Star Spaceport on the western side of the city," Rhett said to Jeshu as he powered up the speeder.

"I know it...meet you there," Jeshu replied as he finished the startup sequence for the speeder.

Bridger and Kase had already made it to the second speeder so Rhett jumped into the pilot seat and took off. After a twenty-minute trek through the city of Zareth, both speeders arrived back at the shuttle *Aviel*. There to meet them was Shayde, Major Kamp, and two more people that took Brae a moment to recognize...two people that had played a critical role in her survival.

"Largo and Foss!" Brae exclaimed. "How...why are you here?" she asked. Old emotions surfaced as she reached for them.

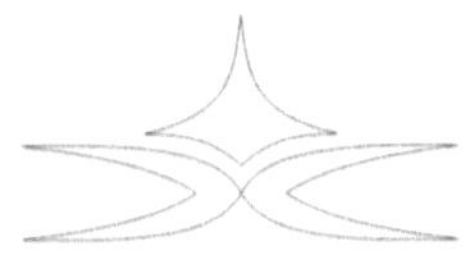

CHAPTER

7

Beginnings

Rhett watched as Brae embraced mechtechs Largo and Foss in turn, but after what he had just witnessed at the sanctum, he felt an urgency to keep their reunion short.

"Rhett told me what you did for me," Brae said, eyes moistening. "I didn't think I would ever get a chance to say this…thank you!"

"The reason Brae and I made it out of the Magnifical Festival alive is because of the help of these two," Rhett explained to the rest of the group. He looked toward Major Kamp. "Thank you for connecting us."

"I don't even know your first names," Brae said with a wince.

"I'm Cilla," Largo said.

"Quill," Foss added. "Seeing what happened…we've been eager to find you ever since. The words of your father gave us such hope."

Brae smiled, looking toward Jeshu then back to Cilla and Quill. "Can you join us? There's a lot to share."

"Yes. That's why we're here. By Ell Yon's hand, we found Major Kamp, fully intending to join ourselves to whatever you were a part of." Cilla's excitement was evident.

"We'll have time for more later," Rhett said, scanning the surrounding spaceport. "I must insist that we keep this brief. There's no telling what the consequences might be for what just happened."

"I agree," Major Kamp said.

"Can you come with us?" Shayde asked the Major.

"I'm afraid not," Kamp said. "I must see to my family and make some preparations."

At that moment, Jeshu stepped forward, still essentially unknown to all but Rhett and Brae.

"This is Jeshu," Rhett offered. "He's the one I told you about."

Jeshu offered his hand to Major Kamp, who readily took it. Kamp's face softened as Jeshu gazed into his eyes.

"Thank you, Major," Jeshu said. "You've given us all a good beginning. Take care of your family."

Kamp didn't respond. Rhett had never seen the stoic man at a loss for a reply.

"There'll be a need for future support," Jeshu said. "Can I count on you?"

Kamp's eyes narrowed as he offered a single nod. Rhett knew Kamp to be an intelligent and discerning man, but even still, it was unusual to see his mentor, a man of consistent authority, submit to Jeshu in a moment.

Rhett and Bridger encouraged the eight of them to board the *Aviel* so they could be on their way. Cilla and Quill each had two large bags that Bridger and Kase helped load into the storage compartment of the shuttle while Rhett requested clearance from the Blue Star Spaceport to depart. He took note that, per his request on arrival, the *Aviel* had been refueled in their absence. In short order they launched and were underway.

Jeshu was sitting in the copilot seat next to Rhett while Brae continued with introductions and conversations with the other five in the passenger cabin. Once they made altitude, Rhett looked at Jeshu.

"It's good to see you again, Rhett."

Rhett was still sorting out how to adapt to his new understanding and belief in Jeshu. Though he had struggled to accept the truth of who Jeshu was, deep in his heart he had known all along. *It's a strange thing to admit to something so grandiose...how does one react?* he thought.

"It's good to see you too, Jeshu." Rhett struggled. "I'm still adjusting...forgive me if I need time to sort things out."

"I understand," Jeshu said. "We have plenty of time, and I'm not going anywhere...at least not for a while."

This statement evoked the strangest of emotions in Rhett. There was a contentment in knowing he had time to adjust. There was excitement in the realization that he was in the presence of the Son of Sovereign Ell Yon. There was a measure of fear also in that same realization, for Rhett would soon be at the epicenter of the explosive intersection of Ell Yon's visit from the Ruah, which was sure to send shockwaves throughout all of humanity. Rhett decided that the best path forward with Jeshu was to shun all previous notions and establish a fresh set of perspectives.

"How are you and Brae getting on?" Jeshu asked. "Are you more amiable toward one another?"

"I see you still don't mince words," Rhett said.

"Life is too short to pretend," Jeshu replied. "The most precious things you can obtain here are the relationships you have with others. Be careful with them."

Rhett was going to have to get used to Jeshu's keen discernment again. Since Jeshu had fully stepped into his position as the Merchant, Rhett imagined that there would be even less he could hide from him.

"We have a beginning that seems to have worked," Rhett replied.

"Worked or is working?" Jeshu asked.

Rhett frowned. Admittedly, he was still offended by the words he had heard Brae say to Shayde the previous night. He didn't answer.

"I want you to know that I'm grateful to you for sacrificing a large part of your life to raise me," Jeshu said, changing the subject. "What I asked of you was difficult."

Rhett offered a weak smile of acknowledgment.

"But you need to know that what I'm about to ask of you now will be even greater. I'm asking you to follow me with complete abandon."

Rhett felt his stomach turn. He knew the words were true, but hearing Jeshu speak them aloud made it all the more real.

"I know," Rhett said. "I've already dealt with my lack of purpose outside of being a pilot for the Raylean Guard. I'm in, and I'm ready."

Jeshu offered a knowing smile. "Yes, you are."

By early evening, Rhett had piloted the *Aviel* back to Brohn and decided to set it down at the designated landing pad nearer to his home. As they disembarked, Rhett noticed that Bridger, Kase, Shayde, Cilla, and Quill couldn't keep from staring at Jeshu. Obviously, during the flight Brae must have conveyed enough narrative regarding Jeshu to begin opening their eyes to his identity. They all seemed unsure how to react to him. Rhett empathized with them for he also was at odds with his own responses. To know and believe that Jeshu was the Son of Ell Yon in the flesh evoked the strangest notions.

As they all walked to the Stryker home, Wescott and Kara came to greet them. Brae introduced Cilla and Quill first, then Rhett brought Jeshu to them.

"Dad…Mom…this is Jeshu, the one we discovered on the merchant ship near the Omega Nebula."

"It is an honor to meet you both," Jeshu said.

The glow in Wescott and Kara's eyes was evident. Rhett marveled at how they could so effortlessly believe in Jeshu, whereas he was only just now arriving at such a place in his heart.

"The honor is ours," Wescott said.

"Our home is your home," Kara added.

"I hope my presence here won't be too much of an inconvenience," Jeshu said.

"Please stay with us as long as is useful to you," Kara said. She then turned to the group. "Come, we've prepared a meal for all of you."

As they walked back to the home, Brae came up beside Rhett. Despite all that had happened during the day, Rhett still felt the barbs of Brae's comments from the night before. It was odd...had those words come from anyone else, he imagined he could have brushed them aside with ease. But apparently not so with Brae.

"Quite a day, wouldn't you say?" Brae asked.

Rhett fully expected to be chided for his earlier stance on not wanting her to come with him.

"Yep," he replied, intentionally looking away. His tone was a bit harsher than he had intended, but he let it stand. Brae said nothing else.

After everyone had a chance to wash up and get their things settled into their rooms, they all appeared for the meal that Kara and Wescott had prepared for them. This time, their large dining room table was full. Rhett remembered what his father had taught them growing up regarding eating a meal together. He had said that it was a time of bonding that cannot be accomplished in any other way. Tonight, that was never more evident as this odd mix of people...pilots, mechtechs, astrotechs and everything in between...shared food and stories together. He could already feel a bond forming between them, and in the center of it all was Jeshu.

Rhett marveled at Jeshu's ability to foster a burgeoning esprit de corps among those who had been strangers just hours earlier. As a former miltech officer, Rhett recognized distinct leadership qualities in Jeshu as he interacted with the group. In the Raylean Guard, men and women went through months of training to learn such things. Jeshu seemed to exude all such qualities with ease and perfection. As stomachs grew full and everyone became comfortable with one another, Jeshu had to field many questions.

"Brae told us how she and Rhett found you," Cilla began. "According to the ancient oracles of Iyhaz, the Merchant will come and cause division among people. If the Merchant is to save us, why must there be division? I've never understood this."

Jeshu, being seated in the middle on one of the sides of the table, allowed Largo's insightful question to ruminate in the minds of everyone for a few seconds. All eyes were on him.

"I can understand your confusion, Cilla," Jeshu said with a thoughtful gaze. "If the purpose of the Sovereign Ell Yon is to save his people from the consequences of Deitum Prime, then how can sending his son to divide the people accomplish this?"

"Exactly," Cilla confirmed.

"Although this is confusing at first, the answer is really quite simple." Jeshu paused to glance around the table, ensuring everyone there felt included in the conversation. "Truth divides."

That simple statement evoked a variety of responses.

"Truth divides people who are willing to hear and follow it from those who want to continue to believe the lies that Dracus has ensnared them with. Without truth there is no ability to save the galaxy, and so the natural and sure result is great division. I am the way to Ell Yon, I am the truth of Ell Yon, and I am the life of the galaxy. For those courageous enough to believe it and follow me, they will see great and marvelous things, but they will be divided from those who are unwilling to accept this truth." He scanned the seven faces looking back at him. "*You* will see great and marvelous things."

"The Keepers and the Builders would have us believe that only the Rayleans will be saved from Deitum Prime because we are Sovereign Ell Yon's special people. Is this true?" Bridger asked.

"It is Iyhaz again that said, 'Beyond the sphere of Rayl, the people in darkness have seen a great light.' And by the oracles of Eziam, 'The worlds of the galaxy will gather to him for they will be his people.'" Jeshu's countenance darkened. "Beware of the pride of the Keepers and the Builders…they belong to the enemy of Ell Yon."

This last statement alarmed everyone at the table except Brae and Rhett for they knew of Jeshu's opinion of the elite Keeper and Builder orders.

More questions came, and Jeshu carefully answered every one until Wescott suggested they give him a reprieve until morning. Rhett had the feeling that they had only scratched the surface in understanding who Jeshu really was and what his purposes were.

After the meal, Brae joined Kara in the kitchen.

"We've really invaded your home," Brae said, coming to stand beside Kara. She grabbed a dish and began loading it into the sanitizer.

"We welcome the interruption. We have front row seats to a galactic event it seems," Kara said, glancing over at Brae. "Westcott and I are deeply committed to the ways of Ell Yon as are Bridger and Kase. Rhett, on the other hand, tends to be a bit skeptical. He's a realist and comes by faith with difficulty. That Ell Yon chose him to help raise Jeshu was more than surprising to us. However, Rhett is fiercely loyal, perhaps to a fault since he expects others to be as well. I'm afraid once trust is lost in a relationship, it may be lost forever because of this expectation."

Brae's heart nearly broke at Kara's words. Kara touched her shoulder. "Your heart is heavy, child. What's the matter?"

Brae looked up at Kara. She was so wise and discerning. "Is it that obvious?"

"Yes…at least to me it is. And by watching Rhett's lack of response to you, I'm guessing it has something to do with him."

Brae's head dropped. "I'm sure he told you how difficult a time we had with each other while we were raising Jeshu. Then when I was injured and in a dark place after watching my father die, Rhett rescued me and wouldn't give up on me. Only then did I come to realize what a loyal friend he had been and still was. Since he brought me here, we've both worked hard on building a friendship." Brae looked back up at Kara. "I think I've ruined it."

"How so?"

"Last night, Shayde insinuated that I might have feelings for Rhett beyond that of our friendship. I emphatically denied it but perhaps went too far, even diminishing the importance of the friendship we had built. I think Rhett might have heard me," Brae said, wincing.

Kara thought for a moment. "Since Rhett was a child, he knew exactly who he was and what he wanted to do—he always had a plan. When Rhett came back to us a couple of months ago, he was so lost. We slowly got bits and pieces of what had happened, who you were, and who Jeshu was. I've always believed that Ell Yon had something significant in store for Rhett, but watching him wander aimlessly for weeks was hard. Then he went to the Magnifical Festival to see you, and I sensed that Ell Yon was calling him there. When he brought you back with him, there was an energy and hope in his eyes I've never seen before." Kara paused.

Brae glanced up, still feeling ashamed for the words that had hurt Rhett. Kara brushed a few strands of hair away from Brae's face.

"Whatever happens between you two, I know this much...he values your friendship as much as you do. Just talk to him. Behind his realism and stoic demeanor, there's a tenderness that you've uncovered—something he'll probably never admit to. Please be careful with it."

Brae reached for Kara, and they embraced. "Thank you," Brae whispered.

Later that night Shayde came to Brae's room.

"Wow...what a day," Shayde said, flopping down on Brae's bed. "How does it feel not being executed?"

Brae shook her head. "I'm telling you, Shayde, nothing has been normal since that trip to the Omega Nebula. And now you're wrapped up in this with me." Brae looked over at her friend. "Are you okay?"

"Yeah...I'm okay, but I sure wish you would have warned me before I said yes to being on your research team," she said with a chuckle.

"Well...I'm warning you now," Brae said rather soberly. "With Jeshu back, you're going to see things the ancient oracles could only dream of. There's a storm coming."

Shayde's smile diminished. "You're just as much of a killjoy as Lieutenant Stryker."

"Huh...I suppose you're right. I see you've taken a fancy to him," Brae said, looking at Shayde out of the corner of her eye.

"Oh, you silly, ignorant girl. Stryker's heart has already been won by another. And with this winning there's no retreat."

Brae was surprised by Shayde's comment. It confirmed what she had suspected. "I suppose you're right...he told me he had a girl in Jalem."

Shayde wrinkled her nose. "What are you talking about? For real?"

Brae nodded. "I'm sure he went to find her when we finished our mission with Jeshu. I've never asked him about her, figuring he would say something when he felt like it."

Shayde looked perplexed as Brae became lost in thought.

"I never thought I'd say this about Stryker," Brae said, glancing out the door portal. "But after three years of despising each other, we finally figured out how to become friends—that is, until I blew it." Brae paused. "Kara told me he was about to ask this girl to be bonded before this all went down." Brae wondered what kind of girl Rhett might have fallen for. "He's a loyal type of guy...I think he felt an obligation to see me through this first," Brae said, rubbing her leg. "He's the kind of guy the Raylean Guard loves to have in their ranks. But now that I'm better, I wouldn't be surprised if he went on with his life."

"I thought for sure—" Shayde began, then stopped. "I've never seen you so concerned about a guy. If I were you, I'd fight for him."

Brae offered a weak smile, realizing that Shayde must have flirted with Rhett just to test her theory about Brae's feelings for him. She shook her head. "It's not like that, and I'm not sure how to explain it. I think that being so intensely frustrated with each other for so long and now finding a true friendship buried beneath our stubbornness is very cathartic. I don't want to do anything to risk losing that."

Shayde gazed at Brae for a long while...silent. "Well, Brae, some risks are worth taking, but okay."

"Can we move on and leave this be?" Brae said, putting an arm around her friend. Shayde smiled, nodding. "Good. Now I have to go try to fix this."

Brae went out onto the deck and walked two doors down to Rhett's room. She lifted a hand to his door portal, hesitating. Finally, she gathered enough courage to knock. When the door portal opened, she was surprised to find Jeshu speaking with Rhett.

"I'm so sorry," Brae said quickly. "I didn't mean to interrupt."

"It's okay, Brae," Jeshu said. "I was just leaving."

Jeshu looked back at Rhett. "Thank you for speaking with me. It seems you're popular tonight," he said. "Good night."

Jeshu exited Rhett's room, closing the door behind him by tapping on the wall panel. Rhett then turned to look at Brae who was still standing out on the deck just outside the door portal.

"May I come in?" Brae asked.

Rhett sighed, motioning for her to come inside. Once she was in, he commanded the door portal to close. He crossed his arms, waiting. Brae looked around his room. She had never seen it before. Images of various space fighter craft flashed across a large display inset in the far wall. Next to it, a vintage display glass with a montage of old photos and memorabilia caught her eye, and she moved in that direction. One image revealed a young boy standing next to an elderly gentleman in front of an older Raylean Guard spacecraft. She leaned over to look more closely at the image.

"Is that you?"

"Yes," came Rhett's terse reply.

"Who is the man with you?"

Rhett huffed. "My grandfather."

"Did he fly in the Raylean Guard too?"

"Yes...what do you want?" he asked. Brae could tell his patience was wearing thin. Just before she turned away from the display, Brae noticed a chain hanging on the corner of the image frame. On the chain was one oddly shaped medallion, its edges worn smooth. She couldn't quite decide what it was supposed to be. She stood straight, turning to face Rhett.

"I want to talk with you."

Rhett looked tired and in no mood to talk. He frowned. Brae walked straight up to him, locking eyes. This face-off reminded her of the first time she'd met him. She had been caught off guard by his stiff countenance and stubborn attitude. It was a meeting that had set them at odds for years. This time, however, Brae was ready. She lifted her chin in the same fashion as over three years ago, then placed her hands on her hips.

"I think you owe me an apology," she demanded, her eyes narrowing to a steely-eyed gaze.

Rhett's eyebrows lifted. "Apology? Why in the galaxy would I owe *you* an apology?" he exclaimed, standing firmly with his arms still crossed.

"Because you're upset with me and you haven't told me why," Brae said coldly. "Friends don't do that to each other."

Rhett's eyes narrowed to slits. "Friends?" he scoffed. "I thought we were 'hardly even friends.' And as soon as you're well, I'm sure you'll move on and be glad for it."

Brae allowed a smile to edge across her mouth as she pointed a finger at him. "You *did* hear me last night. Were you eavesdropping, Rhett Stryker?"

Rhett's face began to flush. "I...I...didn't intend on—"

Brae's countenance softened. "Look, Stryker, when we didn't get along before, I was perfectly okay with it because I didn't want to be around you anyway. But now that we've become friends, I don't like it. I know it's only been one day since we've been at odds, but it feels like a week. Please can we fix this?"

Rhett fidgeted, uncrossing his arms. "When I heard someone on the balcony, I went to find out who was there. I saw you go into Shayde's room and intended to retreat to my own room, but I admittedly stayed longer than I should have. I'm sorry for eavesdropping, but I can't unhear what I heard."

Brae reached to touch Rhett's arm then pulled back, remembering that he didn't like it.

"Listen...Shayde's teasing put me on the defensive, and I said things I shouldn't have, things that aren't true, and for that I'm sorry. Truly I am." She looked up into Rhett's eyes, revealing the warmth that was in her heart. "The truth is that our friendship has become really important to me, and I don't want to lose it. I don't want to lose one of the best friends I've ever had. Please believe me." Brae risked putting her hand on his arm. He instantly softened.

Rhett took a deep breath then nodded once. His eyes warmed to her. "You know, I secretly had a name for you back on Jypton...Thorny Thornton."

Brae smiled. "Oh really...well, I had a name for you too...I just can't remember what it is right now."

Rhett laughed, and so did Brae. She turned, and he followed her as she walked to the deck door portal.

"Am I still as thorny as I was?" she asked as she turned to face him.

Rhett leaned against the edge of the door. "Not so much."

"Good," she said. "Night, Stryker."

"Good night, Starlore," Rhett returned.

Brae walked a few steps then heard Rhett call out from behind her.

"Hey."

Brae looked back at him.

"I'm glad you came to talk."

"Me too," Brae said, turning to face him. Then she took a gamble. "Did Jeshu convince you to stick around, or are you going off to find your Jalem girl now that I'm mostly healed?"

Rhett feigned a weak smile, letting Brae know that she'd hit a sore spot.

"I'm sorry...that's none of my business," she added quickly.

"It's okay. She's moved on...found a chap to be bonded to. I guess I was gone too long."

Brae saw the ache in his eyes. "I'm sorry," she said quietly.

Rhett shrugged. "See you in the morning."

Brae smiled and nodded, then turned away toward her room feeling selfish and guilty that she actually wasn't sorry at all.

CHAPTER

8

Fragments

The next day, Rhett welcomed Brae to the breakfast table with a smile, and she was happy. After breakfast and cleanup, Brae noticed that Jeshu was making it a point to speak to each person in the home one-on-one, and she wondered what message he would have for her. After breakfast, Cilla and Quill approached Brae together.

"Have you got a moment?" Cilla asked.

"Of course, what can I do for you?" Brae asked.

"We have something for you," Quill said. "Actually a few things."

Brae was curious, wondering what either of them could possibly want to give her.

"Please come with us," Cilla implored.

Brae followed them out of the home and to the west side of the garden where Wescott and Kara had a large workshop. As they entered, Brae saw Rhett with two of the bags Cilla and Quill had brought with them on the *Aviel*. Rhett set the bags onto a workbench.

"Should I stay, or should I go?" Rhett asked.

Cilla and Quill looked at each other for a decision, but it was apparent that neither of them felt as though they should offer an opinion.

"I'd like you to stay, Stryker," Brae said. She had no idea what she was going to see, and Rhett's presence always seemed to help these days.

Rhett nodded, crossing his arms as he waited.

"As we've already told you, your father's message had a profound effect on us. When Prefect Terrok conspired with the Keepers and the Builders to have him killed, we were distraught, but we also knew that something spectacular was coming. After helping Lieutenant Stryker get you safely out of the spaceport, Quill and I recovered anything we felt might be important for the mission that Elias had begun."

Brae was confused and curious. "Please continue," she encouraged.

"We had to act fast," Quill said. "Taking advantage of the chaos that followed, we found a tactical bag in a locker that was assigned to your father," he said, pointing to one of the bags on the table.

Brae went to the bag as an avalanche of emotions cascaded through her heart and mind. She gently touched the bag, wondering what her father could have possibly placed inside for her to find.

"I'm sure you'll want to inspect the items in private," Cilla said. "One item in particular you'll find extremely significant. But we also have something else we want to give you."

Quill stepped up to the second bag. Before opening it, he turned to face her. "We were on the cleanup crew after order was restored to the spaceport grounds. Between Cilla and me, we were able to recover as much of...well...here," he said, opening the bag. Brae stepped closer to see the charred and broken pieces of an android...Rivet. Brae covered her mouth as tears welled up. Seeing the shattered form of this noble bot was too much for Brae. It was the unequivocal evidence of Terrok's dastardly hand in killing her father and Rivet.

Rhett, Cilla, and Quill all remained silent and still as Brae lifted Rivet's head from the bag.

"He saved my life," she muttered through tearful words. She gently set his head back into the bag, for it was too painful to see him this way.

"I hope we've done right by you, Miss Thornton," Cilla said.

Brae turned to face them. "Call me Brae, and yes, I can't thank you enough. I am forever indebted to you in more ways than you'll ever know."

Cilla and Quill offered a smile. "Very well. We'll leave you to it then," Cilla said, nodding to the two bags.

Once the pair exited the shop, Rhett stepped up beside Brae. "Are you okay?"

"I think so," Brae said, taking a deep breath. "I might be a while though. Do you mind?"

"Of course not...I'll be back at the home if you need anything," Rhett said, stepping away.

Brae reached for his arm. "No...I mean do you mind staying with me? I don't want to go through this by myself."

"Oh," Rhett replied. "Of course."

Brae turned back to the bag and began pulling out various articles, items one would not normally find in a flight bag. Each item triggered nostalgic memories: a pendant on a chain that Daeson always wore, a small ornate box containing small treasures from Raviel, and a glass tablet with thousands of video entries were the first items she discovered. She held the glass tablet then tapped on one of the entries. The image of a seven-year-old Brae laughing and dancing with her father popped up. Brae bit her lip as she pushed back more tears. She stopped the video after just a few seconds. She felt Rhett's hand on her shoulder. It helped.

"This will take some time to get through," Brae said, looking over at Rhett. "I don't understand...this is all memorabilia from our home that I thought was destroyed when Terrok burned it. Why would Dad have had these in his flight bag—" Brae stopped midsentence, a distressing thought filling her mind. "Unless..."

"Unless he knew that flight would be his last," Rhett finished.

Brae closed her eyes, sorrow killing her one more time. She struggled with rising anger. *Why couldn't there have been another way?* she thought. *Surely the Protector—*

"Brae," Rhett said tenderly.

She opened her eyes to see him peering into the bag. She didn't want to look. "No," she whispered.

When she didn't make a move to come and look, Rhett reached in and lifted out the gleaming form of Daeson Starlore's Protector. Brae clenched her teeth, slowly shaking her head.

"That's why he died...he wasn't wearing the Protector! Why?" she exclaimed.

Rhett silently held the Immortal tech in both hands. As if holding a priceless treasure, he fastened his gaze on the Protector.

"Why, Rhett?" she asked again.

Rhett slowly looked up at her. "I don't know. Maybe he thought it might be destroyed too," he said, offering the Protector to her. She took it.

"This was the first Protector given to humanity by Ell Yon." She looked up at Rhett. "We have to show Jeshu. Perhaps he can help me understand."

"I'll see if he can come," Rhett offered, then quickly left to find him.

Brae ran her fingers along the jeweled Immortal tech once more. She had briefly experienced the synaptic immersion...the mind of Ell Yon. Even now she sensed the power and the peace the Protector brought.

Hold fast, daughter of Ell Yon. There's much for you to do.

The words gently landed in her mind, and although she knew they weren't her own, she still wondered if they had been invented by her subconscious.

A few minutes later, Rhett returned with Jeshu but then exited the shop to give Jeshu an opportunity to speak with Brae one-on-one.

Brae looked up from the Protector, then into the face of Jeshu—hopeful. Jeshu's eyes immediately softened with sympathy. He held her gaze for a moment, spilling compassion into her soul.

"There's pain in this realm that people will never understand, Brae." He reached out and touched her arm. "Your father understood this better than anyone. This realm...this reality is broken because of Dracus and his Deitum Prime. Your father gave his all for Sovereign Ell Yon. And though he loved you with every bone in his body, he was weary and lonely." He looked deeply into Brae's eyes. "Do you understand?"

Ever since she was old enough to grasp Daeson's loss, she had felt the ache in his heart. Of course, there were times of joy and happiness, but his loneliness for Raviel seemed always present in his eyes.

"We will all die, but I have come to reclaim you from death. Daeson knew this, and in the centuries of his life, his preparation for my arrival was the culmination of a life well lived." He placed a gentle hand on Brae's cheek. "I'm sorry for your pain, daughter of Ell Yon. Greater am I than he who has caused you this pain...than he who has poisoned the galaxy with sorrow."

Brae closed her eyes once more, causing two tears to spill down her cheeks. Jeshu had used the exact same wording as the Protector...daughter of Ell Yon. She had never heard him use those words before today.

Jeshu wiped Brae's tears away with his finger. "You must be strong. Becoming a Navi for me isn't going to be easy."

Brae nodded, then lifted the Protector up to Jeshu, and the Son of Ell Yon received it. He took a deep breath, then pressed the Protector onto his left arm. Brae marveled, seeing the Merchant now fully armed with two Protectors. No man had ever worn such power before. It was rumored that decades earlier a Keeper had tried once, but as soon as he touched the second Protector, he instantly died.

Brae searched Jeshu's face but found no arrogance nor false humility in assuming his rightful role as the most powerful man in the galaxy, even if no one knew it...at least not yet. *What does this mean?* she thought.

Jeshu looked at Brae once more. "You'll be okay," he said.

Brae nodded, then Jeshu turned to leave the workshop. A couple of minutes later, Rhett returned to join Brae in resuming their investigation of Daeson's flight bag. Rhett went to the table where Brae had laid out a dozen items from the bag. He reached for the pendant and chain, holding it up for Brae to see.

"What's this?" he asked.

Brae went to him. She lifted the chain and pendant from Rhett's hand. "Dad wore this every day of his life. That he wasn't wearing it and that it's here tells me everything." Brae took a deep breath. "This is one half of a set of Raylean aerotech pilot wings from centuries ago when the aerotech order was still intact. It was given to him by the man that journeyed with him through the centuries, following my mother in her quantum anomaly sickness. My dad said he would never forget him, calling him a true man of honor—a friend closer than a brother."

"What was his name?" Rhett asked.

"My dad called him Tig, but his full name was Silax Tigratinna."

Rhett seemed mesmerized by the broken pendant. He finally looked up at Brae. "I think you should come with me."

"I'm not done here," Brae said.

"We'll come back," Rhett said, as he began walking to the door. "Come on...and bring the pendant."

Brae scrunched her lips to one side, a bit annoyed. She closed her fingers around the wings and chain then followed Rhett. He led her to his room and over to the corner where Brae had earlier discovered some of his own memorabilia displayed. Rhett lifted the chain and worn pendant Brae had noticed earlier from its resting place on the corner of the frame.

"My grandfather wore this his whole life then gave it to me to do the same," Rhett said. "He said it was to bring good luck."

Brae's eyes narrowed. "But I've never seen you wear it."

"Because I can't stand things hanging on my neck, and I don't believe in luck. But that's not the point. Look!" Rhett said, grabbing Brae's pendant from her hand. He put the two pieces together. Although Rhett's pendant was worn and rounded to the point of being unrecognizable, its general shape did match that of Brae's pendant.

Brae slowly shook her head. "Impossible...surely not!"

Rhett looked at her, holding up the two pieces between them. "I don't recognize the name Tigratinna, and this seems ridiculously impossible, but there it is."

Brae grabbed the two pieces of the pendant, turning them over and over as she tried to decide if there was any credence to Rhett's preposterous suggestion.

"It's a stretch, Stryker. How can we find out?"

"My grandfather is still alive. Perhaps he knows more."

Brae looked up at Rhett, a smile spreading across her lips.

"What?" Rhett asked.

"Ell Yon is an Immortal of impossible coincidences. You and I were both chosen to raise and train Jeshu. Is it any wonder that we're connected in more ways than we realize?"

Rhett huffed. He shook his head. "I guess not."

"Dad said that one day the two wings would join back together. In an unexpected way, they already have," Brae said, handing Rhett's pendant back to him. She put hers over her head, tucking the pendant inside her tunic. Rhett did the same.

"I thought you didn't like things hanging around your neck?" Brae said with a wry smile.

"Well...if I'm going to be stuck with you for a while, I'm going to need all the luck I can get."

Brae spent the next few days carefully going through the precious gifts of memory Cilla and Quill had restored to her. Late one night, Brae found sleep elusive. After tossing and turning for over an hour, she rose up from her bed and stepped onto the deck, inwardly hoping that Rhett or Shayde might still be awake, but there were no lights in any of the rooms other than her own. The cool air on her cheeks and in her lungs finalized her insomnia, so she returned to her room and dressed, unsure of what to do until her body allowed her to sleep once more. She quietly descended the stairs, picking up a cool drink on her way out of the home, and stepped out onto the back patio. She wandered about the estate until she found herself at the large workshop.

Something was drawing her there, and she knew what it was. She turned on the soft warm lights then walked to the bag that was sitting on the bench. She carefully opened it, trying hard to stuff away the emotions its contents were sure to evoke. She laid out the shattered pieces of Rivet, one charred and broken fragment at a time. The largest intact portion of the android was the torso with the upper portion of one leg still attached. For one fleeting moment, Brae wondered if there was any remote chance that some portion of his mind had survived, but the gaping hole in his chest and the charred edges of the core processing unit removed all doubt in that regard. The last piece she placed on the bench was his head. With his eyes shut, he looked peaceful in his robotic death. She placed her hand gently on his cheek.

"Oh, Rivet. From the time I was just a girl, I adored you. You saved my mother and my father…you saved me." Brae's eyes moistened as she voiced her pain. "And I sent you to your death when all along my father knew he was going to die that day." Brae wiped away her tears, but more continued to run down her cheeks. "And I think you knew it too, but you still went."

Brae turned away, burying her face in her hands to weep once more for all she'd lost.

"Brae!"

The voice was barely a whisper. Brae jumped, startled and afraid that someone could have come so close to her without her knowing it. She turned about, but no one was there.

"Who's there?" she asked.

Silence.

Chills flitted up and down her whole body. She was convinced that she had heard her name, but with an empty shop it seemed impossible. Was her mind playing tricks on her? *Could deep sorrow do such a thing?* she wondered.

After checking her surroundings a third time, she returned to the bench still somewhat shaken to look once more at Rivet. Then it happened. Rivet's eyes opened for just a fraction of a second. Brae froze, goosebumps rising on her arms and legs until they hurt. Was she actually asleep and dreaming? She slowly backed away from the bench.

"You okay?" a voice behind her asked.

This time Brae yelped as she jumped and turned about. "Oh...it's you!"

"Wow...a little jumpy, aren't we?" Rhett quipped.

Brae's head dropped with a big exhale. She walked up to Rhett, wrapped her arms around his torso, and rested her head against his chest.

"I'm guessing we're not okay," Rhett said, clearly unsure of what to do.

Brae didn't let go. "I'm sorry. I just need something to hang on to for a minute."

Rhett gingerly put his arms around her. "Okay."

Holding Rhett settled her in the best of ways, but she knew she was flirting with the potential of misconstrued intentions. She took one more deep breath then let loose and backed away. Pursing her lips, she looked at him.

"Okay, then. Thanks. Don't get any ideas, Stryker. I was startled and...and..." she pointed to the bench. "Rivet opened his eyes!"

Rhett frowned. "How in the galaxy do you come up with these crazy stories?"

"I'm serious!" Brae walked toward the bench then turned about and came back to Rhett. She looked up into his eyes. "And I think he spoke my name," she said with a grimace.

Rhett's brows raised. "It's just a bot, Starlore. If it did blink and say something, it's probably some nearly dead power module energizing a circuit for a second."

"Rivet isn't just a bot," Brae shot back. "If I didn't imagine it and this really happened, then I have to try and revive him."

Rhett walked to Brae. He put a gentle hand on her shoulder. "I think you need to go back to bed. It's three in the morning—nothing ever looks or feels the same in the middle of the night."

Brae had a moment of déjà vu—of Rhett's hand awkwardly placed on her shoulder at the Magnifical Festival. This time she didn't seem to mind it. She also remembered his awkward attempt at recovery by punching her in the arm. It made her smile.

"I suppose you're right."

Rhett walked her back to her room. At the door she turned to face him. "Thanks," she said, giving him a gentle punch in the arm. Rhett laughed.

"Okay…I get it. That was me trying to be supportive. I pretty much decided to give up after that," he said with a sheepish grin.

"I'm glad you didn't," Brae said with a sweet smile. "Night, Stryker."

"Night, Starlore."

The next morning at breakfast, there was a constant rumble of three and four simultaneous conversations with everyone participating except Brae. Jeshu immediately seemed to notice.

"What's on your mind, Brae?" he asked.

Brae looked up from her food.

"She's seeing android ghosts," Rhett piped in.

Every other conversation stopped, and all eyes turned to Brae. She shot Rhett a sour smirk. Jeshu just kept looking at her. Something about his stare disallowed the option of remaining silent. It was as if he knew her thoughts and was just waiting for her to speak and confirm them.

"Last night I was out in the workshop looking through the pieces of Rivet that Cilla and Quill recovered." Brae scanned the other faces at the table. Everyone was tuned in. "I know this sounds bizarre, but I swear he spoke my name and blinked."

The dining room remained eerily silent. Cilla finally spoke up.

"That android of yours was special," she said. "Never seen another one like it."

Brae looked earnestly at Cilla. No one else seemed to understand what Cilla had figured out in just a couple of exchanges with Rivet.

"I think we should try to put him back together," Cilla said. "Quill and I both have some android tech experience."

Brae's face lit up. It was what she had hoped for but didn't dare suggest.

"Mother, you designed and built engines at the aerotech facility," Bridger added. "Surely you could lend a hand."

"Absolutely. I'll help however I can," Kara said. "I also have access to a state-of-the-art replicator, which I think you'll need based on what I've heard."

Brae's excitement was building with each offer. She looked at Jeshu. He was silent.

"What do you think, Jeshu?" she asked.

He thought for a moment, then offered a hint of a smile. "You won't know until you try."

It wasn't the bolstering enthusiasm she had hoped for, but it also wasn't a no.

Quill jumped up. "Let's do it!"

Cilla smiled from ear to ear and stood to join him. Brae couldn't stop her smile. She stood.

"Kara?" Brae coaxed.

"Let's take a look and come up with a plan," Kara agreed.

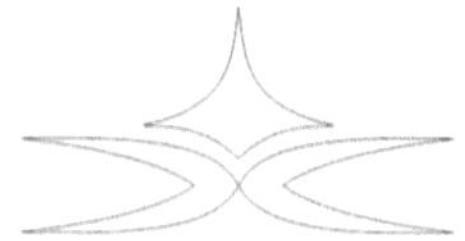

CHAPTER

9

At All Cost

In the realm of the Ruah, deep in Torian-dominated space, two Malakian reconnaissance warriors were risking their lives to discover the plots of Dracus. There were no spies in the Immortal warfare of the Ruah. It was just as impossible for a Torian rebel to pose as a loyal servant of Sovereign Ell Yon as it was for a Malakian warrior who was loyal to Ell Yon to pose as an evil servant of Lord Dracus. But this didn't preclude both the Torians and the Malakians from clandestinely attempting to obtain secret information from each other. Such missions were accomplished by deep interdiction reconnaissance. There was no duty more terrifying for Malakian warriors, for if captured, the Torians offered no mercy in the horror of their torture.

Tahn had risen through the centuries from a laser pick operator from before Dracus's rebellion to one of the key team members of the Malakian Recon Team, MRT7. For the past five years, he had been assigned to Chief Master Sergeant Andrada, a man of great reputation in the world of recon. Tahn had learned a lot from Chief Andrada and was grateful for the honor of being assigned a critical mission regarding their Commander, the Son of Sovereign Ell Yon.

Andrada and Tahn had worked for years attempting to get close enough to one of the key Torian research facilities,

Virant Labs. This facility was comprised of two orbital space stations in close proximity to one another, *Virant-X* and *Virant-Y*. Both research labs were in orbit around the giant gas planet, Far Point, the origin of C'fir Dracus's rebellion against Sovereign Ell Yon thousands of years ago. Although there were other more prominent Torian research facilities, Andrada was convinced that something significant was being developed here, and he suspected that the increased activity they had observed recently had something to do with the Commander's translation into human form as a child on the planet Rayl three years earlier.

"All of our efforts have led us to this time and this place," Andrada said, glancing over at Tahn. Chief Andrada was of average build as far as Malakians went. His dark red hair, short beard, and quiet presence might have indicated a gentle, submissive spirit were it not for his penetrating, fierce eyes, for Andrada was anything but gentle and submissive.

Andrada had piloted their sleek black recon ship, the *Specter,* under their most advanced cloaking tech to the dark side of one of Far Point's twenty-eight moons, Trantis. This precarious position was as close as they dared come to *Virant Labs* in its orbit around the massive gas giant planet.

Tahn looked up from his display as he reviewed recently intercepted telemetry. He was extremely fit and a bit stockier than Andrada, and his dark hair framed his olive-toned face.

"This telemetry intercept confirms our previous conclusion...something very important is being developed at *Virant-X.*" He eyed Andrada. "I've relayed the intercept to HQ."

Andrada seemed more concerned than usual. "What's wrong, Chief?" Tahn asked.

"We'll wait for the analysis from HQ, but from what I can tell, I'm afraid our suspicions regarding the secret initiative at *Virant Labs* may be further along than we thought."

Three hours later, the MRT7 agents were alerted by *Specter's* AI operating system, Sode.

"Chief Andrada, a secure and encrypted communiqué has arrived from headquarters," Sode's calm, pleasant voice announced from the 3D graphics table in the middle area of the pilot command center. Sode was often represented as a holographic torso on the holo table.

"Play the communiqué," Tahn ordered.

"This communiqué is for Chief Andrada's eyes only," Sode replied.

Andrada glanced toward Tahn and wagged his head to exit the command center.

"Seriously?" Tahn asked.

Andrada didn't respond. Tahn suspected the chief already knew what was in the communiqué. Trying not to be annoyed, Tahn stood and exited. *Will I ever know, and why keep something as critical as mission ops info from me?* he wondered.

A few minutes later, Andrada called Tahn back to the command center. Tahn walked in, leaned up against the graphics table and crossed his arms...waiting.

Andrada frowned.

"We have new mission objectives. With the intel we've gathered here along with the other MRT7 teams' intel in this quadrant, HQ was able to piece together something that the Torians are calling, 'The Protector Initiative.'"

"You were right then. *Virant Labs* is where it's happening," Tahn added.

Andrada shook his head. "Not happening...happened. Whatever it is, they've completed it. HQ says multiple devices are already en route to Rayl. A final transport is arriving at *Virant-X* in two days to take possession of the last shipment and deliver it to Rayl."

Tahn fully understood that their mission had just been elevated to the highest level of priority.

"What's the play?" Tahn asked. "The Torians have two fleets protecting this region of space. I doubt HQ is sending a strike force to stop the delivery."

Andrada slowly nodded. "They might have tried if a number of the devices hadn't already made it out. Instead, they need to know exactly what these devices are so the

Commander can prepare for what's coming. That's where we come in."

"And how are we supposed to get that information?" Tahn asked. "*Virant Labs*, especially *Virant-X*, is the most secure facility in the galaxy. That we are even this close is a wonder."

"I'm not exactly sure. HQ is working on it," Andrada said, rubbing his chin. "And we have two days to figure out things on our end."

"You're not telling me everything, are you Chief?" Tahn said, eyeing him closely.

Andrada looked his way...remaining silent. He then picked up a glass tablet and tapped a few commands. "We've exhausted all of our options for long-range recon. As you said, the security here is tighter than at any other station the Torians have, including *DarkWave*. We have to go in."

Tahn's eyes widened. "In?"

Andrada nodded.

"Into the station?"

"Sode, display the *Virant-X* research station on the holo," Andrada ordered.

Sode disappeared and was instantly replaced with a four-foot 3D holograph of the *Virant-X* research station that began slowly rotating in front of them. Tahn turned around to view the 3D model.

"From the information we've gathered, the *Virant-X* lab is where the telemetry originated and where previous transports outside the system arrived and departed," Andrada said, as he maneuvered the display with his hands to rotate and zoom into one section of the large orbiting station. "Section Bravo 11 to be precise. But gaining access to that lab would be next to impossible. The only possible access we have is when they transfer the item to the transport ship." Andrada rotated the model until the main docking bay was displayed.

"Excuse me, but I'm still stuck on the 'in' part of this plan. No Malakian recon agent has ever infiltrated a tier-one security level facility like *Virant-X* and survived, let alone recovered any useful information. We can't just fly into their docking bay and ask to take a look at their super-secret device," Tahn quipped. "Besides, every transport so far has arrived with fighter escorts, and you can bet there are half a dozen security warriors on board the transport if the cargo is as valuable as HQ says."

Andrada seemed undaunted by the impossible objective they had been given. He broke his concentration from the display, turned, leaned back against the table, and folded his arms.

"The Commander's mission on Rayl is just beginning, and based on reports from Admiral Galec, Dracus isn't holding anything back in his attempt to destroy him. In human form, the Commander is vulnerable. If the Torians have crafted a weapon that can take him out...then we have to do everything we can to find out what it is before it's too late."

Tahn drew in a long, deep breath as he considered Andrada's words. "I understand, Chief, but we'll be identified and killed or captured before we get within 20,000 miles of either of those stations."

Andrada stared at nothing in particular...thinking. Tahn had been impressed on multiple occasions by the innovative and detailed plans the chief had developed on previous missions. It was why he was the best of the MRT7 agents.

"Is this the part where you tell me about the secret weapon we took on board when we rendezvoused with Admiral Lucien at Estrada Minor?" Tahn asked.

A slight smirk crossed Andrada's lips. "Come with me."

Andrada led Tahn to the cargo hold of the *Specter*. Inside, they stopped in front of an eight-foot-tall container. Tahn had been curious about this container ever since it was brought on board three weeks ago, but the chief had been silent as to its contents.

Tahn recognized the bio security scanner access panel on the container, but this one had an additional feature—an auto self-destruct for a false scan or if tampering was detected. This level of access protection for the container told Tahn that whatever was inside was something headquarters deemed ultra-sensitive. Tahn hadn't even questioned Andrada about it, knowing full well that this was a need-to-know secret, and limited knowledge was the best protection for everyone involved, including himself.

What could possibly be in a container this size that might help them gain access to a fortified research facility like the Virant-X? he wondered.

Andrada hesitated, then placed his hand on the scanner. After a few seconds, the access panel flashed green, then released a locking mechanism. He pushed open the door to reveal a large one-man mechanized suit with what looked like a miniature slipstream jump-drive engine on its back. Tahn thought it looked both remarkable and ridiculous at the same time.

"What in the galaxy is this thing?" Tahn asked.

"Do you remember centuries ago when Admiral Galec's quantumtech research team designed our first non-gateway slipstream jump-drive engines?"

"Of course," Tahn replied.

"Ever since they completed outfitting our fleets with the new drive, they've been working on a miniature one-man jump-drive-equipped vessel." Andrada opened his palm to the suit inside the container.

Tahn's eyes opened wide. "This suit can perform a slipstream jump?"

Andrada cocked his head. "So I'm told, at least for limited ranges, because of the power required. Our astrotech geniuses wanted to design a one-man suit that could slipstream jump with precision, but the problem with such precise slipstream calculations is that everything in the galaxy is in motion...planets, moons, ships, space stations. In order to use this SS suit, we have to have extremely precise measurements of the departure and arrival locations and their predicted movements, or one might find himself impacting a bulkhead at light speed."

"I see," Tahn said, as he inspected every detail of the suit. "That means we have to expose our ship in order to get those precise measurements."

"Exactly," Andrada confirmed. "We have small probes that we can send out to the moon's horizon and relay the measurements back to our ship and then to the suit. Once those probes are detected—"

"The clock starts ticking," Tahn finished.

Andrada nodded. "I estimate we'll have twenty to thirty minutes at most."

Tahn shook his head. "This is crazy, but I get it...where's my suit?"

"There's only one, and you're staying on the ship," Andrada said, giving Tahn a side glance.

"Chief—" Tahn began to protest, but Andrada wouldn't have it. Tahn shook his head. "How are you possibly going to steal something in a secure facility when you don't even know what it looks like?"

"I don't have to steal it. We just need to know what it is and how it works," Andrada replied. "The telemetry we intercepted is just communication between the *Virant Labs* and the Torian HQ. They would never transmit something as sensitive as the designs of the device, even if it was encrypted. We need to access their secure network, and to do that I have to be physically in that station and access a physical data port."

"Our micro-scan sensor that we were able to attach to the last Torian supply ship gave one good high-res image of the inside of the docking bay before the signal was jammed," Tahn offered. "I think there may be a data port on a control console at the rear section of the bay."

Andrada looked encouraged. "Let's take a look."

Back at the command center, Andrada rotated the holo image then zoomed into the *Virant-X* docking bay. It was a large bay, big enough to receive two large transports at the same time.

"Right here," Tahn said, pointing to a console at the back of the docking bay. "You'd have to slipstream jump to the front of the docking bay because there could be people and equipment located anywhere inside—something we could never predict."

Faster-than-light slipstream travel wasn't magic. The path between the points of departure and arrival needed to be clear of any objects just as it would need to be if travelling at less than light speed. The difference was that the time to travel was nearly instantaneous at such short distances. There were warning systems built into all slipstream engine drives to eliminate the possibility of such spectacular collisions, but neither Tahn nor Andrada knew how much safety was built in to such a compact slipstream travel suit like Andrada was about to use.

Andrada zoomed in further, inspecting that section of the bay closely. "I'd have to slipstream into the docking bay undetected, cloak, get to the data port, and connect a quantum-entangled data transceiver."

"Wouldn't it make sense to enter with the transport then wait in a safe location until the activity in the docking bay diminishes after the transport leaves?" Tahn suggested.

"I don't think so. That suit is heavy," Andrada said, looking intently at the interior design of the station's docking bay. "Just because I'll be cloaked doesn't mean I'll be silent. I'll need the noise and the distraction of receiving, loading, and launching the transport to make my way to the data port console. Sode, will you be able to access the *Virant-X* network once you're connected via the QE data transceiver?"

"Not with absolute certainty," Sode's smooth voice replied. "There is an 83.4 percent probability that I will be able to access the lab's data systems within three minutes."

Tahn looked over at Andrada. The chief shrugged. "It's the best we have. This op must be planned down to the last detail, and timing is everything. *If* I can slipstream in and *if* I can get access to the device and *if* I can relay the data to the *Specter*, you'll need to be here to make sure we get it transmitted to HQ." The chief looked Tahn in the eye. "This is an at-all-cost mission, Tahn. A hundred things must go perfectly for us to succeed, and the future of the galaxy could depend on both of us doing exactly what we need to."

Tahn took a deep breath, trying to accept his secondary role with the appropriate humility.

"I understand, Chief. What about the exit strategy? How are we going to get you out of there?"

Andrada's eyes narrowed. "We'll let the team at HQ figure that out while we work on the infiltration. We have a lot of planning to do. I'll send our initial plans to HQ and see if they concur. With Sode's help, we might just be able to pull this off in the next 48 hours."

The next two days were nearly sleepless for both Tahn and Andrada as they planned the details of the mission down to the last second. As the hour approached for the Torian transport ship to arrive and take possession of this mysterious device, Tahn could tell that Andrada was becoming anxious in a way he had never seen his chief act before.

"Once the Torian transport arrives, the docking bay atmospheric energy shield frequency code will be transmitted to allow entrance," Andrada said, as they recapped the operation. "Sode, is your de-encryption algorithm for the *Variant-X* docking bay still valid?"

Sode's image appeared on the 3D display. "According to the last cargo vessel that arrived, it is valid. However, we have no way of knowing if they will have changed the frequency on the energy field once the transport enters the bay. I would recommend that your entrance coincide with the transport's entrance into the bay once I decipher the code."

"And if they *do* change the frequency before you get in?" Tahn asked.

Andrada tilted his head while raising an eyebrow. "Then I impact the energy field at light speed, and I won't even know what happened. Sode, display my flight path to the *Virant-X* docking bay."

A 3D image of Trantis, the moon they were hiding behind, the *Specter*, *Virant-X* station, and the chief's proposed slipstream flight path appeared.

"Sode, animate sequence of mission events at 10 times real-time," Andrada commanded. The 3D display began with the *Specter* launching two probes to each of the moon's horizons.

"We first send the probes to clear the horizon of Trantis. I'll EVA close behind the one traveling to this horizon,"

Andrada said, highlighting the selected probe. "After the probes attain line-of-sight, they will transmit the critical measurements back to Sode on the *Specter*. Once I get valid calculations from Sode, I'll clear the Trantis's horizon and slipstream jump to a position that will align perfectly with the rotation of the *Virant-X* station and its docking bay. Then I'll set my vector and jump to land here," Andrada said, as he zoomed into the station's main docking bay, showing his jump-drive arrival point. "If I time it with the arrival of the transport, this should be a blind spot for most of the docking bay personnel. All I need is a couple of seconds in order to activate the SS suit's cloaking system."

Tahn looked Andrada's flight plan over. Something felt wrong. "This is extremely risky, Chief. There is no margin for error, and a cloaked mechanical suit inside a manned docking bay could easily be detected. Once they receive the transport, they might close the bay blast doors. Energy frequency code or no code, you'll be stuck inside with no way out."

Andrada looked grim. "It doesn't matter. What matters is that I get that data transmitted out before they stop me. We need three minutes...that's all. It's time," he said, as he turned and exited the command center to head to the cargo bay.

All at once Tahn connected the dots and came to a frightful conclusion. He hurried to catch up to Andrada.

"You're not planning on getting out!" he exclaimed.

Andrada didn't turn or respond—he just kept walking.

"That's what you've been hiding all this time. No, Chief...I can't let you do this...it's suicide!"

Andrada froze as he reached the cargo bay door, his teeth clenched. He turned to look at Tahn with a fierce gaze. "It's not suicide, Tahn...it's sacrifice."

"I don't care, Chief. There's got to be another way!" Tahn protested.

"I've gone through a hundred scenarios—there *is* no other way," Andrada shot back as he pressed the panel to enter the cargo bay.

Tahn followed him to the SS suit, mentally scrambling for an alternative.

"This suit only has enough energy for two jumps. One to line up with the *Virant-X*'s docking bay and one to get inside. Once you receive the intel transmission via the QE data transceiver, you slipstream jump out of this system straight to Admiral Lucien in the Hargate System. When I detonate the self-destruct of the SS suit, it should create enough of a diversion so you can escape the system undetected." He began donning the suit. "I've prepared the probes and their flight paths. On my command, launch ports Tango and Sierra."

Tahn grabbed Andrada's arm. "Please, Chief. There must be something we can do to get you out of there," Tahn pleaded.

Andrada paused, softening. "An entire logistics team at MRT7 has been working on this for days. Everyone is desperate to find an alternative, but there just isn't one, and time is up. This is what *at-all-costs* means. The Commander became human, knowing he was going to die. This mission could mean the difference for *his* mission success on Rayl." Andrada gave Tahn a steely-eyed look. "These are the moments that define futures. A moment that only you or I may ever know about but has the power to alter the destiny of millions. We do what we have to do...got it?"

Tahn stood in awe of Chief Andrada. There wasn't a hint of reservation in the man.

"I've trained you well. Do the right thing and get the intel safely into the hands of the Commander." Andrada glanced at his timepiece. "Our window is closing in fast. Go do your job, Agent Tahn."

Tahn felt like the weight of an entire planet had fallen on his shoulders along with all its crushing pain.

"Yes, sir," Tahn said quietly. "Chief?"

Andrada stopped prepping the SS suit and looked at Tahn.

"It's been an honor serving under you."

"The honor is mine," Andrada replied with his signature crooked grin.

"May Ell Yon be with you," Tahn said, then exited the cargo bay to return to the *Specter's* command center, humbled, frustrated, and...angry. As he walked, he replayed in his mind the 3D animation Sode had constructed. When he arrived back at the command center, he prepared the launching sequence for the probes in ports Sierra and Tango. It would take the chief another fifteen minutes to finish prepping the SS suit and launch. Tahn turned to the central 3D holographic table.

"Sode, do you know the complete mission operation including the destruction of Agent Andrada and the SS suit?"

Sode's holo figure appeared, but there was a longer than usual delay in his answer.

"I am fully aware of all mission objectives," his response finally came.

"I want you to propose an extraction operation for Agent Andrada," Tahn ordered.

Sode looked blankly at Tahn. "That would violate my directives for this mission, Agent Tahn. I cannot comply."

Tahn leaned in to the display. "Sode, I'm not asking you to implement or defy mission directives. I want you to offer a hypothetical extraction operation for Agent Andrada in case he is unable to relay the intel. This is a backup plan."

Sode hesitated once again, his expression conveying one of skepticism.

"Agent Tahn, I am quite adept at discerning ulterior motives, and I suspect that—"

"Sode," Tahn interrupted, "either you help me formulate a backup plan for extracting Agent Andrada, or I will disable your core processor and do it myself. Am I clear?"

Sode's head tilted ever so slightly. "I understand. I've served Chief Andrada for many years. You must understand that all possible extraction operations will put the mission's success, as well as your own life, at risk. If you execute any operation outside of those dictated by headquarters, we will both be decommissioned."

Tahn waited...arms crossed.

"Hypothetically..." Sode began.

CHAPTER

10

The Gamble

Tahn watched as Andrada passed through the air lock chambers of the cargo bay to the *Specter's* docking bay, a plasma rifle in hand and the quantum-entangled data transceiver secured to his waist. One display in the command center was dedicated to the chief's helmet camera so that Tahn could see everything Andrada was seeing via the built-in quantum-entanglement communicator or QEC. This connection didn't need line-of-sight to communicate.

"Telemetry is active. How do you copy?" Tahn radioed on their secure channel.

"Five by," Andrada replied. "Launch probes now."

Tahn brought up the launch ports on his display and tapped on Tango and Sierra ports to activate them. His finger hesitated over the flashing "LAUNCH" icon. This one action would initiate a sequence of unstoppable events. Pushing this button meant killing the chief. His heart quickened, and he could feel his body start to sweat in multiple places.

"Tahn...launch now!"

Tahn closed his eyes. "Ell Yon...save him!" he whispered then pressed the "LAUNCH" icon. The icon turned red, and he felt the gentle rumble in the body of the ship as both probes accelerated out of their port tubes and into space in opposite directions, each one to its respective Trantis horizon.

"Probes launched. They'll be in line-of-site of *Virant-X* in 60 seconds," Tahn reported. As soon as the probes broke the horizon of their moon, it was very likely that the Torian security detection systems would quickly locate and identify them. They could only hope that would take minutes rather than seconds. Tahn watched as Andrada stepped out of the *Specter* and into space to follow the trajectory of Tango probe. His pack thrusters engaged, and Andrada quickly became just a speck on an orbital path around Trantis.

Tahn tapped in the coordinates for the Hargate System in preparation for his slipstream escape exit.

Thirty seconds.

He still had a visual on Tango probe and the chief—both were now moving at high velocity toward the rim of the moon's horizon.

Fifteen seconds.

Tahn watched the probes' telemetry link status... waiting.

Five seconds.

Tango probe's link status suddenly began transmitting measurement data to the *Specter's* transceiver. Two seconds later, Sierra probe telemetry was up.

"I am receiving valid telemetry from both probes," Sode reported to both Tahn and the Chief.

"Tahn, lock their positions to minimize exposure and keep them online until I complete my second jump," Andrada ordered.

"Copy. Calculations for the jump are nearly complete," Tahn replied as he watched an indicator as to Sode's calculation progress.

"Calculations complete...transmitting now," Sode reported.

On Andrada's helmet camera aboard the *Specter*, Tahn could see the *Variant-X* space station slowly edge into view just over the rim of the horizon of Trantis.

"I have line-of-sight with *Variant-X*. Solution locked in. Initiating slipstream jump...now!" Andrada radioed.

For less than a second, Andrada's helmet cam showed a swirl of lights then cleared. A few seconds later, the entire *Variant-X* space station came into full view as Andrada positioned the SS suit to align with the docking bay. It was an ominous view considering the enemy within. Tahn could also make out the arrival of a Torian transport preparing to enter the station's docking bay. Two Torian fighters were holding a distance outside the station in a protective posture.

As soon as the chief had completed his first jump, Tahn brought the *Specter's* engines online and set a vector for the horizon of Trantis.

"I can see the transport and the docking bay of *Variant-X*," Andrada radioed. "Are there any detection alarms?"

"Nothing yet, but those fighters are too close for comfort," Tahn replied.

"Sode, transmit current calculations and synchronize with the Torian transport's arrival through the docking bay's energy shield."

"Updated calculations are being transmitted to your SS suit continuously," Sode confirmed. "Please verify your launch vector is set to 273.4 by 082.1."

There was a ten-second delay as Tahn watched the chief precisely orient the SS suit to the designated vector, the vertical and horizontal azimuth info being displayed on his helmet HUD. Tahn spent seven of those precious seconds verifying the *Specter's* arrival position just shy of Trantis's horizon. He throttled back the engines to bring the *Specter* to a dead stop.

"Confirmed...273.4 by 082.1," Andrada replied.

"Slipstream jump in 5...4...3..."

Tahn found Sode's calm voice irritating considering the chief was about to leap into the jaws of a dragon and die within the next few minutes.

"2...1...jump."

Tahn held his breath as Andrada's helmet cam visual materialized inside the Torian *Virant-X* space station docking bay, not far from the left side of the transport. He exited within five feet of the target coordinates and just a few inches off the floor. He landed with a THUD, but the engines of the transport made the sound impossible for anyone in the bay to hear. The chief had made it through, but would he survive the next few seconds? Chief Andrada didn't move as he activated the SS suit cloak. Three long, intense seconds later, his helmet display flashed, "CLOAK ACTIVE." Tahn noticed that the chief was keeping the plasma rifle close to his chest so it would stay within the six-inch cloaking buffer created by the suit.

Andrada then took advantage of the noise of the transport's engines to move to the wall of the docking bay and begin making his way toward the back, further into danger. Tahn could hardly watch as the chief narrowly missed being hit by personnel, maintenance vehicles, and equipment in transit around the transport. After two minutes, Andrada was only halfway to the back of the dock when the transport's engines began to spool down but didn't shut down completely. Evidently this was a "hot" load where the time in dock was minimal, and the loading of the cargo would happen with the engines still running. The reduced roar of the engine would force the chief to move slower to avoid being heard.

"Sode, I want updated jump calculations for the *Specter* nav system in real time," Tahn ordered.

"Our exit jump has been calculated and needs no update," Sode replied.

Tahn turned to glare at the holo image of Sode.

"I see...telemetry from the probes is still active, and alternate jump drive calculations are being updated," Sode corrected.

Tahn refocused on Andrada and his progress toward the console with the data port. For fifteen long, grueling minutes, Andrada inched his way toward the console. At one point, a mechtech vehicle came within inches of colliding with the chief, the front corner of the vehicle actually penetrating the SS suit's six-inch cloaking buffer and disappearing. Tahn was grateful the driver didn't notice.

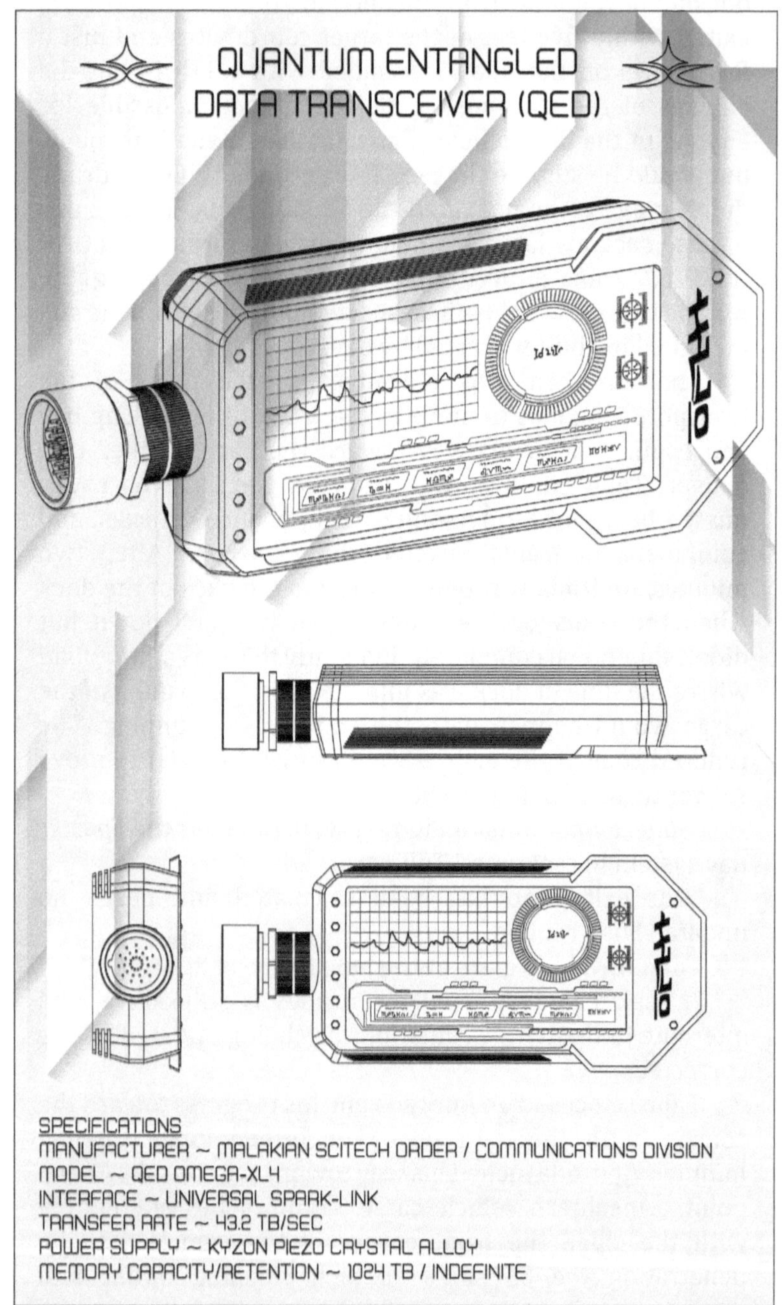

SPECIFICATIONS
MANUFACTURER ~ MALAKIAN SCITECH ORDER / COMMUNICATIONS DIVISION
MODEL ~ QED OMEGA-XL4
INTERFACE ~ UNIVERSAL SPARK-LINK
TRANSFER RATE ~ 43.2 TB/SEC
POWER SUPPLY ~ KYZON PIEZO CRYSTAL ALLOY
MEMORY CAPACITY/RETENTION ~ 1024 TB / INDEFINITE

During the chief's movement, Tahn watched as a hover cargo bin was loaded into the transport under the guard of four Torian warriors.

At last Andrada reached the console just as the cargo ramp of the transport was folding up into the ship.

"Do it, Chief...what are you waiting for?" Tahn said, clutching the edge of the console as he watched Andrada's helmet cam.

As the transport was given the signal to launch, it lifted up and started moving toward the atmospheric energy shield of the docking bay. The chief inserted the QED transceiver and rotated it 90 degrees to complete the link. At that moment, chaos unleashed, and alarms began to sound. Torian mechtechs scrambled as they tried to complete the launch of the transport. Security warriors brought their weapons up to bear but didn't know where to aim. It was only a matter of seconds before they would figure it out though.

"No!" Tahn shouted as he watched six more security warriors rush through an entrance from the main station. One of them held up a special device to his eyes and began scanning the bay.

"They're on to me!" The chief spoke for the first time since entering the bay. He quickly moved away from the console, at which time the QED transceiver became visible. Thankfully, with the distraction of the alarms, it went unnoticed, at least for now.

"I'm going to draw the fire away from the data port to give Sode time to access the network," Andrada said, as he ran along the wall on a path toward the front of the docking bay.

"There!" shouted the scanning Torian warrior, as he leveled his plasma rifle and shot at Andrada.

"Sode, establish a link to HQ with our ship QEC and relay the Torian data directly once you have access," Tahn ordered as he donned his tactical suit and grabbed a helmet.

"The link with headquarters is established," Sode responded. "However, I haven't yet been able to gain access to the station's network. The security measures are significant."

"Hurry up, Sode! The chief can't hold them off long," Tahn exclaimed as he pushed the throttles of the *Specter* up to gain a view of the station.

"I wouldn't advise exposing the *Specter* to the station's scanners. I still don't have access to the network, and the transport and the fighters are still present," Sode announced.

Tahn thought he could hear actual tension in the AI's voice. "You get access, and I'll worry about our ship," he shouted over his shoulder from the pilot's seat as he positioned the *Specter* to perfectly line up with a pre-determined launch vector. He scanned the *Virant-X* station and could see the transport and its two escorting fighters preparing for a slipstream jump, or at least that was what he was hoping for. He figured that even with the alarms sounding, the transport and its escorts would leave as quickly as possible, not wanting to put its precious cargo in jeopardy.

Ten seconds later the transport and the two fighters disappeared in the blink of an eye as they jumped to some unknown destination.

"I'm trapped," the chief radioed. "And they're onto the transceiver." Tahn could hear the desperation in his voice.

"Do you have access, Sode?" Tahn shouted.

"Negative. The station's AI system is reconfiguring and encrypting port access to stop me."

Tahn pulled up the chief's helmet camera to see him pinned down, his cloak disabled, and a half dozen Torian warriors closing in under intense rapid fire. Two more warriors had spotted the transceiver and were moving to the console. If they disconnected it, all would be lost. It was a hopeless situation.

"Try harder, Sode," Tahn yelled. "I'm making the jump now!"

Tahn engaged the slipstream jump engine, and a fraction of a second later, the *Specter* appeared in nearly the identical position that Andrada had after his first jump—

staring straight in the face of the *Virant-X* massive space lab. Tahn could see the flashes of plasma rifles inside the bay just a couple of miles away. What Tahn hadn't expected, however, was the sudden appearance of a Torian frigate and six fighters as they exited out of their slip stream jump just to the rear of the *Specter*.

"Agent Tahn, we are now trapped between the *Virant-X* station and the newly arrived Torian forces. I also do not yet have access to the network," Sode declared.

"What are you doing, Tahn?" the chief's voice blared over the com. "Get that ship out of here! I'm setting the self-destruct on the SS suit."

The fighters were closing in fast, and the first round of cannon fire from the frigate hit the *Specter* with brutal force, but the E-shield held. Tahn made a final adjustment because of the impact.

"Delay that, Chief, and clear the bay—I'm coming in," Tahn radioed back.

"N—" the chief began, but it was for naught.

Tahn engaged the jump drive, and a fraction of a second later the *Specter* was inside the *Virant-X* docking bay. Tahn immediately spun the ship around 180 degrees and set it on the floor in a controlled crash. The arrival of the *Specter* inside the bay had a three-fold impact on the situation. Five of the Torian warriors had the unfortunate consequence of being in the path of the ship and instantly obliterated. The frigate and its fighters ceased firing since they could not continue without damaging the station. The two warriors moving toward the console with the data port were taking cover to avoid being blasted by the *Specter's* engines.

Tahn jumped up from the pilot's seat, put on his tactical helmet, and ran to the cargo hold, grabbing two plasma rifles on the way.

"Sode, drop the cargo ramp and get that network access now!"

Tahn bolted toward the opening ramp at a full sprint, both rifles blasting as he went. He took out one more Torian warrior, but four more were just entering the bay through another door.

"I'll take these four...you take the two at the console and protect the QED," Andrada ordered, renewed by Tahn's arrival.

The fight inside the bay was fierce, and although Tahn and Andrada initially had surprise on their side, there was no way they would be able to survive much longer. More warriors arrived through a third entrance behind Tahn. He was exposed with nowhere to go.

"I have access to the network," Sode announced over his com.

At least my death will count for something, Tahn thought as a plasma round blasted into the armor on his left shoulder, knocking one of his rifles to the ground. He careened over an equipment case.

"I've located the device design files. Transmitting telemetry to headquarters via the QEC," Sode radioed.

Tahn glanced toward the chief's position. He'd been hit twice and was down too.

"Keep low," Sode warned.

Tahn thought that was a strange warning until all at once, the two rapid-fire, turret-mounted class-two plasma cannons on the *Specter* began to rain down holy terror on the Torian warriors in the docking bay. Tahn instinctively covered his head as the ferocious cannons rotated while targeting each enemy. After thirty seconds of plasma fury, the cannons stopped, and a temporary and eerie silence filled the smoky space of the bay. Tahn quickly scanned the area and could find no Torian warrior standing, but he knew more would be coming. Then additional alarms began to blare as the blast doors of the cargo bay started to close. He jumped up and ran to Andrada's position. The chief was hurt but still conscious.

"Come on, Chief," Tahn encouraged while lifting him to his feet. "Let's get out of here!"

The first few steps to the *Specter* were slow, but as the chief gained his bearings, Tahn helped him run to make the ramp.

"Get ready to lift the ramp, Sode," Tahn radioed. "And set a slipstream jump straight out of here 60 light years away."

As they made the ramp, it began to close. "Calculations and course set, but we may not clear the blast door or the frigate in front of us."

"I don't care," Tahn shouted. "Punch it!"

As the *Specter's* slipstream engine engaged, the space inside the *Virant-X* launch bay experienced a micro gravity-well compression shattering most of the supporting structure of that section of the station. The failure caused a massive collapse, destroying nearly one-third of *Virant-X*.

In its light-speed trajectory, the *Specter* narrowly missed the blast door and actually scraped metal off the port side of the Torian Frigate, losing one of its outboard sensor arrays in the process.

Inside the *Specter*, Tahn worked quickly to get the chief out of his slipstream suit to render medical aid. The chief was bleeding badly, but none of his wounds seemed life-threatening. Mid-way through Tahn's work, Andrada grabbed his arm.

"You disobeyed my order," Andrada said with a grimace.

"I did, Chief. I'll submit myself for disciplinary action when we arrive at HQ."

The chief shook his head. "You saved the mission, Tahn. Well done," the Chief finished, emotion uncharacteristically making the last word difficult to hear.

Tahn looked into the chief's red eyes. "*We* saved the mission."

Andrada took a deep breath and closed his eyes. Tahn let him rest while he checked in with Sode.

"That was some great work you did back there, Sode," Tahn said to the green torso at the holo station.

"Thank you, Agent Tahn. Would you like to see the decrypted transmission that was sent to headquarters? I think you may find it...justifying."

Tahn turned to look at the large display in the command center. A model of an odd-looking device appeared next to the text which read...

THE PROTECTOR INITIATIVE

PROJECT SUMMARY:

FIRST INITIATIVE – TO INTERCEPT ORIGINAL PROTECTOR FUNCTION AND INHIBIT ITS EFFECTIVENESS

SECOND INITIATIVE – USE PROTECTOR OMEGANITE POWER TO ENHANCE OUTPUT AND CORRUPT OR DESTROY ITS TARGET THROUGH DEITUM-PRIME-ENRICHED BIO UNITS.

TECHNOLOGY:

NEURO INTERFACE INTEGRATION WITH ANTI-OMEGEON PARTICLES...

CHAPTER

11

A Gift from the Ruah

Twelve cities on the planet of Rayl were granted the high honor of having a Sovereign Sanctum built in the central court of each municipality. Each sanctum was ranked by order of importance and prominence, the Jalem Sovereign Sanctum led by Preeminent Master Keeper Fasa Kylos of course being number one. Although only six sanctums currently had Protectors assigned to them, it was the goal that all twelve cities and their sanctums would eventually host a Protector. Cities that had the honor of hosting a Protector were Jalem, Rea, Joppik, Kaan, Brohn, and Zareth.

The Builders managed the collection of omeganite from their Omega nebula array and were also granted the high honor of replicating the original Protector at Jalem when enough of the precious but deadly substance had been retrieved. Depending on how elaborate the facility construction was, a sanctum vault was built to store its assigned Protector. This vault was located in the center of the building and at the highest level so that the citizens could always be reminded of the promises of Ell Yon. When the Protector was inside the vault, twelve high-intensity blue illumination panels around the periphery of the vault shone outward to signify its presence to the people of Rayl. The sanctum vault and its Protector symbolized the very presence of Sovereign Ell Yon to the Rayleans.

The established Keeper procedure was for the Master Keeper of each Protector-hosting sanctum to don his assigned Protector at sunrise and doff the Protector at sunset. Only the Master Keeper of each sanctum assigned a Protector could enter the vault by means of an extremely secure biometric array to determine his or her identity. On this particular morning, Preeminent Keeper Fasa Kylos of Jalem, wearer of the supposed original Protector, would discover something unique awaited him.

As was custom, two Associate Keepers arrived at Fasa Kylos's chambers at dawn to escort him to the Jalem sanctum vault.

"Good morning, Preeminent Kylos," one of the Associate Keepers greeted as Kylos exited his chamber door in full Keeper attire, his full-length cloak accentuating his rank.

"Morning," Kylos returned. "Let's be on our way."

Kylos enjoyed his position as the Preeminent Master Keeper for all of Rayl. It had taken him nearly forty years of diligent service to attain such an esteemed place of honor. He felt the weighty burden of protecting the position of nobility against the undignified attacks by lesser Rayleans, such as the case recently with this self-proclaimed Navi by the name of Elias Thornton. Kylos knew more would come but didn't expect such a thing so quickly. The rumblings of the incident at Zareth unsettled him for he had hoped that the quelling of Thornton's irreverent accusations would be a lesson for the rest of the world. But alas, it would not seem so.

The Associate Keepers instantly understood the morose state of their leader and kept quiet as they attempted to stay up with his quickened gait. Within a couple of minutes, Kylos arrived with his entourage at the anti-grav platform that would take Kylos up to the vault on the twelfth and highest level of the sanctum. The extreme measures of security designed to keep the Protector safe began here. Kylos entered a secure code, then faced a camera that scanned his face and performed a retina scan to determine his identity. The circular glass wall of the platform rotated ninety degrees, which opened a narrow doorway for Kylos to enter, leaving the Associate Keepers outside to await his return. Kylos placed his hand on the platform control that scanned his handprint. The glass wall immediately rotated back into position, sealing Kylos off from the rest of the world. Five seconds later the platform lifted upward, passing through each twenty-foot-tall level. Kylos arrived on the twelfth level, and the platform wall rotated ninety degrees once more to allow him to exit onto a large, empty but elegant room with glass walls on all sides. Here at this magnificent perch, Kylos took a moment to enjoy the panoramic view of the beautiful city of Jalem. A feeling of pride swelled within him.

"All will be as it should be once again," he said, as he turned to walk twenty paces to the center of the room where the vault entrance was. Kylos submitted himself to another array of identity scanners, including an advanced genetic scanner, and was rewarded with the whirring sound of five ten-inch diameter metal rods being electromagnetically removed from their secure locking positions. There, just a few paces in front of him on an illuminated pedestal, rested the glory of Ell Yon...the supposed original Protector. Kylos took a moment to settle his mind before retrieving it. There were legends of past Keepers found dead within the vault, the cause speculated as their unworthiness or improper mindset before donning the Immortal device. There was enough credence to the fabled stories to cause Kylos to hesitate each morning before lifting the Protector from its cradle.

Kylos took a deep breath, lifted the Protector, and placed it on his right forearm. He closed his eyes, waiting for the rush that should come, but as was the case every time before, there was nothing. He turned about to exit the vault and froze, terror gripping his heart. Just outside the vault doorway stood the form of a man that shattered all shadows of arrogance in the heart of Kylos. As in the fashion of appearance one would expect of Sovereign Ell Yon, this Immortal exuded the power of kings. Kylos fell to his knees. The Immortal smiled, absorbing the adoration of one of his subjects.

"Come, Fasa Kylos...I am pleased with your service... come," the commanding voice beckoned.

Kylos rose on shaking knees then exited the vault.

"My lord, how is it that you are here? Are you truly from the Ruah?

"I am, for there is a threat that has risen up in the midst of Rayl. I come to grant you power to eliminate this threat."

"You speak of the incident at Zareth?" Kylos asked.

The Immortal offered one nod.

"Another false Navi," Kylos offered, his brows furrowing to demonstrate his disgust.

The Immortal opened his cloak and retrieved a device that caused Kylos to gaze in wonder. In his hand was an elegantly woven array of miniature red and amber jewels positioned on a tubular lattice.

"The time for silence and passivity is over. Put forth your arm."

Kylos lifted his right arm and pulled back the sleeve of his tunic to reveal the gleaming Protector. With a great display of solemn ritual, the Immortal slid the jeweled array over the Protector until it joined around its periphery in a seamless fashion. Kylos could instantly feel the presence and power like he had never felt before.

"This is my enhanced Protector that I give to you. The lies of false Navis must be destroyed. This is your duty...this is my command to you!"

Kylos bowed his head in submission. "I shall do as you command, Sovereign Ell Yon," Kylos voiced with determination. When he lifted his head, the Immortal was gone. Kylos took a deep cleansing breath, invigorated by the power on his arm. He lifted the enhanced Protector and let his fingers glide across the jeweled lattice that embraced it. Miniature red flames licked at his fingers as they passed.

"Now is the time of purging," he said with a smile.

In the early afternoon of the same day, the Keepers and Builders of the Protectors gathered at the First Sanctum of Sovereign Ell Yon in the capital city of Jalem. Keepers and Builders from other cities and regions had come to listen to the inquiry regarding the events in Zareth in the last week. Rumors proliferated, especially on the heels of the aftermath of the Magnifical Festival. This gathering of nearly 2,000 Keepers, Builders, and their numerous associates was unusual, but these were unusual times.

In the sanctum's large oration chamber, the assembly of Keepers and Builders watched in silence as a ten-foot display at the back of the platform replayed the recorded events in Zareth. Preeminent Keeper Fasa Kylos stopped the video scene just as the man named Jeshu was in full view, his forearm clearly bearing what looked like an exact replica of a Protector.

Kylos strolled slowly across the chamber platform, his hands folded carefully behind his back. The long cape festooned with the mark of the Keepers flowed elegantly behind him. All Keepers of the Protectors wore capes while serving in their official capacities. The length of the cape indicated the rank and position within the Keeper Order. Kylos's cape touched the ground, demonstrating his supreme position over all other Keepers. For the Builders, capes would hinder their work within the sanctum labs, so their designation of rank and authority was annotated on the lower portion of their uniform sleeves. Krisha Monae, the leading Master Builder, sat in her esteemed position on the chamber platform, along with six other high-ranking Keepers and Builders.

The entire assembly of Keepers and Builders remained silent as they observed the regal contemplation of their preeminent Master Keeper. When Kylos was ready, he stopped, turning to face the constituents of the chamber.

"Do not be deceived, fellow Keepers and Builders. Other than being that of a skilled pilot, Elias Thornton was no Navi, and his fake Protector did little more than give the people a light show designed only to woo and lure them away from us." His eyes echoed the passion in his heart to defend the esteemed orders of Sovereign Ell Yon. "Us...the very chosen Keepers of the Protectors! And now this Jeshu character is simply capitalizing on the emotional hype that Thornton created." Kylos lifted a finger into the air. "Mark my words...just as Thornton was destroyed for his profane words against us, so will this Jeshu of Zareth in like manner be destroyed."

There were rousing cheers from the assembly, but once they fell silent, one Keeper stood.

"But Preeminent, there are rumors that the man at Zareth can perform things even greater than what we saw of Thornton...things like the Navis of old. How can this be?"

Kylos scowled at the man.

"I only ask because the people are asking such things of us," the man continued. "What are we to tell them?"

"Tell them that we have entered a new dawn of Sovereign Ell Yon's commitment to his people. Tell them that Ell Yon has bestowed upon us the power to judge and condemn the lies of those who defame the Sovereign and His Protectors." Kylos glared out across the assembly, capturing their full attention with a dramatic pause in his speech. "Behold!"

Kylos lifted his right arm high in the air while pulling down the sleeve of his tunic for all to see the marvel he now wore. The men and women of the chamber gasped at what they saw. Upon Kylos's arm was a Protector...the same Protector they had seen him wear a thousand times before, but today something was very different. Fastened around the periphery of the Protector was a diamond-pattern lacing of glowing alien technology. Pulsating hues of amber and red rippled slowly across the outer rim of the Protector. It was enchanting to look at.

"This very morning when I entered our impenetrable sanctum vault to retrieve the Protector for the day, this was given to me. This enhanced Protector is a gift from Sovereign Ell Yon to eradicate the lies of men like Thornton and Jeshu. Its power does not lie dormant as before."

Kylos turned his hand to the massive display still showing the face of Jeshu. He closed his hand into a fist and a powerful burst of red energy exploded from the Protector and into the display. It shattered into a million pieces, causing the crowd to gasp in wonder. The esteemed panel of Keepers and Builders on the platform jumped from their seats as a few small pieces of the exploded glass fell near them.

Kylos beamed with pleasure and power. "I have word from the Master Keepers at the other sanctums hosting Protectors that they too have been recipients of this exact same enhancement. No longer do we have to endure the lies of these imposters posing as Navi. Our enhanced Protectors will find them out and destroy them!"

At Kylos's impassioned proclamation, the entire assembly of Keepers and Builders jumped to their feet in riotous applause...all but three.

Thirty minutes later, once the initial thrill of the enhanced Protectors had subsided, Keepers Codemus, Sephner, and Builder Tazra gathered in a quiet corner far away from the ears of their associates. At first, none of them dared utter a word, their eyes conveying the full measure of their concern. It was Codemus that ventured to speak his thoughts.

"Everything Elias Thornton said was true."

It was a simple statement, but the force of it was enormous. It was all that was needed to win an execution, and therefore the bravery of his heart was instantly made known to Sephner and Tazra. They both nodded.

"With severe apprehension, I donned the last Protector we replicated for the Keepers," Tazra said.

Codemus glanced toward Sephner then looked back at Tazra. "Then you know. If you heard the voice of Ell Yon, you know."

Tazra's eyes darkened. "How can they not?" she said, wagging her head toward the hundreds of Keepers and Builders still conversing in the oration chamber.

Sephner frowned. "Truth be told, I didn't know until Thornton appeared. His words brought great conviction to me, and it was then that I dared listen to the whisper of the Sovereign while wearing the Protector. His words frightened me, but I knew they were true. And now..."

Codemus nodded. "And now comes the man named Jeshu," he finished for Sephner. "According to the Keepers at Zareth, his claims are even more dramatic than those of Thornton."

"But what if they *are* true?" Tazra asked, her eyes illuminating with hope.

Codemus and Sephner hesitated.

"We must find out for ourselves. We must talk to him," Codemus said, his eyes reflecting determination. "I'll make that my mission, and you two observe as much as you can."

"Be careful, friend," Sephner warned. "As far as I can tell, there are no others among us."

Tazra nodded her agreement.

"Until our next meeting then," Codemus said. He put forth his hand while touching his thumb to his third finger then opened his palm. Sephner and Tazra did the same. It was their signal to each other that they were in safe company.

Prefect Terrok was sulking on the west terrace of his palace. Wisps of Deitum Prime rose from the vaporators around the lush alcoves and raised gardens surrounding him. He was being fawned over by multiple servants and two mistresses, but neither the attention nor the food and drink seemed to help his demeanor. Aunder, Prefect Terrok's longest employed first advisor, approached the Raylean puppet ruler cautiously.

"Prefect, I have an urgent message for you."

"Don't tell me that treasonous band of Partisans has caused another uprising. I thought we'd executed all of them," Terrok scowled.

"No, Prefect, you've been summoned to Subchancellor Pylok's Skyburough." Aunder purposefully kept ten feet away just in case Terrok was in a throwing-wine-glasses mood.

Terrok froze. His scowl became vapid then slowly transformed to one of great fear. "When?"

"Immediately, Prefect. A Morian transport is arriving at the palace as we speak."

"But I thought Subchancellor Pylok was off world visiting his home planet, Moria."

Aunder hesitated. "He was, Prefect, but he's just returned and evidently wants to speak to you directly."

Terrok shoved consoling offerings of food and drink away from himself, causing the servants to spill their tray contents. He jumped up from off his lounge and began pacing.

"This is bad...this is very bad! That blasted Navi! This is all his fault." He turned his fierce eyes on Aunder. "I should have never listened to you!" he shouted, his neck bulging with muscles and veins. His completely Deitum-Prime-absorbed body was threatening to unhinge with his rising wrath.

"Yes, Prefect, I am deeply sorry for advising you inappropriately, but I would highly recommend keeping calm in preparation for your meeting with the subchancellor. Any display of irrationality will not be well received."

This seemed to settle Terrok slightly as he considered his fate. He stopped pacing, shook out his hands and lifted his gaze to the sky. "Yes...calm...in control. Perhaps he wishes to commend me for sparing the Morian Empire of a rebellion that would have surely spread to their homeworld in time."

"Yes, Prefect," Aunder said soothingly as he placed a gentle arm to Terrok's back, leading him out of the terrace, through the palace, and toward the landing pad. "Surely your brave actions will be praised."

At the door portal adjacent to the landing pad, four large armed Morian commandos were waiting for them. Terrok tried to bring Aunder with him, but one of the commandos held up his hand to the first advisor, making it clear that Terrok was to go alone.

During the flight across the city of Jalem, Terrok could hardly contain his anxiety. He gazed out the window of the transport at his capital city. When the Morian Empire invaded Rayl, Jalem was Subchancellor Pylok's first choice for establishing his governing command center. Choosing the northeastern quarter of the city, he sequestered and renamed the district Skyburough. Over the course of a few years, Skyburough was transformed into a manifestation of Moria, the homeworld of the Morian Empire. The elaborate yet stiff social structure, architecture, culture, and general atmosphere were Morian through and through. What had once been an esteemed Raylean district of Jalem was now despised by its native citizens because of the Morian occupation there.

As the transport carrying Terrok descended toward Pylok's command center, the puppet Prefect felt the suffocating oppression of his captor descend on his wretched soul. Within a few minutes of landing, Terrok was delivered to Pylok by the escorting commandos. Two of the commandos remained stationed on each side of the entrance while Terrok bowed then came to stand before a stern, uniformed Subchancellor Pylok who was sitting at a table with three plates of a variety of Morian cuisine.

Pylok was known to be an ordered man, certain of his duties and committed to excellence in every personal endeavor. Although Terrok's encounters with Pylok were brief, they were always extremely intense. He knew Pylok despised his current assignment, for Rayl was considered an outcast planet in the Morian Empire, far from the esteemed position of rule one of his stature deserved. But success here on Rayl could also bring promotion, and Terrok didn't want to be the reason Pylok was denied such an opportunity, for the wrath of the subchancellor could prove fatal.

Pylok continued to eat while Terrok stood silently before him. He made no offer for Terrok to sit or eat. His omission of speech was anticipatory to the harsh message that was sure to come. Terrok dared not utter a word as he waited in tortuous silence before the man that held his life in his hands. In perfect posture, Pylok placed a morsal of rare smoked meat in his mouth, set his fork on the table, and gave one quick glance at Terrok. The brief but cold exchange nearly put Terrok on his knees. He swallowed hard, waiting. Pylok then lifted a glass of Jyptonian wine to his lips. He swirled the rich red liquid, smelling the sweet fragrance released by the action. Pylok took a sip of the wine then gently placed it back on the table before him.

"Do you know from where I've just come?" he asked without looking directly at Terrok.

"Yes, my lord. From the glorious empire homeworld of Moria," Terrok answered.

It was at this moment that Subchancellor Pylok, Morian governor of Rayl, locked his gaze on Terrok. "Yes, Terrok...Moria, homeworld to the greatest empire this galaxy has ever seen or ever will see. And do you know with whom I spoke while on Moria?" Pylok asked while slowly rising from his seat.

Terrok shrugged his shoulders, managing to offer only a whimper in return.

Pylok slowly walked around the end of his dining room table, his hands folded neatly at his back as his boots clicked on the polished marble floors.

"I was invited to present the status of our occupation on the planet Rayl to First Leader Chancellor Krish." Pylok held up one finger. "...The most powerful man in the galaxy. And do you know what he asked about?"

By now Pylok was directly in front of Terrok, his face white with fear.

"He wanted me to explain why your ridiculous festival turned into a complete and utter debacle where our commandos had to spend weeks getting the city of Jalem...nay...the entire planet under control again."

Pylok's countenance was fierce with hot indignation as he leaned into Terrok's face. "Do I need to appoint a different prefect to keep your people under control?"

"N...n...no, Subchancellor Pylok," Terrok stammered. "I can assure you...p...promise you that this will never happen again. I've purged the planet of all individuals responsible for that abominable uprising. Please...please forgive me. All order has been restored."

Pylok's eyes narrowed as he glared at Terrok. He lowered his voice to a raspy whisper.

"If there is so much as a shout in your streets, I will make sure that the next execution will be yours...a Morian execution. You know how we have perfected the art of killing a man, don't you, Terrok? And as an extra measure, I will mount your head on a pole in Jalem's central court. Do I make myself clear?"

"Yes, Subchancellor...perfectly clear."

Pylok held Terrok captive to his menacing gaze for another ten seconds then turned away. "Leave me and hope I never call you into my presence again."

Terrok bowed low then turned to leave. Just before he exited the door, Pylok called to him.

"And Terrok, keep those ridiculous sanctums and your Immortal-believing fanatics under control...they will quite literally be the death of you if you don't."

Terrok bowed again then exited the room. Outside, he leaned up against the wall and nearly gasped for air. He needed longer to recover his wits, but the two commandos waiting for him outside of Pylok's chamber wouldn't allow it.

"Back to the transport," one ordered, pointing the way with his plasma rifle.

Terrok huffed, forcing himself to regather some dignity and walk with a remnant of poise. All the way back to his palace he plotted ways to ensure such a colossal disaster would never happen again.

"Those blasted Keepers...they coerced me into killing that Navi, and I nearly lost my life for it!"

The next day Terrok demanded that Preeminent Keeper Fasa Kylos and Master Builder Krisha Monae come to see him. In the outer courts of the palace, Terrok attempted to mirror the indignation and the threats he had received at the hand of Subchancellor Pylok, but neither Kylos nor Monae seemed much intimidated.

"Mark my words, Kylos," Terrok scowled, "you had better keep your sanctums and their occupants under control. This incident at Zareth already smells of insurrection. The Morian commandos are ready and willing to eliminate all sources of trouble by any means necessary. And believe me, if I go down, I will make sure that you two go down with me—I swear it!"

Although Kylos looked angry, there were also traces of fear in his eyes. A man in his position wasn't used to being threatened, but the Morians certainly added an entirely new level of credibility to Terrok's threat.

To save face, Kylos lifted his chin, huffed, then turned to leave. Monae followed close behind him.

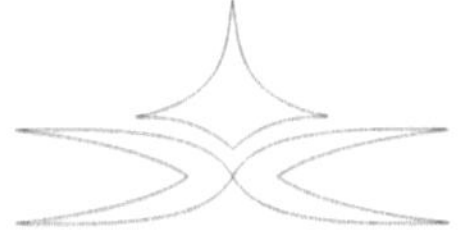

CHAPTER

12

The Gathering Force

One week after Jeshu arrived at the Stryker estate, he gathered Brae, Rhett, Bridger, Kase, Shayde, Cilla, and Quill on the back patio. He asked them to sit while he stood and spoke.

"I've talked to each of you about why I'm here. Now that you've all had time to think over what I shared with you, we've come to a time of decision. After today, any of you who decide to follow me will discover that life is going to change…significantly. If you choose to follow me, know that there will be adversity, but you will also see those things that the oracles of old could only have dreamed of seeing." Jeshu paused, taking a moment to look at each of the faces staring back. "I'm here to change the galaxy, but that comes at a price. Are you willing to join me?"

"I am," Brae said, standing to demonstrate her oath to follow Jeshu.

"I am," Rhett stated, joining her.

One by one each of them stood until all seven had pledged their oath to follow the Merchant. Jeshu looked pleased.

"Very well. From now on, you will be my sectators, the future Navis of Ell Yon."

Just then Kara entered the home and came to Jeshu. She was carrying a case marked "Kaysic Aerotech."

"Ah, Kara. You're just in time," Jeshu said. "Were you successful?"

"It took some convincing, but I was," Kara said, setting the case on the table before Jeshu. "Some of the instruments are quite expensive. I'll need to return them by tomorrow."

"Thank you. I should have them back in just a couple of hours," Jeshu replied. He then turned to his new sectators. "I have some urgent business to attend to, but prepare yourselves. When I return, we start our first mission. Rhett, is the omeganite shielding still functional on the *Aviel*?"

Brae looked at Rhett, confusion evident on his face. "It is."

"Good. I'll be back shortly," Jeshu said, grabbing the case that Kara had delivered and walking to the door.

Brae followed him. "Can you tell us where you're going?" she asked.

Jeshu glanced back at her and then to the others. "To commune with my father. I've received word that Dracus is plotting a way to undermine my mission. I and my Protectors must be ready." He nodded, then exited the home and walked toward the *Aviel*.

Rhett looked at his mother. "What was in the case, Mom?"

Kara hesitated. "Some extremely precise and expensive tools for adjusting the antimatter microtubules in our latest engine tech. He mentioned needing the *Aviel's* shielding to protect this region from omegeon radiation."

"What does that mean?" Kase asked.

"I'm not sure," Kara replied. "Perhaps it has something to do with his Protectors."

"The Protectors are powered by omegeon crystals," Bridger said. "If he opens them, won't the radiation kill him?"

Brae remembered the story of her parents' being marooned on Mesos and nearly dying from the omeganite radiation from the Omega Nebula.

"It would kill us, but him? No," Brae replied. "There's not a trace of Deitum Prime in him. Only he could be exposed to the crystals and not die."

Everyone migrated to the patio hand rail as the *Aviel* lifted off. They watched as Jeshu accelerated the shuttle upward into space.

"There's a certain air of mystery about him, isn't there?" Kase asked of no one in particular as they all stared at the diminishing speck in the sky.

Two hours later, Jeshu was back, his eyes burning bright with the flame of Sovereign Ell Yon.

"Rhett, do a systems check on the *Aviel*," Jeshu said, as he greeted his sectators on the back patio. "We launch in ten minutes."

Brae was excited, wondering where on Rayl, or perhaps even in the galaxy, Jeshu would choose to begin his mission. What facets of government would he engage with? She imagined something similar to the stories of old—a Navi takes command of the political and military seats of power to effect global change.

"Destination?" Rhett asked.

"Take us to the rim," Jeshu commanded.

Brae was stunned. Surely he meant something different than what she was thinking. The rim of every city was where the dregs of humanity lived. Unable but also unwilling to join the rest of society, rim dwellers were the filthy, the sick, the poor, and ofttimes the criminal fringes of humanity. The dark market, along with pervasive immersion in Deitum Prime, was commonplace among rim dwellers. The larger the city, the larger the rim and its population. Rarely if ever would the average Raylean venture into the rim of a major city.

"The rim?" Rhett asked, catching Brae's concerned look.

Surely not, he thought. "As in the Brohn Rim?"

"That's it—let's launch," Jeshu said, undaunted by the looks of consternation he was getting from all of his sectators.

Jeshu and his entourage made the 15-minute trip to the Brohn Rim in silence.

"It's huge," Brae said from the copilot seat as Rhett set the *Aviel* down at the edge of the Brohn Rim.

"I've heard estimates of over 25,000 and growing," Rhett responded as he shut down the engines and completed his post flight checks. "With Terrok as prefect and the Morian occupation, the rim of most cities has doubled in the last ten years."

"I had no idea," Brae said.

Jeshu stood, leaning forward into the cockpit. "Most people don't," he said. "Come...we're needed here."

Jeshu was the first to step out of the shuttle, gaining the attention of many worn and weary faces of adults and children alike. There was little to differentiate the poor and the sick of this generation from the generations of a millennium ago. No matter the technological advancements of a culture, the poor and the downtrodden shared a common bond with those in the same circumstances in all other ages...they had nothing to their names and nothing to live for.

When everyone had joined Jeshu outside the shuttle, there was much silent confusion.

"This is how we change the galaxy?" Kase asked the very question everyone else was too afraid to ask.

"Yes, it is," Jeshu replied.

"And how, exactly?" Rhett asked.

"What don't these people have?"

"Pretty much everything," Brae said. "But I'm guessing you mean hope?"

"Exactly. I am hope. I am life. These people need hope and life more than anyone else," Jeshu replied as he began walking toward a girl and a younger boy who were attempting to salvage a few scraps of metal from an abandoned, rusted-out grav tech vehicle. Brae and the others stayed behind, watching.

"Hi there," Jeshu called as he approached. The girl turned. She didn't frighten, but the boy stepped over to hide behind his older sister.

"What are your names?" Jeshu asked.

The girl just stared at him with dark hollow eyes. "If I were you, mister, I wouldn't stay here," she said, turning to look toward Brae and the others. "Rawders will take everything you have in no time."

Only then did Brae realize that the girl's left arm was shriveled and deformed, perhaps from birth or by an accident that had gone untreated.

Jeshu smiled. "Thanks for the warning, but I think I'll stay just the same." He reached into a pack he was carrying and pulled out a slice of dried meat. "Hungry?"

The girl's eyes immediately lit up, as did the boy's. Jeshu held the meat out to her, and it was enough to entice her to step toward him. She reached her right hand far out to take it then retreated a few steps. After smelling the stick, she tore off a piece with her teeth and handed it to her little brother before taking a big bite for herself.

"Now will you tell me your names?" Jeshu asked again.

"I'm Garson," the boy said between chews.

"My name is Lewenna. What are you doing here?" she asked as she wrinkled her nose.

Brae and the others stepped closer to see what Jeshu would do and say. She watched as Jeshu knelt down so that he could look at the girl eye to eye. Brae watched the face of Jeshu radiate love and empathy toward the two children like they had never seen before...like Brae had never seen before.

"I'm here to help you," Jeshu said, smiling. "Will you let me?"

The girl's brow furrowed as she swallowed a bit of the meat. Jeshu held out his hand to her, and she slowly came to him, the dried meat hanging loosely in her good hand. The little brother stepped out from behind her, apparently encouraged by the meat in his belly and the kindness of

Jeshu. When Lewenna was standing before Jeshu, he reached for her left hand. He carefully lifted her arm.

"What happened to your arm?" he asked, looking sweetly into her eyes.

"Pa said it was crushed when I was little...littler than Garson. He couldn't afford to fix it or get me a bot arm."

"Does it hurt?" he asked.

By now the seven sectators had gathered fully around. The girl looked up at Brae then back to Jeshu.

"Sometimes...when I try to use it much."

Brae looked at Jeshu, his eyes moistening with compassion. He held the girl's forearm in his left hand while placing his right hand on her shoulder.

"Be still, little one," he said quietly.

In hushed awe, Brae and the others looked on as Jeshu closed his eyes. Both Protectors began to pulse in ribbons of energy. Jeshu's hands and the broken little arm he held began to glow as he slowly moved his right hand down her arm. Lewenna's eyes opened wide, but she did not move. Jeshu continued moving his hand down her arm until he reached her hand. He opened his eyes, and Brae thought for a moment she could actually see the same energy flames of the Protector there. Perhaps it was just a reflection. Then the Protectors fell quiet, but the little girl did not. She instantly understood what had happened.

"You...you fixed me!" she exclaimed, turning her hand over and squeezing her fingers into a fist.

Jeshu smiled. Lewenna jumped toward him, throwing her arms around his neck.

"Pa said it would never happen...but you did it!" she said, holding tightly to Jeshu. He gently hugged the little girl, and Brae watched with great conviction. She now understood that this *was* how you changed the galaxy. Not by some military coup or political takeover, but through love and compassion. This was something the galaxy had never seen before.

Before long, word began to spread in the rim, and the people came...hundreds at first, then thousands. Brae, Rhett, and the other five did their best to bring some order to the throngs of people who wanted to see the one called the Merchant. Jeshu was tireless as he spoke to and healed many that day—legs, eyes, hearts, skin, and sicknesses. Many had injuries and ailments because the rim dwellers couldn't afford to have the advanced treatment or replacements needed, but there were also some diseases and disorders that were beyond the capabilities of the state-of-the-art medtech facilities. Jeshu and his Protectors healed them all.

"Bring the food from the *Aviel's* storage compartment," Jeshu commanded when the day was far spent.

"We have food?" Bridger asked.

Jeshu didn't answer, being inundated with the demands of the people. Rhett, Brae, Bridger, and Quill went to see.

"Did you pack this?" Bridger asked Rhett.

"Nope," Rhett said, opening one of the four large cases to see what was inside. Within each case were hundreds of compact, high-nutrition meals. "I'll be," he said with grin. "Okay...let's get after it."

They hauled the four cases to Jeshu.

"Jeshu...there won't be enough. There's got to be over 3,000 people here," Rhett said, as he assigned two sectators to each case.

"Just do what you can," Jeshu replied, continuing to minister to the throngs of people.

Brae worked beside Rhett, feeling more than thrilled at what they were seeing. They passed out the meals as fast as they could, knowing full well that their case would be empty in minutes. Brae's hand brushed Rhett's as she reached for a meal. In that brief touch of hands, Brae felt something flitter in her stomach. She hesitated, looking up at Rhett to see if he had noticed...he had. They exchanged an awkward smile, knowing something small but significant had just happened. A simple touch of hands. Brae heard a child cough in front of her, and Rhett quickly turned to hand a meal to the frail boy. Brae refocused on the ever-growing line of people.

"I hope they don't mob us to get the last few meals," Brae said, looking at a thousand hungry faces eager for a chance to get food.

As they handed out the last meal, Kase plopped another full case down beside them. "You missed a couple cases," he said to Rhett.

"I did not!" Rhett exclaimed.

Kase shrugged. "Well, there it is. I'll go get the other one for Cilla and Quill," Kase said, running back to the shuttle.

Rhett looked at Brae. "I didn't miss any," he repeated defensively.

Over the course of the next hour, sixteen empty cases were left lying on the ground all around, and over 3,000 meals had been given out. All seven of the sectators stood about with gaping mouths.

"What is happening?" Bridger asked, looking around at the others.

Brae glanced over at Jeshu who was using the Protector to make a lame foot whole. "He's changing the galaxy, just like he said he would. This is the beginning of everything!"

When the day was through, they didn't return to the estate, for Jeshu wouldn't leave the rim. They took turns sleeping and helping, but Jeshu worked onward, tirelessly, catching only an hour or two of rest from time to time.

On the third day, word of the Merchant's work in the rim had spread. Citizens from Brohn proper began to show up, some out of curiosity, some out of need. That's when the first broadcast specialist arrived. Jeshu made it clear that the broadcast specialist was not allowed to record his one-on-one interactions with the people. Bridger made it his personal mission to ensure that such recordings didn't happen, keeping the specialist, and any others that showed up 50 feet away. Brae and Rhett had to insist on Jeshu's getting sleep and food at least twice a day, for the masses of Brohn began to overwhelm them.

After one week in the Brohn Rim, Jeshu asked for his sectators to gather the people so that he could speak and be heard by all of them. No longer was the rim just a place for the poor and destitute—thousands came from Brohn and across the region to see and hear the man who was being heralded as the Merchant of the oracles. Three broadcast specialists and their networks were also poised and ready. When all was set, Jeshu stepped up onto the roof of a small hut so that all could see him. The crowd hushed to silence.

Jeshu scanned the mass of people, his eyes conveying the compassion Brae knew he felt for them.

"The realm of Sovereign Ell Yon belongs to the humble and the brokenhearted. For those who weep, you will find joy. For those who forgive others, you will be forgiven. For those who are gentle of heart, you will rule the galaxy. For those who bring peace to the galaxy, you will become the children of Ell Yon. What I have come to teach you is a new way. Learn of me and of my way, and you will be greatly rewarded. My realm will not be won by the edge of a blade or by the fire of a plasma cannon, but by kindness, mercy, and compassion. Do not be deceived, your enemy is not your fellow man…no, your enemy is the enemy of Ell Yon…Dracus the Torian and his Scourge. If you follow me, you will be tried and falsely accused for my sake, but take heart, for your reward in my realm is great. Know that I have not come to destroy the oracles of the ancients, but to bring them to pass."

Brae stood beside Rhett as Jeshu spoke words that had never lighted upon the ears of humanity before—words of hope and words of truth. These new words of hope did not come from the great oration halls of esteemed places, but rather from the lowly ghettos of the Brohn Rim. As bizarre a method as this was to establish a new galactic realm, Brae was being awakened to the true power of the Merchant— his words of hope and acts of love.

"Have you ever heard a man say such things?" Rhett asked, not taking his eyes off Jeshu.

Brae looked over at him, seeing the same glow in his eyes that was in her heart. "No…never."

Jeshu spoke for thirty minutes, and in those thirty minutes he delivered a message to humanity that rippled across space and time to people, nations, and generations throughout the galaxy. In the faces of this crowd, Brae could already see the impact.

The next morning, Jeshu said it was time for them to move on. They spent two days at the Stryker estate to clean up and recover. The seven sectators were exhausted and stunned, unable to fully process what they had just seen and experienced. As they gathered for breakfast on the morning of the third day at the estate, the stories began to fill the dining room with great enthusiasm. Jeshu remained quiet, smiling at the joy of his followers. Finally, Bridger turned to Jeshu.

"What's next, Jeshu?" he asked.

Everyone fell silent, eager to hear him.

"To Zareth and then to all of Rayl."

Rhett sat on the edge of his bed thinking…processing. He had a unique perspective to consider, having experienced the discovery of Jeshu at the Omega Nebula and his upbringing with Brae. But along with that unique perspective came great conviction. His realism and analytical pessimism had nearly cost him the greatest and most significant opportunity of his life. He looked up as if he could see the stars through his ceiling, his heart opening to a whole new dimension of trust and belief.

"I'm sorry, Sovereign Ell Yon…forgive my stubborn pride. If you'll have me…I will go."

When Rhett had left for the flight academy to become a Raylean Guard pilot years ago, he never thought he would ever have any other career or live again at his parents' estate. But as a result of his unusual circumstances, one of the benefits he was grateful for was a chance to reconnect and spend more time with his older brother, Bridger. Growing up, he had always admired Bridger. He was steady, confident, and a protector for both Rhett and Kase.

On their second day back at the estate, Bridger sought Rhett out as he was inspecting the *Aviel*, ensuring it was ready for their next expedition.

"How's she looking?" Bridger asked, ducking underneath the left wing to join Rhett.

Rhett was kneeling as he accessed one of the bottom side panels to check the quark fusion engine charge coils.

"She's in great shape. She's not a fighter but she's the next best thing," Rhett replied.

Bridger was slightly taller than Rhett and a good-looking guy. Rhett had wondered why he wasn't already bonded, but he also knew that his brother was extremely practical and therefore had a particular set of standards for such a relationship. It would have to be just the right kind of girl to win Bridger over.

"What's up, Bridger?" Rhett asked, knowing full well that his brother rarely came to him just to chat.

When Bridger didn't answer right away, Rhett stopped his work, closed the panel, and extracted himself out from under the *Aviel*.

"Uh-oh…it must be serious," Rhett said with a grin.

Bridger let a subtle smile cross his lips. He looked across the top of the *Aviel's* left wing at Rhett. "Not really, but I just thought I should talk to you about something."

Rhett eyed his older brother. This was not like Bridger. "Yes?"

Bridger's eyes narrowed. "You're a great brother, Rhett. Unlike Kase, I never had to work very hard to steer you in the right direction. And not that I need to now, but I just thought it was worth mentioning that despite all that's happening with Jeshu, I've never seen you so…so content. Not even when you were with Quilla."

"But I'm not *with* anyone," Rhett said, eyeing Bridger.

Bridger stared at Rhett for a few seconds. "That's kind of my point. If you hadn't noticed, Brae is special, brother. If you don't do something about it, you'll regret it."

Rhett wasn't sure how to respond. Bridger was a man he respected and considered to be wise beyond his years.

"I'll have to think that through some, but I appreciate your words," Rhett said.

Bridger pursed his lips. "That's all. Do you need a hand?"

"No thanks. I'm just about finished," Rhett replied.

Bridger turned to leave.

"Hey…thanks," Rhett called after him.

Bridger nodded then left. Rhett might as well have been finished because after Bridger's visit, there wasn't much he could concentrate on other than what his brother had said. After a few minutes of unfruitful work, he wiped his hands and put his tools away.

"Huh."

As with any group, people sort themselves out into different roles to which they are well suited. Shayde was the encourager, Cilla and Quill the helpers, Bridger the pragmatic, Kase the communicator, and Brae was the visionary. Rhett found himself in a role not necessarily by his choosing but rather by the need to keep everyone focused and moving the direction Jeshu intended. Rhett's military background had equipped him to lead people, and so he did...carefully and in submission to Jeshu's agenda. Bridger seemed to accept the role reversal with grace. As they traveled from city to city, Jeshu added to their numbers until there were twelve. In Zareth, Jeshu invited the ardent Jaym and the meticulous Salara. In Leeam, the financially astute Dahj joined, as did the brilliant-minded Mazon and the resourceful Lubin in Joppik. Each new sectator that Jeshu chose had unique abilities and a personality that balanced everyone else.

The impact of Jeshu's visits to the city rims was profound, and his popularity among the masses grew exponentially. After visiting the rim of a major city, Jeshu made it a point to visit the court of the Sovereign Sanctum as well, where crowds of thousands and tens of thousands gathered to hear him speak of Sovereign Ell Yon and to see the power of the Protectors. Never in the history of the Raylean people had a man wielded such power and moved the hearts of so many by words so profound. But with Jeshu's rise to fame, he also drew the attention of all officials and authorities everywhere, including those of the Morian Empire.

Jeshu and the twelve sectators were offered significant support from some of the wealthier Rayleans that had come to believe that Jeshu was indeed the Son of Ell Yon. Besides the offering of food and lodging by many in whatever city or region they visited, one extremely helpful contribution was a second shuttle for transportation by an anonymous person. Major Kamp played a role in facilitating the transfer to Jeshu and his followers. Now when they traveled, Rhett piloted the *Aviel,* and Brae piloted the newly acquired *Endeavor.*

Within a couple of weeks, there was heightened excitement and activity by many people no matter where they landed. Rhett, Brae, and the other ten sectators worked hard to organize, assist, and even protect Jeshu from the masses. With each city they visited, Rhett became more energized, more exhausted, and more stunned by what was happening. Although he often worked side-by-side with Brae, whatever growing friendship they'd had before this all started was eclipsed by the incredible mission of supporting Jeshu as he transformed Rayl and eventually the galaxy. Rhett missed having both meaningful and trivial conversations with Brae, but there simply wasn't time for such things...at least not now. The days were long and hard, demanding maximum effort from everyone.

In the Rea Rim, Jeshu and his sectators were overwhelmed by the needs of the people and, in this case, the darkness that seemed to linger there. Here, and as was becoming commonplace everywhere, the people who gathered to see and hear Jeshu fell into one of three categories... those that were in desperate need of healing and hope, those that were healthy but were simply curious about the one people began calling the Merchant of the oracles, and those that were looking for an opportunity to discredit or ridicule Jeshu, such as the Keepers and the Builders. It was now common to see at least three or four Keepers and Builders at every rim Jeshu and his sectators visited. In their long cloaks and pious demeanors, the Keepers and the Builders looked completely out of place in a rim.

As Jeshu's influence with the common people increased, the Keepers and the Builders' influence decreased. Prefect Terrok was of no help since he dared not touch Jeshu for fear of another uprising by more than just a few Partisans.

Therefore, the Keepers and the Builders, emboldened by their enhanced Protectors, plotted to diminish his rising influence by publicly demonstrating their superior power before it was too late.

Usually after a day of watching Jeshu heal the sick and deformed, the discouraging spirit of seeing such overwhelming destitution began to lift, but not so here. Throughout the day, Rhett had noticed a grim-looking fellow standing far off, his arms crossed. The figure set Rhett on alert, wondering if he might attempt something vicious toward Jeshu. Rhett also noticed that the people all gave the man a wide berth. Late in the afternoon, Rhett spoke to the father of a boy who was hopeful that Jeshu might restore his son's eyesight.

"Excuse me, sir, who is that man?" he asked.

The man glanced toward the grim figure in the distance then back at Rhett.

"That's Bane, but most just call him Beast." The man swallowed hard. "He's a terrifying thing. We've petitioned the Keepers and even the Raylean Guard to do something with him, but they refuse." The man looked toward Beast once again. "I think they're just as afraid of him as we are. Some say he is Lord Dracus in the flesh, sent to torment us. He even wears a Triad. Where he got it...nobody knows."

Rhett instantly felt justified in his apprehension, knowing that he would need to alert Jeshu to the danger. When Jeshu was taking a few minutes to drink water and eat something, Rhett went to him. Brae, Bridger, Cilla and Jaym were there also.

"Jeshu, you need to be aware of the man over there in the distance. They call him Beast."

"I wondered about him too," Brae added. "According to the people here, he has terrorized them for years."

Jeshu glanced toward the man then took another drink of water from his container. "Yes...he's one of the reasons we're here." He stood. "Come, let's go talk with him."

Before Rhett or any of the others could protest, Jeshu began walking directly toward the man. The Keepers and the Builders seemed very interested in this new development. Once it became evident what Jeshu's intention was, the clamor among the people fell to an eerie silence as they turned to watch. It was as if everyone knew that the forces of good and evil were about to collide. When Jeshu and his five sectators were within twenty feet, the man uncrossed his arms, revealing the glowing green orb of the Triad attached to his chest.

"Stay away, Son of the Immortal! I'll have nothing to do with you!" Beast's body seemed to swell as the Deitum-Prime-engorged muscles throughout his body expanded in powerful convulsions.

"But I have something to do with you," Jeshu said, stepping forward three more paces, his sectators cautiously following. But Beast would not have it. The man let out a bloodcurdling scream while unleashing a powerful broad burst of Torian energy from the pulsing Triad. Rhett put up his arm to shield his face, but the onslaught of energy collided painfully with his body, throwing him backward twenty feet. He hit the ground and tumbled another three feet before recovering to his knees. Brae and the other sectators had experienced the same assault. Rhett made an attempt to help Brae, but the agonizing energy stream was undiminished, pinning him in place. All he could do was look to see what had happened to Jeshu. There stood the Merchant fully immersed in the red storm of Torian power, his right leg behind for support, his chest forward, and both arms at his sides.

Was he paralyzed...overcome by Dracus's power? Rhett wondered. The moment lingered as the people looked on in great fear, cowering to the corners of buildings and behind debris. Then with his hands lowered at his sides and palms forward, Jeshu called upon the Protectors. It was not an explosion of power that would crush and perhaps kill Beast. Instead, Immortal blue flames began to slowly emanate from his hands, pushing back against the continuous Torian wave of red energy. Slowly, the front edge of the blue flames of power began to invade the space of the Triad's energy. Rhett instantly felt the release from the Triad's paralyzing force. Jeshu continued to push back against Beast and his

Triad until the colliding wavefront of energy began to collapse on him. The man's face became taut with fear, his eyes opening wide as the power of the Protectors surrounded him. With eyes filled with panic, Beast screamed again, but there was no release from the invasion of Jeshu's authority. The blue sphere of Sovereign Ell Yon's power crushed down on Beast until all at once, the Triad exploded outward from the man. Then it ended. He fell to the ground in a heap as Jeshu called back the force of the Protectors.

Ten thousand people looked on, stunned by what had just happened. No one on Rayl had ever seen such a thing...such power under such control. Even the Keepers and the Builders seemed dazed as they looked on with mouths hanging open. But the encounter with Beast was not over.

Jeshu walked toward the prone figure, but as he did, Beast tried to scoot away while still on his backside, his face filled with terror.

"Stay away from me, Son of Ell Yon...stay away!" Beast exclaimed in a deep, unholy voice.

By now Rhett, Brae, Bridger, Cilla, and Jaym had recovered and were at Jeshu's side. The other sectators were gathering close by as well. Beast continued to back up until he was stopped by a short retaining wall. Jeshu knelt down, holding his right palm out to the man.

"Be still," Jeshu said calmly as he reached for the man.

Rhett and Jaym cautiously knelt down on each side of Beast, ready to help if needed. Jeshu placed his left hand on the man's chest where the Triad had been then reached with his right hand past the man's right ear and around to the back of his neck. The Protectors began to glow with soothing ribbons of energy as Jeshu held tightly to the man's neck and chest. Beast's face contorted with pain, then all at once, everything terrifying about Beast disappeared. His deep lines of fear and fury gave way to peace. His arms and body fell quiet as Jeshu purged him from Deitum Prime and its horrible effects. The transformation was beyond remarkable. When Jeshu pulled back his right hand, he was holding a miniature tech implant that he'd removed from the man's cerebellum. He held it up between his forefinger and his thumb, anger lacing his eyes. He crushed the implant to dust.

"Give him some water," Jeshu ordered.

As he attempted to stand, the man reached out and clung to Jeshu's arm. "Don't leave me, Master. What if he comes back?"

Jeshu knelt back down, looking compassionately into his eyes. "Follow me, and you will never see such darkness again."

Bane's eyes filled with great tears. He nodded, too choked up to speak but still clinging to Jeshu's arm. Jeshu lifted him up then pulled him in closely, wrapping his arms around the man. Bane held on as if his life depended on Jeshu...and it did.

"Navi Jeshu," Salara interrupted. "The Keepers come."

Jeshu handed Bane over to Lubin and Mazon. "Take care of him. See that he gets food and water."

Four Keepers and two Builders walked through the crowds to get to Jeshu. The people cleared a path, knowing they were not to touch the garments of the Keepers and the Builders of Sovereign Ell Yon's Protectors. The Master Keeper wore a look of disdain as he stopped just a few feet away from Jeshu. He lifted his chin slightly before speaking.

"Who gives you the right to practice such treachery and such trickery among our people?" he demanded.

Rhett and Brae stood just to Jeshu's right, watching. The other sectators, along with the entire crowd of rim dwellers, were also gathered close by.

"For which treachery do you accuse me?" Jeshu asked bluntly. The Master Keeper struggled to reply.

"Take off those fake Protectors," the Keeper diverted. "You're not authorized, nor are those authentic. What you've done here is by the hand of Dracus."

Jeshu looked down at the Protectors fastened around his forearms. When his gaze returned to the Keepers, his eyes held an Immortal flame that clearly affected the Master Keeper and his entourage. Jeshu took a step toward them.

"How can Dracus fight Dracus?" Jeshu rebuked. His eyes turned fierce. "I am given all authority in this realm by my father in the Ruah. *You* have made a mockery of his name among the people, and the Protectors you claim to possess of Ell Yon are of your Master, C'fir Dracus!"

At Jeshu's rebuke, the Master Keeper's face flushed red with anger. He lifted his arm, pulling back the sleeve of his cloak to reveal a pulsing red lattice about the periphery of his Protector.

"Feel the power of Sovereign Ell Yon in his wrath for your blasphemy," the man shouted then clenched his fist. The enhanced Protector exploded forth a blast of energy that would have obliterated any mere mortal, but Jeshu was not such. He held up his right hand, and his Protector instantly engaged, spilling out a blue shield of energy that absorbed every joule of energy from the Keeper's Protector. Jeshu's face remained calm and undaunted by the Keeper's attack. He began walking toward the Keeper until the concussion of energy between the two Protectors was just inches away from their hands. The other Keepers and Builders backed away, leaving their master to deal with Jeshu alone. The Master Keeper tried all the harder to push back against Jeshu and his blue energy of judgment. Finally, when the heat of the colliding energies was too much to bear, the Keeper relented, and his beam of red energy dissipated. Jeshu's Protector instantly fell silent as well.

Jeshu was staring at the man eye to eye. He then turned to the people.

"Beware the lies of the Keepers, for their ways are not the ways of Ell Yon."

The Master Keeper scoffed to hide his shame and humiliation, but he was powerless in the presence of the Merchant. Jeshu looked over the shoulder of the Master Keeper and into the eyes of another Keeper and a Builder beside him then turned his back to return to the people.

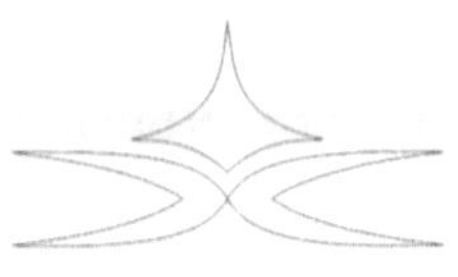

CHAPTER

13

The Light and the Dark

"I wish you had been at the Rea Rim with us, Codemus," Sephner said. "I've never seen anything like it—Rayl has never seen anything like it." The Keeper turned away, walking a few paces with his head down...thinking. "The power he wielded through the Protectors—"

"And you, Tazra...you saw this too?" Codemus asked the Builder.

Tazra's eyes lit up. "Yes. I wanted to ask him a hundred questions, but the Keepers we were with would have surely had us expelled from the orders." Tazra looked over at Sephner who spun about and came back to them.

"I'm telling you, Codemus, Sovereign Ell Yon is with him. The other Keepers said that what he did with the man at the Rea Rim was by the power of Dracus, but Jeshu put them in their place."

"'How can Dracus fight Dracus?' he asked them," Tazra added. "His rebuke of the Master Keeper at Rea was bold...daring."

"And truthful?" Codemus asked.

Tazra nodded. "Yes...truthful. And when Master Hodad tried to attack him with his enhanced Protector, Jeshu's Protectors pushed back against Hodad until he relented in humiliation." Tazra fell silent as she remembered the moment. "Then he looked right into my eyes," she said, nearly trembling. Her eyes transformed from excitement to worry. "He's making enemies in high places. If he is indeed the," She hesitated. None of them had dared speak such specific speculations until this very moment. "—the Merchant, why would he risk making such powerful enemies? How could he possibly win the world...the galaxy if he can't win over those in power?"

Codemus seemed lost in thought. "Maybe Sovereign Ell Yon's idea of saving the galaxy is different than ours."

That single statement revealed a possibility that they had never considered before. The three secret Keeper and Builder dissenters stood in silence for a moment.

"What was Preeminent Keeper Kylos's response to the incident at Rea?" Sephner asked.

"I'm sure you can imagine," Codemus said, shaking his head. "Anger, but I think he believes that Hodad failed because he wasn't strong enough to take on Navi Jeshu. Should the Navi and his followers come to Jalem, Kylos is planning his own confrontation. He still believes that Jeshu's false claims and power can be exposed and undone by an enhanced Protector wielded by a more powerful Keeper like himself. Should that day ever happen, I shudder to think of the outcome...either way!"

"Have you figured out a way to speak to him...the Navi?" Sephner asked.

"I'm close...I have a name."

Sephner and Tazra nodded. "Until next month then."

"Until next month," Codemus said, offering their secret sign.

It took Codemus two weeks of careful questioning and investigation before he had come upon a name...Major Edison Kamp, a Raylean Guard pilot. He secretly sought him out. The man seemed trustworthy, but in this game of secrecy, misplaced trust usually ended with blood. Could he truly trust the man?

Codemus sat across the table from Major Kamp at an eatery in a small village ten miles south of Jalem. This was not the time for uniforms. Both men wore the clothes of the average Jalem citizen, and they spoke in hushed tones.

"Hypothetically, let's say I could arrange for you to meet him. How do I know this isn't a ruse to capture and execute him?" Major Kamp asked.

Codemus nodded. "I can see why you might suspect that from a Keeper." He looked at Major Kamp, wondering how much he dared share. "Let me just say that my visit with him would not be in an official capacity. I would earnestly prefer the meeting happen late at night and in a discreet location."

Kamp eyed Codemus for a long time. "That still smacks of trickery...perhaps more so."

"Please, Major Kamp. There are things I must know, and the only way to know them is to speak directly to him. I don't know how I can convince you other than to swear before you and before Sovereign Ell Yon that my intentions are honorable, and I wish him no harm. If this man is more than just a fanatic making wild claims about his identity, we must not miss it!"

Kamp's eyes narrowed. "I can't promise anything, but I'll try. I'll contact you as soon as I hear something."

Codemus looked relieved. "Thank you, Major. That's all I ask."

Three weeks later, Major Kamp was flying a small shuttle with one passenger to a remote location near the edge of the rim at Kaan. The twilight sky with its retreating orange and yellow hues softened the dingy reality of an impoverished section of the city. Outside of a rundown cafe, Jeshu, Navi and Son of Sovereign Ell Yon, met with Codemus of the Jalem Keeper order. Brae, Rhett, and Bridger were nearby but far enough away to give the two men a sense of privacy. At first Codemus just stared at Jeshu, eager, excited, and afraid.

"Keeper Codemus," Jeshu said softly, "Major Kamp informs me that you sought me out a few weeks ago. What can I do for you?"

Codemus took a moment to gather his thoughts and form the right words.

"I know that you have come from Ell Yon, for no one can wield the power of the Protector as you do unless this is true. The things you have done and the words that you speak...we have not seen or heard before."

Jeshu looked at the man, discerning a truthful heart and purpose for his visit. "What is it that you want to ask me?"

Codemus looked Jeshu in the eyes. "Why are you here?"

Jeshu gazed back at Codemus...loving him. "I am the Merchant—I have come to purchase the souls of humanity."

Codemus swallowed hard. Wherever he fell with his belief, this night would change him forever. That singular statement by Jeshu shattered all speculation as to who others claimed he was. It forced Codemus to choose—to choose to believe Jeshu meant abandoning his role as a Keeper and suffering the very likelihood of being expelled and persecuted by his own. To choose not to believe Jeshu meant risking opposition to Sovereign Ell Yon and his own future existence.

"There are two births and two deaths," Jeshu continued. "Though the first death destroys the first birth through Deitum Prime, the second birth destroys the second death through me."

"How is this possible? What do you mean by a second birth and a second death?"

"How is it that you are a Keeper of the Protector for the people of Rayl and you don't understand these things? All who believe me and accept the gift of my sacrifice are given a second birth, and the second death cannot touch them. Without me, no one shall see the realm of Sovereign Ell Yon, for he loved humanity so much that he sent his one and only Son to save them from the second death. Whoever believes in me and follows me will not die but will live with me forever in the Ruah. In my blood is the cure for the consequences of Deitum Prime. You must understand that there is a war between the dark and the light. I am the light and will overcome the dark."

Codemus rubbed his forehead at hearing such things, struggling to absorb the deep words of Jeshu. "The things you speak are hard to hear."

"And yet?" Jeshu prompted.

Codemus's brows furrowed as he looked into Jeshu's eyes. "And yet, there is a truth in them that can't be denied." He glanced down at one of Jeshu's Protector. He reached to touch it, and Jeshu allowed it. As his fingers landed on the silky metal surface, micro arcs of blue flame danced across its surface. "Your Protectors are unchanged," he nearly whispered.

"Ell Yon doesn't change, Codemus. You know this to be true."

The furrows in Codemus's brow eased. He withdrew his hand, sitting straight. "Thank you for your time this evening, Navi Jeshu. I'll not forget it."

"Neither will I," Jeshu said with a smile.

After Major Kamp and Keeper Codemus left, Brae, Rhett, and Bridger were joined by three other sectators as they came to talk with Jeshu.

Brae looked over at Rhett and Bridger, wondering who would lead the conversation. She nodded toward Rhett, and he shot back a subtle smirk then mouthed the words, "Okay."

"Jeshu, everywhere we go, thousands...tens of thousands come to see you and hear," Rhett began.

"Yes?" Jeshu asked.

"Many of them never leave," Rhett said, pointing to a makeshift encampment a few hundred feet from their shuttles.

"And many want to follow you, Navi," Bridger added. "What are we to do with them?"

"That is the point of my presence here," Jeshu said with smile.

"But how, Jeshu?" Brae asked. "Every time we move to a new city, the number of people and shuttles that follow us increases. There must be 60 different shuttles and crafts out there. The ones that don't travel feel abandoned when we leave. How do we manage all of this?"

Jeshu seemed lost in thought.

"What do you suggest?" he finally asked.

Brae was a bit surprised, thinking that Jeshu had an answer for every dilemma.

"What do *we* suggest?" Brae replied.

"Yes, come up with a solution," Jeshu said, standing up. "Now, I'm very tired and need to rest for a few hours. Let me know what you come up with."

Brae, Rhett, Bridger, Kase, Jaym, and Shayde looked at each other, quite at a loss. Jaym stood with an enthusiasm that everyone else seemed to lack. "Well...let's find the others and come up with a plan."

Jaym disappeared to find the other sectators.

"Jaym the optimist," Shayde said with a grin.

Before long, the twelve sectators were deep into a hundred different ideas on how to manage Jeshu's increasing popularity and his enthusiastic followers. Three hours later when Jeshu returned, Rhett was chosen to present their idea, for it had originated with him.

"I can see by the looks on your faces that you have a proposal for our situation," Jeshu said with a yawn and a stretch. "I'm eager to hear it."

"What's happening with your growing popularity is unsustainable. I believe that what we need is a base of operations—a place for us to plan, equip, and launch each mission. For those that want to help and follow you, we would set up living quarters and even dining facilities to feed them. It can be a place where you can rest and commune in peace."

Jeshu thought for a moment. "Where would this base of operations be?"

"There's an abandoned Raylean Guard aerotech facility and spaceport 120 miles west of Jalem. I think it would make an excellent place to set up ops."

Jeshu nodded. "Very well. That will work. Find out who we need to get permission from to occupy the abandoned base and start making plans. We must visit Kaan, Leeam, and Reekojah before traveling to Jalem." Jeshu scanned the faces of his sectators. "Well done, everyone. By the way, Rhett, what's the name of the base?"

"Olea Station."

Jeshu seemed lost in thought for a moment. "I have plans for Olea Station."

Over the next few months, Brae worked with Rhett and Major Kamp to secure the permission they needed for Olea Station. They discovered that a wealthy landowner had purchased the abandoned facility many years ago. Once the man heard who it was that wanted to use it, approval happened quickly. Major Kamp discovered that the man had a wayward grandson that his family had lost to the underbelly of Joppik and who eventually landed in the rim there. Evidently the grandson found new life in a stranger that had visited the rim, and he came home completely changed. The words of this stranger, a Navi foretold by the ancient oracles, had saved the grandson's life.

The global impact Jeshu was having on Rayl was unprecedented. Yet the irony of it all was that he never visited any of the seats of power. In fact, he purposely avoided them. When asked about his political ambitions, his response was simple:

"I come for those without hope, for those imprisoned by Deitum Prime. I come for the sick, the hungry, the destitute, and the brokenhearted. My realm will not be found in the halls of government or in palaces high above the plains. I am from the realm of my father, and with me comes freedom and peace. The office I hold is far above that of any prefect."

The day came when Jeshu gathered his sectators together. "Prepare yourselves for we travel to Jalem."

When Brae heard this, she couldn't help but grow excited. Knowing the power of Jeshu, she was anticipating his accomplishing what her father could not. Others, including Rhett, seemed significantly less enthusiastic about their journey to Jalem.

"There's danger there, Navi," Rhett said. "The word is that Preeminent Fasa Kylos is extremely upset with your influence among the people, and he has the ear of Prefect Terrok and even Morian Subchancellor Pylok."

"Shall we withhold the hope of life from the citizens of the capital of Rayl?" Jeshu asked. "Danger or not, tomorrow we travel to Jalem. The rim there is the largest on the planet, and so the need is great."

"Yes, Navi," Rhett replied.

The moment they arrived in Jalem, people began to gather to Jeshu by the thousands. Because they hadn't yet officially occupied Olea Station and because it was a fair distance from Jalem, they landed at a private spaceport on the western edge of the city. But word had clearly reached the people before their arrival. There was no time to set up any reasonable venue, so Brae and the other sectators tried to organize what they could on the tarmac by the landing bay they had been assigned to. As Brae and Rhett did their best to organize the other sectators in the ensuing chaos, Jeshu stayed in the *Aviel*, communing, as he called it, with Ell Yon through the Protectors in preparation to meet the people. Brae stole a glance toward Rhett as they worked to set up a space for Jeshu to begin meeting the people. She knew he was concerned. *Was it for Jeshu or for her?* she wondered. He caught her looking at him.

"How are you doing, Starlore?" he asked.

"This is exciting, isn't it?" she responded.

"Exciting?" Rhett asked.

"Yes...exciting. Jeshu in Jalem, the people loving him, his influence growing every day." She was disappointed at his lack of reciprocated enthusiasm. "There's nothing to stop him!"

Rhett looked out at the waiting crowd. She followed his gaze, locating his concern. There had been Keepers at other cities, but here in Jalem, there did seem to be an added level of intensity in the solemn faces of a dozen Keepers, Builders, and Raylean Guards standing a short distance off to the side.

"There's everything to stop him," Rhett said.

Brae didn't respond. With Jeshu, it seemed to her that nothing could stop them, but she had to admit that Rhett was keen about seeing danger where she did not at times. About then, a throng of people pressed in on them. Just when it looked like they would lose control, Jeshu stepped out of the *Aviel* and came to them. Brae was amazed at how Jeshu had the capacity to not only to calm the masses, but also to genuinely care about every person he encountered. His concern and care seemed inexhaustible, although his physical strength waned at the end of a long day.

At the end of the third day at the spaceport, Jeshu insisted they relocate to the Jalem Sovereign Sanctum outer court, which Brae could tell made Rhett extremely uneasy. That evening, the sectators rested, insisting Jeshu eat and restore his energy as well. They were all gathered together between the two shuttles underneath a brilliant display of billions of stars. Brae noticed that Rhett had taken a place next to her. In all the recent wild activity, they rarely had a moment together. She missed that. She looked up at the night sky in wonder.

"You do love the stars, don't you?" Rhett asked quietly.

"Yes, I do. I hope that someday I can carry his message to them all," she said without looking his way. A few seconds later, she turned to him, catching a glow in his eyes that she'd rarely seen. Something about that look quickened her heart. He flashed a quick smile then diverted his eyes to Jeshu.

"Are you sure about going to the Sanctum tomorrow?" Rhett asked Jeshu. "I don't think the Keepers and Builders are going to roll out the red carpet for you."

"I have to agree with my brother," Bridger piped in. "We have a hard enough time helping and protecting you out here in the open."

There were a few nods of agreement from the other sectators. Jeshu thought for a moment before answering.

"My friends, the Merchant didn't come to be sheltered and protected. I'm here to heal the brokenhearted, deliver truth to all of humanity, and expose the lies of Dracus. There is no corner of the galaxy I won't go to in order to accomplish this, including my father's sanctum in Jalem."

Brae could tell that Rhett felt foolish for expressing his concern, but she understood. Being in Jeshu's presence was a perpetual lesson in humility and understanding. She watched Jeshu place a hand on Rhett's arm.

"Don't worry, Rhett...all will be well."

By the time they arrived the next morning, it was as if the entire city of Jalem had been stirred up into a frenzy. Brae remembered Rhett's concern when they arrived and now took it to heart. She could imagine what kind of discussions and precautions were taking place in the halls of Terrok's palace and even in the governing chambers of Morian Subchancellor Pylok. For the Keepers and Builders, there was little guessing as to what they felt was necessary. When they arrived, the people parted for Jeshu to enter the large and ornate outer courtyard of the sanctum. Preeminent Keeper Fasa Kylos stood guarding the entrance to the sanctum with his glowing enhanced Protector. Beside him stood three more Keepers from other city sanctums, each brandishing an identical enhanced Protector. Although the courtyard was packed with over five thousand people, they pressed into each other further so that an empty space of fifty feet was cleared between Jeshu and the Keepers. Kylos stepped forward.

"You shall not enter into this place of honor, for you have defiled yourself by associating with people fully immersed in Deitum Prime. The false Protectors you wear are not sanctioned by the established order of the Keepers as mandated by Sovereign Ell Yon himself."

Thousands looked on, wondering how the proclaimed Navi would respond to Kylos's accusations. Jeshu stood still, strong, tall.

"You condemn others for partaking in Deitum Prime, and yet you consume and enjoy its pleasures. Your hypocrisy is detestable in the eyes of Sovereign Ell Yon. I come to fulfill the command of my father in the Ruah."

Kylos glared at Jeshu, insulted that one as lowly as a rim dweller would address him with such arrogance and imply such great association with Sovereign Ell Yon.

"Do you then claim to be the coming Merchant of the ancient oracles?" Kylos shouted, laying before Jeshu an accusation that would fully reveal his preposterous claim.

"For thousands of years the Merchant's arrival has been foretold, but because your hearts are hardened by Deitum Prime, you are blind and ignorant. Think what you want, Kylos. I have no need to answer you."

Jeshu turned his back to Kylos, looking to speak directly to the people.

"You insolent rim dweller!" Kylos shouted while lifting his Protector toward Jeshu.

"Jeshu, watch out!" Brae shouted, but it was too late.

Kylos unleashed the fury of his Protector on Jeshu with a brilliant and powerful beam of enhanced red power. With the people packed in so close and nowhere to go, many were going to die no matter what Jeshu did, or so Brae thought.

Jeshu spun about quickly, the Protector on his right arm emanating an impenetrable blue wall of protection through the fingers of his spread hand. The collision of energy threatened to expand outward in a fatal cacophony of steady explosion. The people all gasped, falling over while trying to retreat from the white-hot searing energy collision. But before a single person was scorched, Jeshu engaged the second Protector on his left arm, containing the energy in a conical shield emanating outward from his hand. Kylos screamed in fury when he saw that his attack was not successful. The three other Keepers immediately engaged their enhanced Protectors, adding to the ferocious power of Kylos's Protector. Brae felt Rhett grab her arm to pull her away from certain death, but Jeshu stood firm. The resulting explosion seemed brighter than the sun, and the sound was deafening, like that of a star cruiser's roaring engine just a few feet away. For Brae, the encounter seemed to last forever even though she knew it had only been a few seconds. The crowd of people began screaming in panic. Broadcast specialists were trying to record the event, but the intensity of the moment seemed to threaten every life there, including those of the spectators. Yet the containing power of Jeshu's Protector held firm, shielding every single person from the reckless assault of the Keepers.

For five long seconds, Jeshu held firm, unshaken by the attack of four Keepers and their enhanced Protectors. Then he began moving toward the Keepers, one step at a time until he was just ten feet away. Jeshu began to close the fingers of his right hand, and as he did so, the red beams of energy from each Keeper's Protector began to fade until at last they were no more. But the blue flame of Jeshu's Protector was not done. Frozen in place and stunned by the power of Jeshu's Protectors, the Keepers gasped in fear as Jeshu's beam of energy engulfed each of their extended arms. Jeshu finished by forming a fist then opening his hand in one final burst of energy. The red technological mesh around each enhanced Protector instantly dissolved away to dust, and the confrontation was over.

Jeshu glared at Kylos with the eyes of an Immortal judge.

"Those who pervert the Protectors of Ell Yon will be judged. If you dare look behind the veil...if you dare look into the vaults of your Protectors, you will see me there looking back. Before you were, I was, and long after you are gone, I shall still be." Jeshu held his ground a few seconds longer. "I will be back, and I will speak to the people in the court of the sanctum, for this is the will of Ell Yon." He then turned and walked away.

Jeshu and his sectators exited the courtyard, allowing the people to recover from the intense exchange. As they went, Brae stepped up beside Rhett. "I see what you meant," she said, still shaken by what had happened.

Rhett looked over at her as they approached their transport speeders.

"I see what *you* meant," he replied. "Seems we were both right and both wrong at the same time."

Brae raised an eyebrow. "Agreed. See you back at the shuttles."

The encounter at the Jalem Sovereign Sanctum produced a variety of effects. After that day, none of the Keepers dared attack Jeshu or hinder his efforts again. However, Preeminent Keeper Fasa Kylos, Master Builder Krisha Monae, and all their subordinate associate Keepers and Builders began planning how they might destroy Jeshu.

CHAPTER

14

Olea Station

When Jeshu and the sectators left the Jalem sanctum and arrived back at their shuttles, Jeshu gathered the twelve of them around himself.

"Don't be frightened by what you saw. The things you have seen me do, you will do and even more so."

Rhett saw Brae's eyes open wide. She looked at Shayde and then back to him. He was just as stunned as she was by Jeshu's words.

"How's this possible?" Salara asked. "You're the Merchant—we're just your sectators."

"There's coming a day when the Protectors I wear, you will wear, and Ell Yon will be with you to the ends of the galaxy. Trillions of people must hear my message and learn my way. You will be my mouthpiece, and you will show them my way."

Rhett felt both thrill and fear at his statement. The Keepers and the Builders were powerful people. No one had dared stand against them until today.

"Tomorrow we'll return to the sanctum to talk to the people once again, but now it's time we see Olea Station. Come—Rhett...Brae...take us there."

Flight time from the private spaceport at Jalem to Olea Station was only 22 minutes. From a distance, Olea Station looked remarkable. It wasn't until they were within a quarter of a mile that the facility began to show the scars of its abandonment. They set the shuttles down near one of the larger hangars in a wash of dust and pebbles. After everyone had exited the shuttles, they gathered to look at their new base of operations.

"You said you have plans for this place...mind telling us what that means?" Kase asked.

Jeshu scanned the twenty or so buildings and the acres of concrete surrounding them.

"We train an entire generation of Navis, and we build a fleet."

Rhett couldn't help the grin that spread across his face, and by the look on Brae's face, she had noticed as well.

Over the next six months, the transformation of Olea Station from an abandoned aerotech facility to an operational base was remarkable. Skilled individuals from each of the tech orders came from all around the planet of Rayl, eager to join in the cause of the chosen one of Ell Yon. Financial support and resources arrived from some of the most unexpected people and organizations. Jeshu assigned different divisions of the operation at Olea Station to each of the sectators, encouraging and expecting each to manage them well. Rhett was given operations, Brae training, Shayde personnel, Bridger production, Kase interdivision communications, Cilla and Quill tech development, Dahj finances, Jaym fabrication and manufacturing, Mazon and Salara data systems integration, and Lubin acquisitions. But Jeshu made sure that each sectator and their support personnel understood that the single greatest priority regardless of any project development was the care and well-being of every single person they encountered, whether at Olea Station or in a city rim on the other side of the planet.

On one sunny morning, Rhett was on his way to see Dahj. Jaym had let him know that the manufacturing team needed several large graphic displays, and as sectator in charge of operations, Rhett had spoken to their contact in the city but needed to run the numbers past Dahj for financial approval. As Rhett was transiting one of the interconnecting walkways from his complex to finance, he glanced down to his left to see that Brae was conducting a basic defensive training course for some of the new arrivals. Her leg was now fully healed, and he was glad for it.

Rhett paused to watch as she patiently demonstrated the proper stance for one of the maneuvers. Although the hectic activity of developing Olea Station had precluded them from spending much time together over the last few months, something was changing between them.

Brae turned, her face catching the morning rays of the sun in just the perfect way. Rhett was struck by her beauty and poise—and not for the first time. What had once been easy to dismiss now captivated him. He felt an undeniable attraction to her in a way that certainly transcended their original friendship agreement. This surprised him since Rhett was a guarded man, and the lingering pain of losing the woman he'd loved to another wasn't something he wanted to experience twice. When he overheard the hasty words Brae had spoken to Shayde regarding him, he hated how much it hurt—evidence that he was losing the battle for control of his heart. These growing feelings for Brae concerned Rhett in another way. A deeper relationship between the two of them would most certainly bring distractions that could prove to be a liability not only for him but for Brae as well.

Brae glanced upward to see Rhett, and her face instantly lit up. She waved as he smiled and waved back. Oddly, in a feeble attempt to quench his growing feelings for her, he tried to remember Brae as the annoying, arrogant woman he thought her once to be, but couldn't. Her injury and the loss of her father had crushed her pride and her spirit to such a degree that Rhett couldn't help feeling sorry for her...at least at first. After that, however, her newfound humility and gentle words began to capture Rhett's heart over time, even though he fought against it. The first time he held her, something deep inside him shifted, and the eventuality of losing his heart to her had been set in motion. A part of him was hoping Brae would become difficult and bitter toward him once again after she had healed, for he knew that love had the power to make the bravest of men vulnerable in the strangest of ways. But that was not the case, and every time she touched his arm or smiled at him, he fell a little further. Today was no exception—his gaze lingered, and his heart quickened…falling a little further.

Rhett turned to press on, annoyed with himself.

"Come on, Stryker," he mumbled as he fixated on the glass he was holding, trying to make the figures mean something again. "Get your head straight. You have too much to do to be distracted now."

He took a deep breath, pushing down the feelings he didn't want to deal with yet as he arrived at the door to Dahj's office. A final thought landed on his mind.

Does she have any feelings like this for me? he wondered. *Probably not*, he concluded.

Brae and the other sectators followed Jeshu as he continued to visit cities and regions throughout the planet, and all the while Olea Station grew and developed. And although the Keepers and the Builders seemed to have been subdued for a time, Brae understood that their political power was still very much a threat to the missions Jeshu had in store for them. She knew they were watching from a distance and perhaps even had spies within their ranks at Olea Station. When this possibility was brought to Jeshu's attention, he was quite dismissive.

"We have nothing to hide here at Olea Station," he'd replied. "All are welcome, even our enemies."

Of the twelve sectators, that philosophy was most difficult for Brae, Rhett, and Bridger to submit to. But watching Jeshu lead the most irregular and odd assortment of people from every walk of life was simply astonishing, so they kept any further reservations they had to themselves.

Brae was also concerned over the ever-present and watchful eyes of the Morian Empire. Much to her surprise, they had not interfered with the development of Olea

Station, although they were never far away. At least once a week on random days and at random times, Morian patrol ships would appear out of nowhere to conduct inspections of the entire facility. Their search for class-two weapons or greater and any tech relating to such always came up empty-handed. In fact, this was the very reason Brae began to struggle with the purpose of it all.

One day early in the evening when she had a few minutes after her last training session, Brae went to check on the progress with the rebuilding of Rivet. Although the intense pace and requirements of the development of Olea Station had slowed her efforts, the combined technical prowess of Cilla, Quill, and herself had resulted in a nearly perfect replication of the ancient bot that Brae had come to love and trust.

She entered the small lab that was devoted to Rivet's rebuilding. Along the walls were benches and shelves filled with bot tech, computational workstations, and bins of mechanical hardware. Currently, no one was present except for the perfectly still form of her mechanical childhood hero at the far end of the lab. A dozen interface cables were connected to his circuitry through the access panel in his back and through the base of his cranial port. Behind him, multiple displays depicted diagnostics reports and a constant stream of data indicating Rivet's status. To Brae, it looked as if Rivet should open his eyes, stand up, and ask if he could be of assistance, but that didn't happen. Every attempt that she, Cilla, and Quill had made to power up his cognitive core system had failed. She walked over to the bot and placed a gentle hand on his shoulder.

"Oh, Rivet...it hurts to see you so whole and yet so absent. Did I destroy you forever?"

Brae felt the emotional tug on her heart as she remembered all the gallant stories her dad had told her about Rivet. The android seemed to always know more than he should have, as if he were privy to the deep knowledge of Ell Yon—mysterious, brilliant, loyal, and intimidating.

"He still won't talk to you?" a voice said from the doorway, jolting Brae out of her moment of reflection. She looked that way. Rhett was leaning against the doorpost with his arms crossed.

"Hey, Stryker. I didn't expect you."

It had been a while since Brae last talked with Rhett, and she missed him. For some reason, his confident pose and gentle smile caused her heart to flutter.

Rhett hesitated then uncrossed his arms and came to her. She turned back to Rivet.

"I really thought we could put him back together," she said, not hiding her disappointment.

"It sure looks like you have. What's the problem?"

"Cilla, Quill, and I were able to either repair or replicate nearly every component. We had to rely on a lot of our current tech for the mobility processing and actuator controls, but the core processing unit and memory modules had to be original or it wouldn't be him." Brae frowned. "They were damaged some, but I thought we could recover them. Building the interface circuitry was extremely difficult...maybe we got it wrong."

"Or maybe the processing unit and memory modules were too damaged to be functional?" Rhett asked.

Brae turned and looked at him with sorrow in her heart. "Yeah. It's hard to be so close...to have him look so perfect and yet—" Brae said, looking back at Rivet. Her head lowered in defeat. "I think I should have never tried."

Rhett came close to her. "Don't say that. I know he was special to you and your dad. He deserved a chance, and I think you needed to try." He placed a gentle hand on her shoulder.

Brae looked up at him. *When did he become so kind?* she wondered. It was difficult to deny the growing feelings she'd been having for Rhett. *Does he have such feelings for me?* she wondered. *Probably not*, she concluded.

Brae couldn't help herself. She leaned into him, resting her head on his shoulder. He gently wrapped his arm a little further around her shoulders. In his embrace she felt such peace...such contentment.

"You always know what to say to encourage me...and you're always there when I need a hug, even if you don't like it."

Rhett huffed. "I didn't say I didn't like it."

In that one sentence, something changed between them. Comfort shifted to affection, and peace transformed into preference. Brae felt her heart flutter as she wrapped an arm around him. This was the moment she had dreaded and longed for. No matter how hard she tried to deny the rising feelings she was having about Rhett, they came anyway and despite their minimal time spent together. Lately, it was becoming impossible to suppress those powerful feelings, both to herself and to Shayde. They were becoming difficult to bear, and if she were completely honest with herself, they scared her. She had never had romantic feelings about any man before. For Brae, this was uncharted territory, and she wasn't sure how to respond.

They held each other for a few more seconds, then she leaned her head back, daring to look into his eyes. She allowed her affection for Rhett to spill out through her smile and the gaze of her eyes. It was new, slightly awkward, and wonderful. He reached with his hand to push a few strands of hair from the corner of her eye, brushing them back behind her ear.

"No matter how hard I try, I just can't help liking you more and more," Rhett said. "I hope you're okay with that."

Hearing Rhett confess his feelings for her was like tasting some new exotic fruit. She had no idea how delicious such a thing could be.

"I am...more than you realize," Brae replied. "I just hope you'll be patient with me. I've never felt like this about anyone before. Can we go slow?"

Rhett's eyes warmed with a gentle smile forming on his lips. "The longer we take, the more memories we'll have."

"Thanks."

"I'm truly sorry about Rivet. I remember that a walk always used to cheer you up. Shall we?" Rhett said, motioning to the door with his head.

Brae smiled and nodded. "I'd love to. I think I need it."

They released each other and walked toward the door. As soon as they exited the building and began making their way toward the border of the complex, Brae felt her discouragement about Rivet lighten. She took a deep breath.

"This helps...thanks."

Rhett nodded. "I have to ask you something. Do you think that anything here is...off?"

Brae looked over at him, not sure what he might be alluding to. "You mean here, as in Olea Station?"

Rhett nodded.

"Perhaps. What are you thinking?"

Rhett pursed his lips. "It just feels like something is missing."

Many acres of forested land surrounded the complex. One place at the northern edge of the station was Brae's favorite place to walk and think since it reminded her of her life as a child. She had instinctively begun walking in that direction.

Brae sighed. "I'm so glad you said something. I thought I was the only one."

"It feels like we're gearing up a high-tech manufacturing facility with nothing to build." Rhett added, running his hand through his hair.

"Or that we're training a generation of Navis that are never supposed to fight anyone," Brae added.

"Exactly!" Rhett exclaimed in frustration. "When we first arrived, Jeshu talked about building a fleet...was that a metaphor for something we don't understand?"

Brae stuck her hands in her pockets, and shrugged her shoulders, unable to answer his question. They walked in silence for a few minutes, entering the edge of the forest where the trees and mossy undergrowth soothed the borders of a sea of white concrete that surrounded Olea Station.

"The work we're doing out in the rest of the world is still significant," Brae finally said, looking over at Rhett.

He nodded. "No doubt. Olea Station is supposed to be more though, don't you think?"

"It sure seems like it. I think we should talk to him and straight up ask," Brae said.

"Agreed. It's just nice to know I'm not the only one thinking this."

Rhett turned to face Brae. "We haven't been able to see each other much these past couple of months."

"I know...I've missed you," she said with a quick smile.

"I've missed you too," Rhett replied. "I think I was avoiding you because I wasn't sure about us...does that make sense?"

Brae nearly laughed out loud. "Completely."

"Well, Starlore...if you don't mind, I'd like to rectify that and see you more often."

"I'd like that," Brae said.

Rhett looked pleased.

"On one condition," Brae added, lifting a finger in the air.

Rhett raised an eyebrow. "Our walks and conversations have a condition?"

"Mm-hmm. You have to start calling me Brae."

Rhett gazed into her eyes. "I think I can handle that."

They turned back toward the complex to find Jeshu, and as they did, Rhett reached for Brae's hand, and she took it, palm to palm. Brae marveled at how natural it felt to hold his hand.

"Do you think our friendship can handle this?" she asked, glancing over at him out of the corner of her eye.

"This is the best kind of friendship there is," he said with a grin.

The last vestiges of their tumultuous beginning finally faded completely away as she leaned into him...happy. She was dreading telling Shayde that she had been right about the two of them all along.

When they were nearly back to the complex, Brae realized something. She turned to face Rhett.

"Hey, just so we're clear...we're both training to be Navi, and you can't jeopardize yourself or anyone else on my behalf. No extra protection, okay?"

Rhett offered a crooked grin. "You're a little late with that. I was obligated to protect you even when I *didn't* like you," he said with a wink. "But that goes both ways you know."

Brae hadn't thought of that, but he was right. *That's what love does,* she thought...*sacrifice.*

When Brae and Rhett located Jeshu, all the other sectators were already with him.

"Ah...good. Now that we are all together, I want to show you something," Jeshu said, as he led his sectators to a lab in the research facility that Cilla, Quill, and Mazon had been working on for the past two months.

"I've been waiting for this research and design lab to be completed," Jeshu began. "Well done, Cilla, Quill, and Mazon."

The other nine sectators whistled and cheered with mild applause, congratulating their accomplishment...and what an accomplishment it was. Two of the four walls were massive displays with motion-controlled human interfaces. Half a dozen design stations with holographic 3D displays were positioned in a semi-circle around a larger central interactive holographic display hub. Two sides of the lab were glass view ports that looked out onto the surrounding forest. Brae marveled at the technological beauty of the lab. After scanning every detail of the exquisite lab, her eyes fell on Jeshu. He was looking back at her.

"You've all done an excellent job with the responsibilities I've given you. And I know that you're all wondering—why?"

Brae looked over at Rhett. He glanced back at her, a knowing look in his eyes. Jeshu walked to the center holographic design table, tapped on the edge of a panel to activate the display, then manipulated various icons floating in the space before him until all at once, a space fighter craft appeared in perfectly rendered detail. It was a sleek dual-cockpit fighter with broad canards, forward swept wings, and dual vertical stabilizers. Two large engines with a slipstream jump drive gave the impression that this craft was fast and advanced. Brae couldn't help getting excited about what this meant. She exchanged wide grins with Rhett.

Rhett stepped up close to the holographic display. "Now this is something to get excited about," he said with a gleam in his eye.

"I thought you might like this, Rhett," Jeshu said with a grin on his own face. "It's called the Spacehawk. I've been working on this ever since we arrived at Olea Station."

"It looks fast yet has minimal weapons," Rhett continued as he intently analyzed the design.

"Keen observation," Jeshu said, rotating the display so they could see all sides. "This craft isn't designed to destroy things. It's designed to get you across the galaxy… undetected if necessary."

The rest of the sectators joined Rhett in a closer evaluation as Jeshu turned the craft about, zooming in to some of the features. Brae recognized some identifying tech like three anti-grav pods and a cloaking transmitter, but other features were completely foreign to her. Brae was once again amazed not only at Jeshu's intellect, but also at his creative ability.

"It's remarkable," Brae said. "Do we get to build it?"

Jeshu left the Spacehawk holographic slowly spinning as he turned to face Brae and the rest of the sectators. "Yes."

"So this is the fleet you were talking about," Rhett said. "Does it have any weapons at all?"

"No…only defensive systems," Jeshu replied. Rhett's countenance fell.

"None?" Bridger asked.

"Sectators, I'm not here to teach you how to conquer other worlds," Jeshu scolded. "I'm here to teach you how to love and care for them. I thought you would understand that by what you've seen me doing these past months."

"But the training," Brae protested. "I'm training people to learn the ways of the Navi…hand-to-hand…weapons combat."

"And this!" Rhett exclaimed holding out his hands to the powerful form of the Spacehawk. "Surely this is designed for combat."

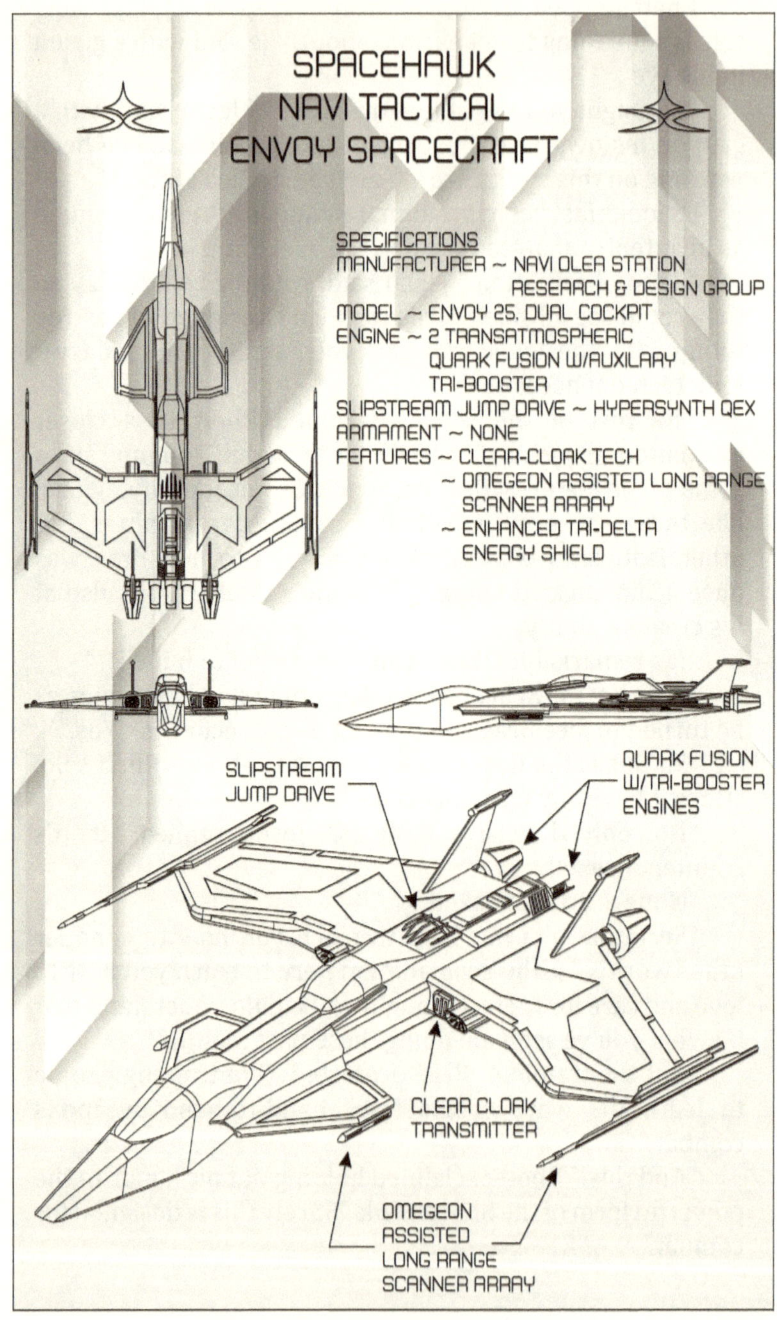
SPACEHAWK
NAVI TACTICAL
ENVOY SPACECRAFT

SPECIFICATIONS
MANUFACTURER ~ NAVI OLEA STATION
RESEARCH & DESIGN GROUP
MODEL ~ ENVOY 25, DUAL COCKPIT
ENGINE ~ 2 TRANSATMOSPHERIC
QUARK FUSION W/AUXILARY
TRI-BOOSTER
SLIPSTREAM JUMP DRIVE ~ HYPERSYNTH QEX
ARMAMENT ~ NONE
FEATURES ~ CLEAR-CLOAK TECH
~ OMEGEON ASSISTED LONG RANGE
SCANNER ARRAY
~ ENHANCED TRI-DELTA
ENERGY SHIELD

SLIPSTREAM
JUMP DRIVE

QUARK FUSION
W/TRI-BOOSTER
ENGINES

CLEAR CLOAK
TRANSMITTER

OMEGEON
ASSISTED
LONG RANGE
SCANNER ARRAY

Jeshu hesitated, appearing slightly frustrated as if he were trying to explain a simple concept to children who could not comprehend it.

"It is, but not in the way you're thinking," Jeshu answered. "What I need to teach you...to show you...you're not yet ready for. You must trust me and have enough faith in me to follow my lead. Can you do that?" Jeshu looked longest at Rhett and Brae.

Brae turned her eyes back to the Spacehawk. "If I get to help build this, I'm in for anything," she said with a smile.

"Please tell me I get to fly this one day," Rhett said with a crooked grin.

Jeshu laughed, putting a hand on Rhett's shoulder. "You will all fly this one day."

"But Jeshu...what about those of us that aren't pilots?" Salara asked.

"You will be. Some of you for combat and some of you for transport. Others of you will be Advanced Marines for ground assault. Others will be advisors and weapon support."

Rhett scratched his head. "Combat but with no weapons...I'm sorry, Jeshu, but you aren't making any sense to me at all. Are we warriors or are we peacemakers?"

"You are both."

Brae could see Jaym's mind turning as he considered all the fabrication and manufacturing processes necessary to pull off a project of this scope.

He gave a low whistle. "This is going to take some time."

"Yes, but don't get ahead of yourself, Jaym. Before we build the Spacehawk, we will build its simulator."

Jeshu manipulated the hovering icons to make the Spacehawk disappear. It was immediately replaced by a sophisticated simulator cockpit with pages of technical specifications.

"This may not look as exciting, but it is absolutely necessary and a prerequisite. You will understand the Spacehawk's systems and capabilities once you build these simulators and train in them. I showed you the Spacehawk first so that you would see the purpose for the simulators."

"Brae, Cilla, Quill, Salara, and Mazon will be our primary design team. Work closely with Jaym and Bridger since they will be fabricating and manufacturing both the simulators and eventually the Spacehawks. Shayde, I need you to identify qualified personnel for each phase of the project. Dahj and Lubin, as directors of finance and acquisitions, you will have your hands full ensuring each division has what they need to proceed with the designs. Kase, communication between divisions must be timely and efficient. Rhett, as the different phases of the designs are complete, I want you to thoroughly test and evaluate each system."

Jeshu spent the next two hours outlining tasks and timelines for the simulator and Spacehawk fighter design projects. Despite Jeshu's words about not conquering other worlds, Brae couldn't help the thought she had about casting off the yoke of servitude the Morian Empire had placed on her people. And the Morians weren't their only enemies. *Surely a fleet of Spacehawks would initiate a new order of power and freedom for the Raylean homeworld, especially if it was led by the Son of Sovereign Ell Yon and his Protectors, wouldn't it?* Brae wondered...hoped.

When most of the questions had been answered and the initial plans had been laid out, Jeshu dismissed everyone. The Spacehawk project would begin tomorrow, and all the sectators had a lot to think about and plan for. Rhett looked toward Brae, and she smiled. Things between them were already different. As everyone exited the design lab, they found each other and walked out of the facility and on toward their quarters together.

"I guess we have our answer," Brae said.

"Yes, and I'm excited."

Brae laughed. "Nobody could tell," she teased.

"Sure...sure. Don't deny it—you were just as excited as I was," Rhett countered.

"I won't deny it. What a gorgeous fighter," Brae said.

"Is it a fighter?" Rhett asked. "No weapons."

"Right...Jeshu isn't telling us everything yet," Brae agreed. "Some things don't add up, but building and learning to fly the Spacehawk helps a lot."

"No doubt. Did you look at the simulator specs that popped up?" Rhett asked.

"Not really. Why?"

Rhett hesitated, not sure if he should divulge his speculations just yet.

"Come on, you tease," Brae said, leaning into him while nudging him with her shoulder.

Rhett shook his head. "This is why I didn't want you to touch me before," he said with a pleasant smirk. "You pretty much disarm me."

Brae smiled. "Oh."

Rhett stopped walking and turned to face Brae. He glanced around them to see if anyone was within listening distance. "That Spacehawk may not have any weapons on it, but the simulator for it is loaded with them...weapons I've never seen before."

Brae's smile faded. "Are you sure?"

Rhett recalled the quick glance he got at the specs. "Yes. Ever heard of a laser-guided arc disrupter? Or a phase-enhanced ion burst cannon? It doesn't make sense, Brae. And Jeshu didn't talk about it, so I didn't ask."

Brae seemed lost in thought, looking off into the distance. Rhett just watched, allowing himself to enjoy the subtle and captivating nuances of her face that he hadn't dared to appreciate before. She glanced up at him, catching his admiring gaze. She looked pleased.

"Well, I'm sure we'll find out soon. It's impossible to build a weapon system and not know it's a weapon," she said, looking into his eyes.

"Sure enough. I guess this is where trust comes in...something I'm still working on," Rhett admitted.

They resumed their walk toward their quarters. When they arrived at Brae's entrance, Rhett felt an awkward goodbye coming, not knowing what to expect or to offer. She turned to face him.

"Hey," Brae said, reaching for his hand. "I just want you to know that I'm glad we're here at this place with each other. I really like you, Rhett. And with us being sectators for Jeshu, I think we have some pretty intense days ahead. I'm just glad I get to experience them with you."

"And I with you, Brae Starlore," he said with a smile.

Rhett reached for her, and they embraced for a couple of seconds, then Brae kissed his cheek.

"See you tomorrow, Stryker," she said, as she turned away and tapped the code to enter her quarters.

"I thought we were doing first names now," Rhett called out.

"You agreed to that...not me," she said with a sly grin then disappeared into her quarters.

Rhett laughed. Brae always surprised him in some way, and he loved it. He was already looking forward to the next time they could be together.

Over the course of the next five months, Olea Station continued to be a base of operations for Jeshu's missions to the cities of the planet. Development of the Spacehawk project also commenced and was making excellent progress. Four Spacehawk simulators were being built simultaneously, along with the fabrication and manufacturing of the actual craft. Jeshu never called them fighters. He dubbed an entirely new category for the Spacehawk, called a tactical envoy spacecraft. Rhett's first go at one of the simulators was thrilling. The only operational systems so far were avionics, flight control, and navigation, but he could tell multiple systems were on the cusp of development.

After exiting his first simulator flight, Mazon and Salara met him in the design lab to debrief the flight.

"What did you think?" Salara asked enthusiastically.

"Incredible," Rhett replied. "As realistic as I've ever seen for a simulator. Great job on the programming."

"That's not us," Mazon said. "Salara and I integrate all hardware for the sim, but the software is all Jeshu."

"No kidding?" Rhett asked. He didn't remember teaching any programming to Jeshu when he was in his development ages. "Well, it's flawless, and it seems to me there's a lot more coming."

Mazon and Salara looked sideways at each other.

"You two know something, don't you?" Rhett pressed.

"A little, but not enough to say much. Jeshu only gives us what we need in time for the next stage of development," Mazon said. "I don't think there will ever be an end to what he can teach us or for what he has in store for us."

"I've learned that any mystery about him is for our own good," Salara added.

Rhett thought about Salara's words and realized that she was right. It helped him to be patient and to trust. "Good reminder. Thanks."

After the debrief, Rhett stood up to exit.

"Just a heads up, Rhett," Mazon said. "Something's happening tomorrow, and whatever it is may give you some of the answers you're looking for."

Rhett wasn't sure how he felt about that. As a pilot for the Raylean Guard, he was trained to be prepared ahead of time. Not knowing critical information was more than frustrating for him. But it seemed to be Jeshu's way, and Rhett realized he would need to get used to it.

Rhett nodded. "Very well...tomorrow then."

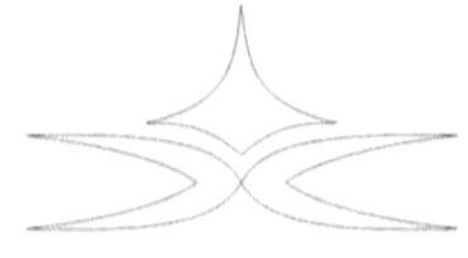

CHAPTER

15

Children among Gods

In the realm of the Ruah, Kalem was saturated with situation reports relaying the status of critical fleet missions throughout the galaxy. As the First Admiral of Ell Yon's Aurora Galactic Fleet, the responsibility of strategic positioning of resources and orchestration of mission directives weighed heavily upon Kalem's shoulders. But once the Commander of Ell Yon's Malakian Forces, the Son of the sovereign himself, had translated into fully human form and began the mission of reclamation, those weighty responsibilities increased ten-fold. Kalem doubted that he would ever fully understand the "why" of such a dramatic and dangerous move by Sovereign Ell Yon and his son, but that was irrelevant now. Jeshu was on planet Rayl, exposed and vulnerable to the onslaught of Dracus's dark forces.

Because of the potential galactic impact on both realms, the war between the Malakians and the Torians had escalated to an entirely new level, with Rayl at its epicenter. Admiral Kalem would not delegate such critical protection of the planet to any fleet other than his own during such a desperate time. From the command deck of his star cruiser, *Advent*, he watched and coordinated the entire war while also keeping a massive ground force contingent engaged with Dracus's Scourge on the planet's surface. Kalem made sure that at least one of the other four fleets was always on alert should Dracus launch an unexpected offensive beyond their normal operations. Kalem quietly admitted that he was most at peace when Admiral Galec's fleet was on alert. Despite their tumultuous beginnings, the rebellion that their mutual friend, C'fir Apollus Dracus, had led against Ell Yon had forged a friendship between Kalem and Galec that would last through eternity.

Kalem retreated to his bridge quarters to contemplate a recent secure dispatch from Tsiyyon—the message disturbed him. After finding no solace in his own reflection, he initiated a secure hyperlight communication link with Admiral Galec. Thirty seconds later, Galec appeared on his display.

"Yes, Admiral. What can I do for you?" Galec asked, apparently expecting fresh orders.

Kalem hesitated. As the leader of millions, he didn't have the luxury of many friends. Galec was one of three, and of the three, his best.

Galec's eyes narrowed. "What is it, Kalem? I'm alone."

"Galec, I just received a directive from Tsiyyon to support the Commander in a way that has never been done before."

Galec frowned. "Why is this a problem? We would do anything to protect him—you above all."

Kalem shook his head. "Of course, but this is different. Take a look," he said, transmitting the Tsiyyon directive to Galec via their secure link.

Kalem gave Galec a couple of minutes to read through the directive. When finished, the admiral looked up with confusion and concern in his eyes.

"This is...extremely unusual. I didn't know the Protector could even do such a thing. I don't understand." Galec said

"Nor do I, my friend. I'm not sure why I even called you other than to see if you saw some logic in this directive that

I don't see," Kalem said. "It is going to require resources that are already stretched thin and expose the Commander to even greater risk."

Galec stroked his chin, thinking. A moment of silence passed as Kalem allowed Galec to reflect. Finally, the admiral pursed his lips. "I don't know what counsel to offer, Kalem. We both know that Dracus seems to be winning throughout the galaxy. But there on Rayl, with the Commander taking on the form of a human—we just have to trust that he has a greater plan in regard to his human followers than we can see right now."

"I'm going to the surface myself to brief Colonel Ruger. He's going to be even more confused and concerned than we are."

Kalem could tell that Galec didn't approve of his decision to deliver the directive to Ruger on the front line in person.

"Be careful, Kalem," Galec said.

Kalem offered a quick nod then ended the transmission. Thirty minutes later, Kalem was on a transport with an escort of six ground warriors. They set down three miles south of the current line of conflict near the abandoned base that Jeshu had chosen for his training. Ground Assault Force Commander Colonel Ruger was there to meet him. In the not-so-far distance, the sound of fierce battle was evident. A steady burst of plasma fire reverberated through the air followed quickly by three concussion rounds.

"How goes the fight, Colonel?" Kalem said after a quick exchange of salutes.

"It's brutal, sir," Ruger replied, nodding toward a bunker that he had set up as his tactical headquarters.

Inside, the sounds of battle were muffled but still very evident.

"Why the visit, Admiral? If the Scourge knew you were here, I'm not sure what they would do to get to you." Kalem could see annoyance in the Colonel's eyes for the extra burden his visit brought.

Kalem shot Ruger a harsh look, and the Colonel immediately responded.

"Forgive me, sir," Ruger said, dropping his gaze briefly. "This fight is fierce. I've never seen the Scourge fight with such tenacity. Clearly, they understand what the Commander's presence here on Rayl means."

"I'm here, Colonel Ruger, because we just received a new directive from Tsiyyon, and it's going to affect your ground operations significantly in the coming years."

"Years?" Ruger said, his eyebrows furrowing to indicate his alarm.

Kalem tapped a sequence on his arm control then flipped the directive onto the nearest display for Ruger to read. As the colonel took a minute to digest the directive, Kalem walked toward the large tactical 3D holographic display in the center of the command center. Three Malakian strategists were around its periphery issuing status and intelligence reports to warriors and their field commanders in real time. One of the strategists looked as if he were about to cease his operations to address the admiral, but Kalem shook his head, not wanting to distract from what looked like a dire situation for a squad of twelve Malakian warriors in a fierce engagement. Kalem returned to Colonel Ruger to find a man wrestling with the extra burden of responsibility that had just been given him. He turned to face Kalem.

"Sir, I know the Commander is training a new era of Navis, but how could any human have any significant role in our battle here?" Ruger said, his countenance laced with concern and skepticism. "You've seen what we're facing. This will only burden our warriors and resources more than they are already...and for what gain?"

Kalem knew better than anyone that solidarity among military leadership was paramount to success. Therefore, though Kalem might inwardly agree, he dared not show even the slightest hint of empathy for the colonel because of the new challenges he would face.

"Develop a plan on how you're going to implement this new directive and transmit your strategy to me by morning. I'll do what I can to direct additional resources your way. Are we clear, Colonel?"

Colonel Ruger stood straight and saluted. "Aye, Admiral."

Kalem returned the salute and turned back to the holographic display. "Take me here, Colonel Ruger. I want to visit with our warriors there. They'll be the first ones impacted, and I want them ready."

"But, sir, that's extremely close to some of our most fierce fighting. I—"

"This isn't a request, Colonel," Kalem said with narrow eyes.

"Aye, sir."

Within a few minutes, Admiral Kalem, Colonel Ruger, and a dozen heavily armed warriors were making their way to the front line in the battle for Rayl.

Jeshu led his sectators to an abandoned building on the eastern side of Olea Station. This building had been deemed too difficult to recover when they took possession of the station. A section of the roof had collapsed, so they had condemned the building and forbidden everyone from entering. Brae could tell by the look on the faces of the others that they were as confused by this excursion as she was.

Inside, they stepped across fallen beams and a mess of debris as they navigated through one of the larger open areas, finally arriving at a dusty chamber, the air musty and old. Jeshu stopped, turned, and looked at the twelve of them. A sliver of sun was streaking in from a lofty window, illuminating the floating dust particles that had been stirred by their entrance. The haze within the room seemed to accentuate the serious demeanor of their leader.

"You've heard me say that the Morians are not our enemy, Terrok is not our enemy, nor is anyone that takes up arms against you, yet I train you for battle. You must understand that your fight is greater than anything you will experience here in this realm. Your fight is against the evil of dark empires beyond this dimension," he said, lifting his hands outward and motioning to the world around them. "Most of humanity has no idea that galactic wars are being fought for the sake of their futures." Jeshu lowered his hands, gazing with eyes of fire at each of their solemn faces. "I'll not be with you forever, and you must carry on in this worthy fight...a battle against the evil empire of Dracus and the Scourge."

Brae realized that she was barely breathing. Jeshu's words were heavy, but what did he really mean, and why bring them here to this forgotten chamber?

"Through the Protector, you've seen me commune with Sovereign Ell Yon. I am going to teach you to do the same, for in communing with him, there is power. You will need his power to survive and advance my mission across thousands of planets. Today your eyes will be opened to the reality of this galactic war against evil."

Jeshu singled out Brae, nodding for her to come to him. Brae swallowed hard as she stepped forward. All of the other sectators watched on with bated breath. Standing before the Son of Ell Yon, Brae was once again humbled by his choosing her to be a Navi in training. Whatever he was going to do now, would she be able to bear it? Would she be worthy? Jeshu pierced her thoughts of doubt with a brazen look of courage. He lifted his right hand, pulling back the sleeve of his tunic to reveal the brilliance of one of his Protectors. Even now, subtle wisps of flaming blue power flitted up and down the length of it. Brae's fear rekindled, but Jeshu reached for her hand, his touch calming her. He then placed his left hand on top of the Protector as if to remove it from his arm. Brae had worn Daeson's Protector once before when Jeshu was a child in need of its healing. That encounter with the mind of Ell Yon was glorious and terrifying all at the same time. *Is Jeshu about to initiate another encounter, placing his Protector on me?* She trembled at the thought of it.

Jeshu lifted his Protector up and off his arm. It was the startled response of the other sectators that hinted that something extraordinary was happening. Brae then realized that as Jeshu lifted his Protector off his own arm, it appeared to have instantly replicated itself, leaving the original Protector securely in place as if nothing had changed, and yet, in his left hand was another gleaming Protector. Chills flitted up and down her spine when she realized that what she and the others were witnessing had never been seen by any member of humanity before. *Is there no limit to the power of Ell Yon, Jeshu, and the Protector?*

Jeshu placed the replicated Protector above Brae's arm, pausing for just a moment, then pushed it downward, propelling her into an avalanche of synaptic infusion. She gasped as the Protector melded with her mind.

"Focus on my voice and on my face," Jeshu said calmly.

The strength of his words lifted her out of the threatening cacophony of extreme power, steadying her. She took a breath, strength spilling into her bosom. She stood straight, her eyes now reflecting the eternal wisdom of the Immortal Sovereign Ell Yon.

Jeshu let loose of her hand. "Rhett," Jeshu called.

Brae turned to look at the rest of the sectators. Rhett stepped forward, moving toward Jeshu, but he stopped to look into Brae's eyes.

"I've seen this fire in your eyes once before," he said.

Brae looked at Rhett and then down at the Protector pulsing with Immortal power. "It's indescribable, Stryker. Just keep your eyes on him."

Rhett nodded then went to stand before Jeshu. Once again, Jeshu's Protector replicated, and soon Rhett was immersed in overwhelming Immortal power. When he returned to Brae, she was stunned by his visage. His eyes held a glimmer of the nobility that she saw continually in Jeshu. His face radiated wisdom and strength. *Is this what I look like when wearing the Protector?* she wondered.

One by one, each sectator received a replicated Protector until they all stood in a semicircle, now christened with Jeshu's Immortal power. One particular aspect of wearing the Protector was obvious to everyone in the chamber, and that was the perfect knowledge of the supreme rank and position of Jeshu in the realm of the Ruah.

Standing in the presence of the Commander of the Malakians was now starkly and undeniably humbling.

"Kneel down with me," Jeshu said, as he bent to one knee.

Brae, along with each of the other eleven sectators, followed suit. Jeshu seemed concerned.

"I'll teach you how to commune with Sovereign Ell Yon and how to see into the realm of the Ruah. Prepare your hearts," Jeshu commanded. He lowered his head and closed his eyes.

Brae did the same, waiting.

"Through the Protector, hear the whisper of Ell Yon in your hearts. Seek Him and you will find him for he is not far from you."

Brae quieted her mind, letting the voice of Jeshu lead her to Ell Yon. Jeshu continued to speak, guiding them toward the distant light in their minds. She could hear Jeshu walking behind them, patiently encouraging them in their communing with Ell Yon. In the solace of a dusty, abandoned chamber, Brae began to feel the warmth of Ell Yon's love spill into her soul. Within a few minutes, she had arrived at the foot of the Sovereign, bathing in the power of his might... safe, protected, instructed, loved.

"Lift your heads and stand up," she heard Jeshu's gentle voice call out. "Keep your eyes on me."

By this time, Jeshu had moved a few paces to a different part of the chamber. Slowly, Brae stood up to see him calling her to him. She walked his way, feeling not quite herself. She arrived before him, along with each of the other sectators, taking a position between Rhett and Shayde. Things were different than just a moment ago...much different, but she didn't understand why. With each passing second, she became acutely aware that her senses seemed to be in overdrive. She could hear a distant rumble, its origin unknown, as well as feel a tremor in the ground beneath her feet. The smell of the chamber was powerful, much more intense than when they had entered. She could feel every square inch of clothing pressing on her skin. She dared to look past Jeshu, realizing then that her optical acuity was dramatically improved. It was as if the world had all of a sudden become more. She glanced at Rhett and the rest of her companions, seeing clearly that they too were experiencing the same sensations. However, they also looked different...they appeared thin and weak, lesser versions of themselves. It frightened her.

"What's happening?" she asked, as the others also awakened to some new reality.

"Don't be afraid," Jeshu said, his voice now booming in thunderous power. Then Brae realized that Jeshu was different too, but not in the same way they were. He was taller, stronger, greater—a magnified version of who he had been a moment ago. His clothing had been replaced with that of a reinforced battle suit. The very image of his stature was ominous.

In all the stories Brae had heard from her father about the Protector, he had never described anything even remotely resembling the effect the Immortal tech was having on her and her companions. This transformation was unprecedented.

"Turn around and look back to where you were kneeling," Jeshu commanded.

Brae turned about, her new eyes beholding a spectacle so bizarre that dreams could never invent. Still kneeling in absolute perfect stillness was Jeshu and all twelve of the sectators, including herself! Many of her companions let loose expressions of disbelief as they beheld this strangest of sights.

"How is this possible, Jeshu?" Rhett asked, walking toward the kneeling statuesque figures.

"Go no further, Rhett," Jeshu said. "My sectators, you have entered the Ruah by means of your essence. Here your projection is directly correlated to your wisdom and to your strength of faith in Sovereign Ell Yon and in me."

Everyone fastened their eyes back on Jeshu. As Brae gazed upon the powerful form of their leader, she was amazed once again. This is who Jeshu really was! He had no equal in either realm. She knelt before him as did all the others.

"Rise up, sectators, and know that here is where the battle for the souls of humanity is fought. Do you understand?" he asked.

Brae looked down at her frail form, wondering how she could possibly fight in such a pathetic state. As if reading her mind, Jeshu spoke to her thoughts.

"As Navis, you will grow in your skill and strength to take the battle against evil into the Ruah. And when you're ready, you must make Navis of all people on all worlds. All your training is for this battle. Here is where you fight!" he exclaimed.

Brae saw Shayde pinch her arm, wincing as she did. "If we're just projections of ourselves, why do I feel pain?" she asked.

Jeshu stepped toward them as if to make sure they would all understand his next few words.

"This projection is not a dream...it is not some flimsy holographic representation of your body. The Protector has endowed your Ruah projection with the very essence of who you are. This existence is every bit as real as, even more so than, your existence in the realm of humanity. Deitum Prime dulls the senses and your life experiences there. But here you can already feel how those blinds have been removed. Make no mistake, your actions here will have dramatic consequences in both realms. That is the whole reason I've brought you here."

Rhett was looking at his hand, turning it over as if to evaluate its authenticity. "So if we are injured here, what happens to us in the realm of humanity?" he asked, looking back toward his kneeling body.

"The pain you will feel is real. Though that body will not endure the actual injury, your mind will believe it to be so. If you die here, you will die there," Jeshu said, nodding to the thirteen kneeling vessels. "When the mind dies, so does the body."

Brae and every one of her companions stood in solemn silence, contemplating Jeshu's words. None of them were prepared for such an initiation into Jeshu's world. Brae had always known that he was a man from a different world, but watching him translate from one to the other with such authority was simply stunning.

"How do we return?" Kase asked.

"For now, you return to your body and resume the state of communing. The Protector will merge you back into yourself. As you become more adept and stronger in this realm, there is another way, but you are far short of mastering the technique."

Just then the entire building shook from some distant explosion.

"Is that the sound of battle we hear now, my lord?" Bridger asked.

"Yes," Jeshu nodded. "Come and see, but don't wander from my side. You're not yet able to bear long in this realm."

Brae needed no encouragement to keep from wandering from Jeshu's side. She felt extraordinarily small and vulnerable.

Jeshu turned and exited the chamber. Brae, Rhett, Shayde, and the other nine sectators followed close behind, but just outside the chamber door they all froze. A few paces away were four towering warriors in tactical battle gear. Their appearance was unnerving for they were clearly vessels of great might and ability. Brae felt as though they had entered into the presence of gods.

"Malakian warriors," Brae whispered over her shoulder to the others.

Jeshu approached the warriors, being more than their equal. All of the mighty warriors bowed their heads as Jeshu came to them, instantly revealing the transcendent authority and power of this man they called their leader. Two of the warriors began handing Jeshu advanced tactical combat gear including an in-ear com transceiver, what looked like an extremely advanced class-one blaster, a Talon-style bladed weapon, and a sleek-looking power module that slipped over his left hand. Brae could only guess at the functionality of this final piece of equipment. When Jeshu's accoutrement was complete, he looked like the commander of worlds he was.

One of the warriors looked toward Brae and her companions, a muted look of displeasure on his face. He came toward them, carrying a large tactical gear bag, and stopping just a few feet away. In their diminished form, the warrior towered above them by over two feet. He said nothing as he dropped the bag in front of them, then turned to rejoin his fellow warriors. Rhett knelt to open the bag. Inside were advanced protective armor kits. Rhett looked up at Brae and toward the rest of the sectators. He removed a chest plate, holding it up to his torso. At first contact with his body, it molded itself to him, expanding clear around his upper body but stopping just short of his hips and arms. He smiled.

"I like it."

Rhett began handing the different kits to each of the others, and within a couple of minutes, they were all fully outfitted from neck to feet with protective composite battle armor that didn't hinder their motion in the least.

"No weapons," Rhett said with disappointment after examining the empty bag.

Brae looked over toward Jeshu and the other Malakian warriors. The one with obvious authority entreated Jeshu to step away from the others. With her now acute hearing, Brae could just make out some of their conversation.

"Are you sure, Commander?" the large warrior said, glancing their way. "They're hardly more than children here. My men will be burdened to protect them. I don't see how they could possibly contribute to our cause in the least."

Jeshu looked at the mighty warrior with patience. "You see them as they are, Admiral Kalem. My father sees them as they will be. Take heart...one day you will see as we do."

The man he called Kalem nodded, taking one more glance toward Brae and the other sectators. He frowned. "Yes, Commander...as you wish."

He saluted then turned and left with the other three warriors following behind. Jeshu returned to his sectators, scanning each one to take an inventory of their protective gear.

"Weapons?" Rhett asked.

"Tactical packs and weapons will be provided to you when the time is right and your Navi training is complete," Jeshu replied. "The battles here are like nothing any of you have ever seen…including you, Rhett."

As they maneuvered through the shambles of the building, they came to the doorway they had entered less than an hour earlier, but the world they now looked upon was not the one they had left. The sound of fierce alien battle was everywhere.

"This is madness," Rhett whispered to Brae and Shayde. "We're unarmed and have the strength and capabilities of school children."

"You're not here to fight," Jeshu said, glancing toward Rhett. "Your first mission here is to see and to believe. Dracus and his Scourge search the galaxy for easy prey, but he focuses especially on those who are devoted to serving Ell Yon."

"How?" Jaym asked.

"By a hundred different ways, but it always starts with Deitum Prime. His ultimate goal for humanity is death…death at every level. On a galactic scale, he incites worlds and nations to war and is responsible for the deaths of billions. On a personal level, he revels in the death of anything good, driving one to ruin and despair."

Jeshu led them out of the building, taking up a position behind a large concrete abutment that had toppled. The twelve sectators gazed out on the distant battle in wonder and fear. The sound of plasma fire, concussion missiles exploding, and laser bursts filled the air. Brae glanced toward Rhett and saw him looking to the skies above.

"Even in the skies," he said.

Brae could just make out the wisps and flashes of fighters engaged in desperate air battles.

"Is it like this everywhere?" Shayde asked. "Throughout the galaxy?"

"At times, such battles take place throughout the galaxy, but not to this extent," Jeshu said, turning toward his followers. "It's like this here because of me...and because of you."

Chills flitted across Brae's arms and legs. The thought of Jeshu's warriors fighting on her behalf instantly silenced any pride in her heart. Her soul began to ache for the violence to cease, for peace to reign in the galaxy. She looked toward Jeshu, seeing the same ache in his eyes. The world of the Ruah was terrifying with an enemy so great as Dracus. She hoped she would never set eyes on one so evil. It was then that she realized that her own world was just as terrifying and perhaps more so because Dracus was just as present but unseen. Those without eyes for the Ruah were fodder for this creature of hate and death. Ignorance and blindness led the foolish to their demise. *But how can one live with such stark awareness of the darkness and not be paralyzed by its devices of evil?* Brae wondered. She glanced at the faces of her fellow sectators and saw the same morose contemplation.

The piercing sound of an assault vehicle's engines throttling back assaulted Brae's ears, jarring her out of her contemplation. With frightening speed, the vehicle crested the rooftop of the building they had exited.

"Get down!" Jeshu commanded while drawing his class-one blaster. He radioed an urgent message of some sort then activated the power module in his left hand.

The Scourge assault vehicle quickly descended to within fifty feet of the ground in the open court in front of them. It hovered only a few seconds, just long enough for five of the most fearsome battle warriors Brae had ever seen to jump the remaining distance to the ground, firing their deadly weapons as they went. Miniature jet packs on their backs ignited to soften their landing. Jeshu didn't hesitate. He ran toward Dracus's assault force, drawing fire away from Brae and her companions. The Scourge took up positions behind various fallen structures. As they returned fire, Jeshu dodged and maneuvered with uncanny skill. When two plasma rounds came at him simultaneously, he juked left to avoid one while an emerald energy shield from his left hand absorbed the impact of the other.

With precision fire from his blaster, Jeshu eliminated each grisly warrior one by one. As the last fell, the assault vehicle that had delivered them circled back and began to unleash an endless barrage of deadly fire from its front-mounted class-two plasma cannon, sweeping from Jeshu to Brae and her fellow sectators. The ground exploded sending dirt and concrete debris into the air with each successive burst as the rain of destruction came swiftly toward them. Jeshu knelt to one knee, held up his right hand, and commanded his Protector. With the twelve sectators just a second away from certain death, Jeshu's Protector unleashed one powerful blast of brilliant blue energy that instantly ended the assault. The Scourge vehicle exploded into a thousand pieces of flying debris. Everyone ducked behind the abutment. Brae felt an arm cover her. She looked up to see Rhett offering himself as a shield then quickly retreating as the threat disappeared.

A second later, Jeshu was back with them. "Sector Alpha Three is neutralized," he said over his com link, "but I suspect more on the way. Deploy a squad to our location and provide additional support for Admiral Kalem's exit. He is located one mile east of our position." Jeshu then looked to his sectators. "Is everyone okay?"

After a quick confirmation from all, Jeshu commanded them to follow him.

"In both realms, it is the Protector that gives power over the darkness of Dracus," he said as they walked. "Never forget this."

Jeshu led them east, away from the ensuing battle. As they came around one of the buildings, Brae spotted a small transport with its engines running. They approached, and the rear access opened to them. Jeshu led them aboard. The pilot and copilot were warriors of equal stature to those they had seen earlier. After a brief exchange with Jeshu, the transport lifted off, making a 120 degree turn to a southeast heading.

Brae glanced once more at the faces of her fellow sectators...solemn, tense, reflective. Little was said between them. There was too much to process to give voice to any reasonable conversation yet. Rhett was sitting across and over two seats. She caught his eye. There was concern there. She gave him a thumbs up, and he nodded.

In just a few minutes, the transport was setting down inside a large hangar. Moments later Jeshu ushered them out. Here, away from the intense sounds of battle, there was a distinctly different feel. The twelve of them gawked at a squadron of elegant yet powerful fighter craft as Malakian crews performed maintenance, repairs, and inspection of the same. The gentle whirs of equipment complemented the purposeful actions of the crew. The entire hangar and all the equipment were immaculate. Brae saw Rhett smiling from ear to ear, then realized that she was doing the same. The flying machine near them was one of twelve fighters, its sleek form revealing power, agility, and advanced technology beyond anything Brae could have ever imagined possible.

Jeshu guided them to the nearest craft. He ran his hand along the leading edge of its wing as if to soothe its eagerness to launch and fight.

"This is the Starstreak, our premier fighter in the battle against Dracus and the Scourge. This fighter has extremely advanced avionics, sensors, navigation, and weapons. The avionics control system has an integrated pilot neurolink to help deploy the full capabilities of the craft, nearly anticipating the pilot's next move."

Rhett and Brae moved forward to touch the fuselage of the sleek craft. The silky-smooth metallic skin was unusual, and Brae wondered if it had something to do with its cloaking system. The rest of the sectators began examining the craft as well.

The Starstreak's dark gray-and-white color scheme accentuated its sleek design. On its struts, the nose and cockpit were lower to the hangar floor than the rear section of the craft, giving the impression that it was poised to launch at any moment. The canopy of the cockpit was open, and Brae could just make out the advanced glass instrument panels that nearly enveloped the pilot.

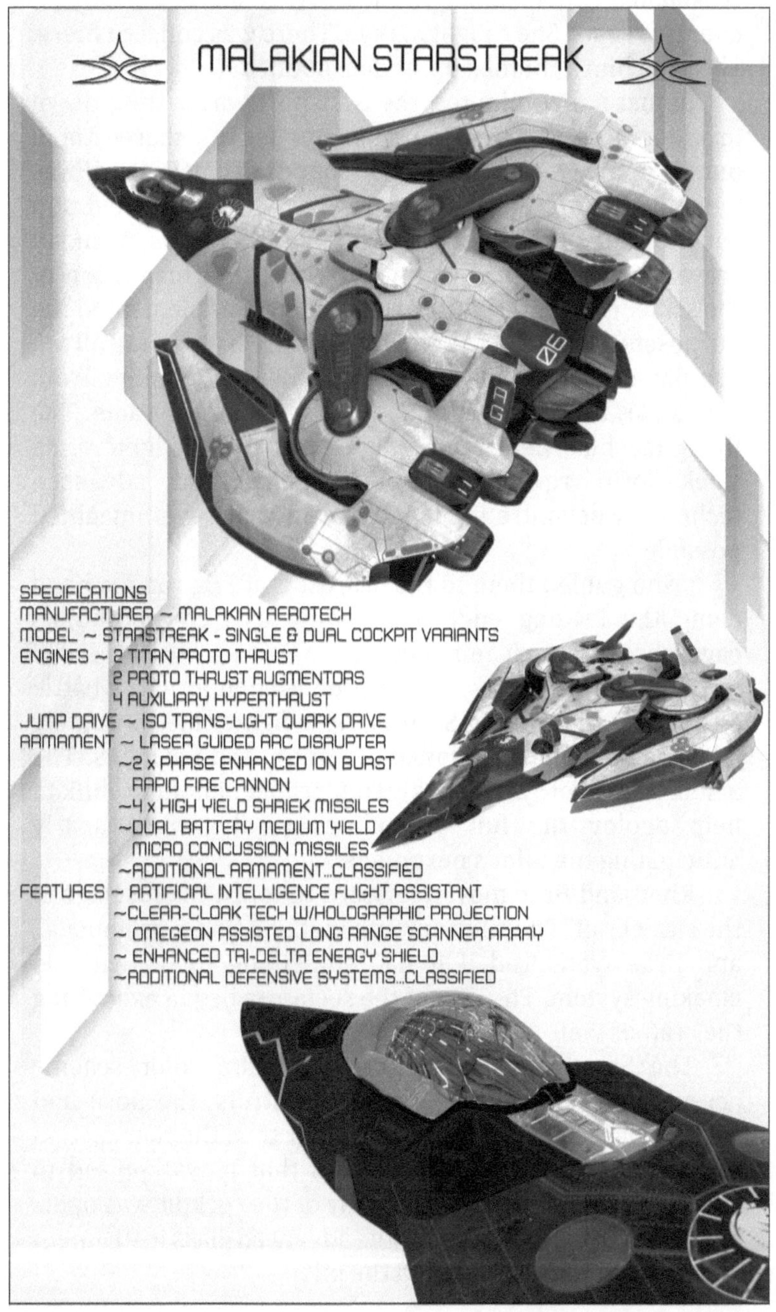

SPECIFICATIONS
MANUFACTURER ~ MALAKIAN AEROTECH
MODEL ~ STARSTREAK - SINGLE & DUAL COCKPIT VARIANTS
ENGINES ~ 2 TITAN PROTO THRUST
          2 PROTO THRUST AUGMENTORS
          4 AUXILIARY HYPERTHRUST
JUMP DRIVE ~ ISO TRANS-LIGHT QUARK DRIVE
ARMAMENT ~ LASER GUIDED ARC DISRUPTER
          ~2 x PHASE ENHANCED ION BURST
            RAPID FIRE CANNON
          ~4 x HIGH YIELD SHRIEK MISSILES
          ~DUAL BATTERY MEDIUM YIELD
            MICRO CONCUSSION MISSILES
          ~ADDITIONAL ARMAMENT...CLASSIFIED
FEATURES ~ ARTIFICIAL INTELLIGENCE FLIGHT ASSISTANT
          ~CLEAR-CLOAK TECH W/HOLOGRAPHIC PROJECTION
          ~ OMEGEON ASSISTED LONG RANGE SCANNER ARRAY
          ~ ENHANCED TRI-DELTA ENERGY SHIELD
          ~ADDITIONAL DEFENSIVE SYSTEMS...CLASSIFIED

"Look at the cockpit," Rhett whispered in her ear. "It's nearly identical to the Spacehawk, especially the simulator version with the weapons systems I told you about."

"Now it begins to make sense," Brae said.

The wings of the Starstreak swept forward from the rear in a curved fashion unlike anything Brae had ever seen. She saw weapon bays on top, on the sides, and underneath the main fuselage, as well as on the two outboard wing sections. Inward-slanted vertical stabilizers hugged closely to the main fuselage. What she really found thrilling was the engine array at the back of the craft. Everything about it exuded power. Brae and Rhett couldn't help exchanging giddy grins with each other as they inspected the alien war machine's aerodynamic genius. Everything about the Starstreak screamed, "Let me fight!"

"Jeshu, since you've invited us to see this fighter, does this mean what I think it means?" Rhett asked with a grin.

Brae knew exactly what he was getting at, and she was just as eager for the answer.

Jeshu offered a smile. "Yes, but there's much to teach you before you're ready for this," he said with a nod toward the Starstreak. "Just like the Spacehawk, there's a dual cockpit variant for specialized weapon deployment."

Brae could tell that Rhett was bridling his excitement as best he could.

"Sectators...listen closely," Jeshu said, as the others gathered about him. "Some of you are warriors," he began, glancing toward Rhett and Brae. "Some of you are peacemakers," he said with a warm smile as he glanced at Shayde and Kase. "You must all learn to be both warriors and peacemakers, but above all you must love the people for whom I came...people of all worlds across the galaxy. Your roles in both realms will depend on this. Do you understand?"

Brae nodded but noticed that Rhett was still mesmerized by the Starstreak. She wondered if he had heard anything Jeshu said.

"Why is there a seam in the fuselage here?" Rhett asked.

Nope, Brae thought. *Not a word.*

"It tracks clear around the front cockpit and forward fuselage," he continued.

Jeshu looked only slightly perturbed. "Rhett, all will be revealed in its time. For now, we must return."

Brae grabbed Rhett's arm, pulling him along with the rest of the retreating sectators and away from the enchanting Starstreak.

"Okay…okay, but you have to admit—getting to fly that thing one day is going to be the greatest thrill in my life. Yours too, I'll bet," he added, nudging her.

She glanced back at the elegant fighter bathing in the soft glow of the hangar's lighting. It was a glorious machine indeed. She wondered how it would compare to the Malakian-enhanced Starcraft that Daeson had flown a thousand times.

"I won't deny it," she said with a smile.

Rhett's smile grew even broader. "You can be my co-pilot."

"Ha!" Brae snorted. "You can be mine!"

"The Starstreak doesn't have a co-pilot," Jeshu said, as they stepped back on board the transport. "At least not in the way you're used to thinking about it."

"What's that supposed to mean?" Rhett asked. "You said some variants have two cockpits."

Jeshu just smiled as he gave the transport pilots the all-clear signal to spool up the engines.

Fifteen minutes later, Jeshu and the twelve sectators were back in the abandoned building looking at their kneeling selves. It was more than peculiar, almost like a bizarre dream.

"Resume your position of communing," Jeshu guided as he knelt into his body. "The Protector will lead you back."

Brae knelt into her body, allowing the Protector to lead her home. Within a few moments, she felt the tether of the Raylean world pull hard on her legs and arms. She hesitated, then relented and fell back into herself. Suddenly she opened her eyes as she felt the full impact of her experience nearly crush her. She fell over onto the ground, wondering what had happened to her strength. She felt pinned to the ground, nearly unable to move. It was as if her arms, legs, and torso were trapped in concrete.

"Calm yourselves," Jeshu said, standing over them. "Be patient and allow your strength to return. Entering into the Ruah can tap all of your energy. Feel the Protector strengthen you, and when you are ready, rise."

After another ten minutes, all twelve of the sectators had risen and were now standing before Jeshu. He touched his Protector and Brae instantly felt the connection with Ell Yon fade away as the Protector on her arm dissolved to a molecular wisp. She was instantly lonely.

"But why, my Lord?" Bridger asked, feeling his arm where the Protector had been just a moment ago.

"Don't fret, my friends. There's coming a day when the Protector will never leave you, and you will do even greater things than I. The galaxy will know me because of you." Jeshu paused, taking in the gaze of every follower.

"But Jeshu," Jaym began. "How could we possibly have any positive impact in the Ruah? I felt like a child among those warriors."

"With Ell Yon, all things are possible," Jeshu said, placing a hand on his shoulder. "You must trust and continue to grow as my Navis, and one day you will be mighty and feared as warriors of the Ruah. Now go...rest and prepare for tomorrow."

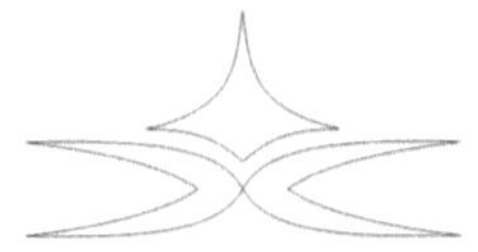

CHAPTER

15

Navi Training

After having experienced the realm of the Ruah, the training Jeshu was giving to his sectators as future Navi became extremely relevant and purposeful. They embraced their instruction with vigor. Two months later the simulators were complete, and the fuselage structure of the first six Spacehawks began to take shape. Additionally, Jeshu commissioned another project to enhance their tactical ground assault training—four holographic simulators with real-world adaptive visualization. The labor force that had come to Olea Station to accomplish such lofty projects was impressive. Resources and financing were always tight but ever sufficient, not only for their research and design projects but also in fulfilling the humanitarian needs of such a growing community at the station.

Rhett began evaluating the Spacehawk flight simulators with great enthusiasm. He discovered that along with the usual complement of two plasma canons and six internally mounted high-yield concussion missiles, the simulator version of the Spacehawk had an extra arsenal of weapons. Two eight-bank, medium-yield micro missile launchers and an enhanced laser energy weapon were recessed in the upper side of the fuselage that, when extended, had a 270-degree, targeting laser-burst cannon that doubled as a laser-guided arc disrupter, a weapon Rhett had never heard of before. The fighter also had two triple-phase-enhanced ion burst cannons that were recessed on the underside of each curved wing. The defense systems, which Rhett understood to be in both the simulator and the actual Spacehawk craft, included a powerful holographic transmitter capable of projecting both visual and radar images, an advanced full cloak system, a powerful energy shield, and a counter electromagnetic pulse-dampening system for energy weapon defense. Once the Spacehawk simulators were commissioned, Rhett and Brae began working side-by-side to implement a training program for potential pilots.

At the end of each day, Rhett found it difficult to disengage from his training. The systems were so advanced and thrilling to learn and deploy that there didn't seem to be enough hours in the day to accomplish what he felt was necessary. Jeshu also gave Rhett and Brae the task of identifying which sectators had the potential of being Navi pilots and which would be ground-assault Navis. Jeshu made it clear that this specialized training would eventually transcend the 12 sectators and included thousands of followers of Jeshu.

Once Rhett and Brae had become proficient on the simulator, they began to train the other four sectators that they had selected with Jeshu's approval—Bridger, Jaym, Salara, and Lubin. After each pilot trainee had learned all the systems of the Spacehawk simulator, including the weapons systems, Jeshu personally conducted intense flight and weapons deployment training. All of this was accomplished in the four simulators that had been designed and built for such training.

For the other six sectators, Jeshu utilized the newly constructed holographic simulators for advanced ground assault and reconnaissance training. Sectator Mazon seemed to have an instinct for this and fell into a natural leadership position for the ground assault team. In the realm of humanity, there wasn't a single real-world weapon to deploy, which is why the Morian Empire seemed content with their activities. After all, Jeshu's labor to feed and care for the city rims took a significant burden off Subchancellor Pylok so that he could focus on capturing the resources and income from the well-off citizens and industries of Rayl.

What helped Rhett disengage each day from the rigors of training was the joy of spending a couple of hours unwinding each night with Brae. They loved to walk just within the edges of the woods bordering the station. A clearing along this path was where Rhett had been invited this evening. Being twenty minutes late, he hurried across the pavement and ducked into the woods, trotting along their favorite trail. At last, he came to the clearing that Brae had prepared for them. There, in the middle of a forest haven, was a delightful picnic spread of some of Rhett's favorite foods.

"I'm so sorry, Brae," Rhett said, as he knelt beside her on the blanket.

"It's all right. I've just barely set things up," she said, reaching over to give Rhett a quick hug.

After giving thanks to Ell Yon, Rhett and Brae spent the next hour eating and relaxing as much as was possible, but the events surrounding their work for Jeshu were never far from their minds.

"I see you're up for a two-hour simulator ride with Jeshu, Bridger, and Salara tomorrow," Rhett said after taking a bite of his favorite Raylean fruit. The sweetness filled his mouth with flavor, a wonderful finish to Brae's delicious meal.

Brae looked a little disappointed.

"What's wrong?" Rhett asked.

"I like flying with you," Brae said. "It kind of reminds me of flying with dad. You fly like he did."

Rhett smiled. "Really?"

Brae nodded as she took a bite out of a bright orange hand-sized melon.

"Wow...that's quite a compliment," Rhett said.

"I didn't say you were as good as him, just that you fly like him," Brae qualified with a grin.

"Oh...I see," Rhett said, appearing to have his feelings hurt. "That's only because you've never seen me in real combat."

"Is that so?" Brae asked. "Well just remember that my dad won the Magnifical Festival competition with a 1,500-year-old Jyptonian Starcraft fighter. You do that, and I'll believe you."

Rhett laughed. "Okay, you win." He moved closer to Brae. "It's incredible what Jeshu has done here in just a couple years. Next week I'm scheduled to make the maiden flight of the first Spacehawk." Rhett eyed Brae to see what her response would be.

"So I've heard." She looked at Rhett with warm eyes. "Don't push it, okay? I need to know you'll be safe."

Rhett still wasn't used to having someone be so concerned for him. He reached for her hand. "I will...I promise."

Brae seemed content with his promise. "Remember when we were concerned that we were training with no enemy to fight?"

"Yes," Rhett said, lowering his hand to hers again. "After getting a glimpse into the Ruah, that pretty much changed everything." Rhett shook his head. "Seems hard to believe we could ever make a difference there against such fierce warriors like the Scourge."

Brae looked concerned. "We have a long way to go, but can you imagine the galactic impact if Jeshu can pull it off?"

"Wow...I hadn't thought of that," Rhett said. "If the battle in the Ruah impacts humanity the way Jeshu says it does, then enlisting an army of trained sectators to help fight the war would be substantial."

"What I don't yet understand is how Jeshu is eventually going to rule our realm without weapons like he's training us to use in the Ruah," Brae added. Her brows furrowed. "According to the oracles, he will come to rule all worlds of the galaxy. It's still very confusing."

Rhett nodded, tossing the remnants of the core of his fruit into a waste bag. "It is confusing...Jeshu's words are becoming more ominous and more cryptic with each passing day. However, imagine if he had taken us into the Ruah on day one...none of us would have stuck around. I think his vision is too big for our puny brains."

Brae chuckled.

As the hour passed, late afternoon gave way to twilight, and their forest haven became a place of enchantment. Brae scooted closer to Rhett so she was face to face and just a few inches from him. She seemed to be searching his eyes for something.

"Do you remember that day after the Magnifical Festival when I was so despondent, and you held me?" Brae asked.

"Yes...I do. You surprised me," Rhett said, as he lifted his hand to touch her cheek. "It's something I think of often."

"Me too...I didn't quite dare think it yet, but now I know...that was the moment I never wanted to be away from you." Brae's eyes glowed with affection.

Although Rhett had yet to kiss Brae, he wanted to. She was so close to him. He felt his heart quicken. "If you get too close, I might just kiss you."

Brae tilted her head ever so slightly. "Why haven't you?"

"You said you wanted to take it slow," Rhett replied.

Brae's left eyebrow lifted. "This slow?" she said, leaning into him.

Rhett felt the warmth of her breath on his lips. "Well...we only get one first kiss, and I want to make sure it's one we remember forever." Then Rhett realized that in the beauty of a lush forest with the evening lumin flies dancing their soft light across leaves and enchanting their surroundings, it probably wouldn't get any more memorable than right now.

"Rhett?" she whispered, their lips nearly touching.

"Yes?"

"We're being watched."

Rhett froze. "Seriously?"

Brae gave one subtle nod. Rhett had no idea how Brae knew, but she had proven to have an uncanny ability to just know such things.

Rhett slowly reached for his blaster, and so did Brae. When his hand found the grip, he spun about on one knee, leveling the blaster at whoever was nearby. Thirty-five feet away, the underbrush rustled, then something bolted. Rhett ran in that direction, but whatever had been spying on them was fast. After scouting the area, he returned to Brae who had been searching in the opposite direction.

"Did you get your eyes on it?" Brae asked.

"Not really. You see anything?"

Brae hesitated. "Not exactly, but there was more than just one, and they were big," Brae said, her eyes conveying a measure of alarm.

"Okay...our picnic is over. Let's pack up and get back," Rhett said, continuing to scan the area.

"No arguments from me," Brae agreed.

Rhett walked Brae back to her quarters. He wrapped his arm around her.

"You okay?" he asked.

"I'm good, but it would probably be a good idea to let our people know to be on the watch if they venture into the woods. Just in case."

"I'll take care of it," Rhett offered.

Brae turned and leaned into him. They held each other for a few minutes then pulled away. As Rhett stepped away, Brae grabbed his hand.

"Hey...can I have my kiss now?" she asked, a sweet smile on her lips.

Rhett looked left and right to see if they would be too conspicuous. He returned to her, holding her close. "Here? Doesn't seem too memorable."

Brae wrapped her arms around his neck. "It wouldn't matter to me if we were in the middle of a desert. I'll never forget kissing you for the first time...I promise."

For some reason, Rhett became nervous. Their first kiss would create a sacred moment...one that he would never retreat from. Loyalty was woven into the core of his being, and although he wasn't afraid of committing to such loyalty, he didn't know if Brae realized what this would truly mean. He held his heart carefully but more than that, he cherished her heart with a depth of respect that no other human had ever earned from him. This kiss would bind their futures together forever.

He leaned forward and gently kissed her. When they parted, Brae looked up at him, a knowing in her eyes. They would never be the same.

"Goodnight, Stryker."

"Goodnight, Starlore," he countered with a subtle grin. The façade of distance from calling each other by their last names now became a token of deep fondness. Brae turned and walked away. He watched until she had entered her quarters.

Rhett loved being with Brae. Seeing her disappear saddened him. *Perhaps one day I will never have to leave her,* he thought.

CHAPTER

17

The Fight to Die

Prefect Terrok had devolved into a constant state of paranoia and frustration, and no amount of cajoling from his first advisor or any of his royal staff could even slightly deter his mental collapse. The intense pressure he was receiving from Morian Subchancellor Pylok was no small contributor to his dismal state. A visit from Preeminent Keeper Fasa Kylos and Master Builder Krisha Monae wasn't going to help in the least. When Terrok refused to meet them in the courtyard of his palace, the two leaders of their orders acquiesced and entered his throne room. Terrok didn't rise to meet them.

"Terrok...how long must we endure the impudence of this man they call Jeshu? You must enlist the Raylean Guard to arrest and imprison him once and for all!" Kylos insisted as he and Monae approached.

Terrok sat sulking on his royal bench. With head drooped, he glared at Kylos.

"For what?" Terrok hissed. "Making you out to be the hypocrites that you are?"

Kylos clenched his jaw in anger. "Your abdication of your responsibility to keep this man and his fraudulent activities under control will bring the indignation of the Morian Empire on our heads!"

Terrok scowled, rising up slightly, his muscles and veins bulging from the ravaging effects of a nearly 100 percent Deitum Prime absorption. Gone was First Advisor Aunder's previous confidence as Terrok's soothing agent. He and three of his attending staff instantly recognized an impending tirade and backed away a few steps.

"I am already experiencing the indignation of Pylok and the Empire," Terrok said through clenched teeth.

Terrok's heinous transforming visage caused Kylos to hesitate. Monae stepped forward. "This man must be stopped before it's too late, and we don't have the authority to do what must be done."

"What are you talking about?" Terrok exclaimed. "You both have the authority to arrest anyone that defies the precepts of sanctum order, which I understand you feel has happened many times already," Terrok rebutted.

"Arrest, yes, but not—" Kylos stopped short.

"Ah-hah!" Terrok exclaimed, his first indication of a pleasant thought. He pointed a crooked finger at Kylos. "You mean execution! You don't have the backbone to even speak your dastardly schemes."

Kylos's face flushed slightly at Terrok's accusation. "It's the only way to stop him. He's bewitched millions of Rayleans, and it will be the doom of them...of all of us."

Terrok sank back into the cushions of his bench, eyes narrowing as he considered Kylos's words. After a moment of reflection, he scowled.

"If what you say is true and this Jeshu has won the favor of millions, then my arresting him would surely incite another insurrection, and that would be the end of me...Pylok has made that clear. No...this man is your problem. Elias Thornton attacked my reputation, and I took care of it. This man is attacking you, and you come cowering to me for help. Deal with him yourself!"

Kylos fumed in frustration. He stepped forward to protest further, but Terrok lifted his chin while turning his head away from the Keeper as a show of disinterest. Krisha Monae turned toward Kylos.

"If the prefect won't help us, then we will simply enlist the help of those who can," she said with a gleam in her eye.

"And who might that be?" Kylos asked.

"The Morian Empire."

The hour was drawing close even though the sectators didn't realize it. Jeshu led his twelve followers up to a wooded knoll that overlooked the city of Jalem. Here they found an ancient ruin, its marble floor and columns cracked and shattered. It held the ambiance of a once significant but now abandoned structure.

Jeshu stood in silence, looking thoughtfully over the city of Jalem. His sectators gathered near, each one seeming to understand the solemn heart of their commander. The night was far spent, and although Brae was feeling the pull of sleep, Jeshu seemed unwilling to stop the day.

"Oh, Jalem and the inhabitants of Rayl, if you could know the good that was planned for you, but instead you will see destruction because you did not know me when I came to you." Jeshu turned to face his sectators.

"Destroyed, Jeshu?" Brae asked. "When will this happen?"

Jeshu scanned the faces of his sectators. "Soon after I've gone, and you will see the day. Dracus is coming to destroy this city and all of Rayl with powerful forces, but don't despair. The destruction of Rayl will ignite the flame of truth that will carry my hope to the four corners of the galaxy."

Brae struggled with this message from Jeshu. She could see on the faces of her companions that they too found his words hard to hear. Rhett was right, Jeshu's words were becoming more ominous and more cryptic with each passing day.

"But today is not that day, and we must fight to maintain superiority over Jalem for my mission to be fulfilled." Jeshu looked up into the night sky as if he could see a raging battle. *Could he?* Brae wondered. All she could see was the peaceful and serene evening sky hovering like a blanket over the glowing city of Jalem.

Jeshu gathered the 12 sectators in a circle in the center of the ancient ruin. "Please sit," he said, but before Dahj could do so, Jeshu caught his arm and pulled him aside. Jeshu looked at him with fierce eyes. "Depart and do what you must do."

Brae and Rhett were close enough to hear the quiet words. They exchanged confused looks. Dahj seemed surprised at first, but then his countenance turned dark. He pulled away from Jeshu, turned and left. Jeshu's gaze lingered for a moment in the direction Dahj had gone. He looked back at his remaining 11 sectators then stepped into the middle of the circle.

"In preparation for what is to come, I gathered these on our journey here." Jeshu removed a dozen Wild Crimson Roses from his pack. "Just as in the days of Daeson Starlore on the planet Jypton, anyone with the mark of the Crimson Rose on the forehead and temple was spared from the death of the Mist."

Jeshu took the first rose and knelt before Brae. As he stacked the petals of the rose, Brae remembered teaching the tradition of reclamation to him when he was just a boy. Now there was the sense that something supremely significant was about to happen. Quietly, Brae held her hand out. Jeshu twisted the layered petals until a single drop of the red fluid landed in the palm of her hand. With his forefinger, Jeshu swiped the red dye across her brow and down each side of her temples then kissed her forehead. After performing the ritual of reclamation on each of the eleven sectators, Jeshu returned to Brae.

"Commune with me," he said, replicating his Protector so that each sectator could follow him into the Ruah. When they were ready, Jeshu knelt in the middle of them and the sectators followed suit.

Within a couple of minutes, Brae rose up with Jeshu and her eleven companions into the frightful world of the Ruah. The night sky was filled with brilliant flashes of a great battle. Some regions of the city and beyond hosted greater battles, but it seemed as if the entire area was embroiled in continual war, both on the ground and in the skies above.

"What is happening?" Rhett asked, stepping forward to stand beside Jeshu, whose eyes reflected the flashes of this eternal war.

"The Torians are trying to keep the final Reclamation from happening. They're desperate to do so." He pointed to seven tactical bags that were placed just a few yards from their communing bodies. "I know you aren't fully trained in the ways of Ruah warfare yet, but I need you to be courageous tonight. Don your gear and take up positions around this ancient hall of meditation to protect our bodies from the attacks of the Scourge. If you're injured, rejoin to your bodies and wait for me here."

"But there are only seven bags," Rhett said, being the first to investigate the gear.

"Rhett, Brae, Bridger, and Jaym, your missions are different," Jeshu said. He looked at the other seven sectators. "Don't be afraid. You're not alone here. Just remember your training and do your best."

As the seven moved toward the tactical bags, Jeshu came to Rhett, Brae, Bridger, and Jaym. "Follow me." He led the four of them another mile further from Jalem. As they crested a hill and entered into a shallow valley, Brae could see activity ahead.

"Quickly," Jeshu urged. "Tonight you must be stronger than you have ever been in your lives."

Brae felt her heart quicken. Such an entreaty from Jeshu was alarming. She looked over at Rhett, but the darkness made his face indeterminate. In just a few more minutes of a quickened gait, they arrived at a tactical bare base with nothing but a few pieces of equipment to support the launching of their awaiting craft—three fully weaponized Starstreaks. Three Malakian mechtechs awaited. As they approached, each Malakian snapped to a full-attention salute. Jeshu responded then pointed to the tactical gear bags positioned at the forward strut of each Starstreak.

"Master...we've only simulated air combat in the Spacehawk," Brae said.

She glanced toward her three companions, and although they didn't voice it, she could see the concern in their eyes as well. Jeshu turned to them, placing a hand on Brae's shoulder.

"Time is short, and there's no way that I can give you everything you think you need to accomplish the weighty missions before you, but take heart...the Protector will guide and keep you. Trust in Ell Yon and in me." He looked to the skies above Jalem. "We fly to fight Dracus for air superiority over Jalem. My Malakian warriors have secured enough of the global airspace, but I've received word that Dracus himself and a small squadron of fighters have penetrated our defenses in an effort to stop me. They're cloaked, so I have to draw them out. What we do tonight will determine the futures of many." Jeshu's eyes turned hard with steely determination. Brae felt her heart strengthen with his gaze. "Jaym, you're with Rhett—Bridger with Brae. Don your flight suits and prepare to launch."

Jeshu turned to his Starstreak. Rhett, Bridger, Jaym, and Brae glanced from one to another, offering looks of solidarity and confidence. Rhett held up his forearm to Bridger.

"Navi!" he exclaimed.

Bridger crossed forearms with Rhett. "Navi," he replied.

Each in turn encouraged each other with the same gesture, and as they did so, their Protectors flashed with pulses of Immortal power at contact. When Rhett crossed forearms with Brae, he grabbed her arm with his free hand.

"You can do this, Brae...you're a Starlore—don't forget that."

Brae nodded. "See you in the sky...Navi!" she exclaimed. The brilliant flash of light between them gave Brae all the assurance she needed to press on into the fray that awaited.

She turned to follow Bridger to their Starstreak, its glorious form of stealth, speed, and power poised to launch.

She stroked the nose of the craft, feeling the power systems already online and reverberating in a way that almost made Brae believe the Starstreak was trembling with excitement for the battle that was to be fought. The Malakian assigned to their Starstreak was busy doing a final inspection and externally arming all weapons systems.

Brae and Bridger opened their tactical bags and began donning the armored flight suits. Brae placed the chest piece against her body—it expanded and molded to her torso. Although the donning of the flight suit gear was similar to donning the ground tactical suit, this version was designed to interface with the Starstreak's flight systems and its neurolink. When finished suiting up, Brae glanced over at Bridger. The fully formed armored flight suit was impressive, and she wondered if she looked as intimidating as he.

"I'll be your co-pilot, Brae. Your piloting skills are superior," he said, then moved to climb up the rear cockpit ladder.

Brae looked over at Rhett and Jaym. Both were just stepping up on their ladders. Rhett offered a quick salute then mounted his Starstreak. Brae did the same, for Jeshu was already spooling up his engines.

Brae climbed the ladder and stepped into the cockpit, carefully placing herself in the seat so as to avoid damaging any of the instrumentation. Once seated, she pressed the "ACTIVATE HARNESS" button, and the five-point harness automatically secured Brae to her seat. She powered up the electrical systems, and the cockpit came to life. Flashing in pale blue letters on her main display was the message, "ACTIVATE NEUROLINK?"

Brae pressed the "CONFIRM" selection, and her suit instantly connected with Starstreak's Artificial Intelligence Flight Assistant or AIFA. The sectators called her "Ayfa" for short. In an odd way, she felt the presence of AIFA connect to her mind.

"Welcome aboard, Navi Starlore," a calm female voice said, although there were no actual sound waves generated through a headset. This voice came from the neurolink and spoke directly to her mind. "What level of neurolink do you desire?" AIFA asked.

Brae needed to have more hands-on control to start with. A fully functioning neurolink took extreme discipline of the mind, and she wasn't there yet.

"Sensors, weapons, and defense systems deployment," Brae spoke in her mind.

"Confirmed," the Starstreak's AIFA responded.

Brae clicked the inter-cockpit mic button. "Confirm ready."

"Ready," Bridger responded immediately.

"Focus on sensor and visual IDs and relay pertinent info through your neurolink," Brae replied.

"Copy," Bridger said.

The neurolink interface for a pilot-copilot mission was extremely helpful. AIFA filtered and relayed messages specific to their respective responsibilities. The inter-cockpit audio com was always there for them as a backup and for non-Starstreak, systems-related com, but eliminating verbal communication decreased response time significantly.

Brae heard her headset click on.

"Engines clear and ready to start," came the voice of the attending Malakian mechtech on the ground.

Brae made eye contact. "Copy. Engine start commencing," she said, as she offered a visual thumbs-up signal. She tapped the engine control icon and a display of the Starstreak's engine array became visible. She then tapped on the image of the six engines and the two sub-engines, highlighting each one before selecting "INITIATE STARTUP."

Thirty seconds later, Brae's Starstreak was humming with more power than she had ever felt while strapped in a fighter.

"Engine startup sequence complete," AIFA announced.

Brae finished the rest of her startup checklist just as her headset clicked again.

"Navi flight check," Jeshu's voice rang out.

She waited, not sure what position she was to be. Finally, she heard the mic click.

"Navi Two, check," Rhett radioed.

"Navi Three, check," Brae followed.

"Launch now," Jeshu commanded.

Brae saw Jeshu's Starstreak lift smoothly into the air, its anti-grav pods fully engaged and causing the grass beneath the craft to instantly flatten to the ground. Rhett was next, followed quickly by Brae. She activated the anti-grav pods, controlling the level of power with her left thumb while pushing the main engine throttles forward to initiate forward movement. The launching of the three Starstreaks initiated a rush of adrenaline for Brae. Until this moment, there had been the intensity of the preflight and launch requirements, but now that she was lifting into the air, the reality of the mission hit hard. She was literally flying a Malakian Starstreak in the Ruah to engage Torian fighters in defense of her beloved city, Jalem.

How did I come to this place? she thought.

"Information inadequate," AIFA responded.

Disregard, Brae replied with her thoughts. *Oops…not that part of the mind,* she scolded herself.

It had taken months of training to cordon off that one section of her thinking that would interface with the Starstreak neurolink. If not careful, the link would pick up unintentional commands, and during the intensity of a dogfight, the risk became greater.

"Keep a tight formation to 20,000, then execute a one-mile tactical split," Jeshu radioed.

"Two copy."

"Three copy."

The first hints of approaching dawn came with silvered streaks of light shimmering off the undersides of high cirrus clouds. Brae was thankful—she discovered during her training that she really didn't like night combat missions. The Spacehawks they flew in the realm of humanity were close approximations of these craft, but there was an energy in the Ruah Starstreaks that superseded their trainers. The power of this Immortal craft was absolutely exhilarating if not intimidating.

Brae focused on keeping her formation flying tight. Jeshu was moving fast, and she had to force herself to stay close, as uncomfortable as it was. Rhett was flying off Jeshu's right wing, and Brae was off his left.

"Passing 20,000. Spread to tactical formation and initiate cloak," Jeshu radioed.

"Two copy."

"Three copy."

Rhett and Brae banked opposite directions to find their tactical splits. Brae initiated her cloaking system while looking over her right shoulder at Jeshu's Starstreak. As she did, his craft shimmied then disappeared.

Activate ally projections, she commanded in her mind. Her visor immediately displayed the visual for both Jeshu's and Rhett's Starstreaks to account for their cloaking.

They were now passing 25,000 feet, and the battle for Jalem from this perch was mesmerizing. Brilliant flashes of intense battle were everywhere. Brae could even see the distant streaks of plasma fire and an occasional explosion above them in space.

How do I find cloaked Torian fighters in all this chaos? Brae thought, but she didn't have to wonder long.

Just as they passed 27,000 feet, the air around Brae's Starstreak exploded in a vicious onslaught of laser and plasma fire.

Two bandits—four o'clock high! Bridger alerted through AIFA.

The first hit nearly took Brae out, but the Starstreak's AIFA system dropped cloak to divert energy to the E-shields so they could survive. Brae rolled, inverted, and pulled hard on the stick, narrowly missing the next salvo of attacks.

"Navi Three is defensive!" Brae radioed. "Two bandits four o'clock high."

"Navi One is engaged," Jeshu radioed. There would be no help from him for the next 60 seconds. Brae wondered if they would last that long. Rhett and Jaym were two miles away, but could they help?

"Navi Two is engaged."

No help there either. She and Bridger had to survive long enough for Navi One or Two to break away. Brae began jinking to avoid the Torian's rapid fire cannons, but with two of them, there was little hope. She was aware that AIFA was deploying defensive countermeasures including a holographic projection of her Starstreak 100 feet away to confuse the attackers. Brae knew that a dogfight with sophisticated craft like the Torians typically lasted less than two minutes, but she started out defensive, so the odds of their survival for that long were grim.

Another rapid-fire salvo screamed just above her canopy, the last shot slamming into her right wing. The craft ratcheted but held together. Brae knew she was going down, so she decided to do so with her guns blazing.

"Hang on, Bridger," she said over their audio com link.

Brae pulled hard on the stick, forcing their Starstreak into a pure vertical climb. The two Torian fighters split left and right, following in the 5,000-foot climb. Brae then cut engines, engaged her nose thrusters to whip their Starstreak completely around so that she had a passing shot at one of the Torian fighters. She smashed the plasma cannon trigger, sweeping the nose of her craft in a last-ditch attempt to maim at least one enemy. The maneuver worked. Two rounds impacted into the fuselage of one of the fighters. She saw the E-shield of the craft engage and deflect much of the energy of the first round, but at such a close range, the second round did some damage. Just how much, Brae couldn't tell, for her Starstreak was now falling out of the sky like a sitting duck.

Bandit Two is positioning to fire! The message from Bridger through AIFA was urgent, but there was nothing she could do to stop it.

The second Torian fighter repositioned to put them in the lethal cone of its weapons. Brae slammed the throttles to max, but there wouldn't be enough time to regain maneuvering velocity to avoid the imminent death blow. Time slowed. Brae's heart pounded against her chest as she prepared to be obliterated. She dared look into the cockpit of her enemy, catching a glimpse of the visored evil warrior poised to destroy her and Bridger.

Out of the corner of her eye, Brae saw something flash, then the sky lit up in a blaze of fiery judgment. Two Starstreaks unleashed plasma cannons and laser fire at the same time on Brae's unsuspecting executioner. The combined energy tore through the Torian's E-shield in an instant, exploding the fuel cells in a brilliant flash of crushing power. *Was that Jeshu and Rhett?* Brae wondered. Although the adrenaline of battle distorts time perception, she was certain they couldn't have made it to her in time.

"Navi Three, this is Saga One—take trail and prepare to engage," came a radio call. The voice caused Brae to hesitate. She glanced at AIFA's arena map and saw that Rhett was in trouble too. She stifled any peculiar thoughts she was having and obeyed.

"Navi Three, copy."

The two savior Starstreaks accelerated toward the distant fights with Brae and Bridger flying trail. Brae's arena map began to light up with another six Torian fighters as they uncloaked to engage. In seconds, the dawn of this day was herald to one of the most ferocious air-to-air engagements Rayl had ever seen. Brae felt like she was just hanging on for her life as Jeshu and these two new Starstreaks began unleashing their holy fire on the enemies of Ell Yon.

Brae picked up Rhett and Jaym's fight and maneuvered toward them, ever wary of picking up a tail.

Watch our six, she said to Bridger via AIFA.

Copy.

Brae broke into the fray just aft of a Torian fighter that was unleashing on Rhett.

"Navi Two, I'm hound dog on your bandit—break right," Brae radioed, hoping she was in time.

Rhett's Starstreak banked hard right, and the Torian fighter followed, which put him right within the lethal range of Brae's weapons. Two seconds later, Rhett cleared her line of fire as she unleashed a three-second burst of her rapid-fire plasma cannons followed by a high-yield shriek missile that AIFA had locked on. The Torian fighter's right wing exploded, causing the rest of the craft to tumble wildly out of control.

"Thanks, Navi Three," Rhett radioed.

Over the next 20 minutes, Rhett and Brae provided support when possible, but the tactics and maneuvers they saw Jeshu and the other two Starstreaks perform watered their eyes. On the com link, Jeshu identified them as Saga One and Saga Two. Brae couldn't help but wonder about these two additional Starstreak pilots...were they Jeshu's equal in the Ruah?

Jeshu is my son, Commander of all in the Ruah. Listen to him!

Through the Protector, the voice of Ell Yon shattered Brae's foolish thoughts. She was ashamed.

When only two Torian fighters remained, they bugged out to the south, unwilling to continue the fight over Jalem with Jeshu, the supreme warrior of the galaxy. Brae was awestruck by what she had seen the Merchant accomplish that morning.

"Well done, Navi flight and Saga flight," Jeshu radioed. "Saga One and Saga Two, thanks for the help. You're cleared off."

"Saga One, copy," came that same voice. This time shivers flowed up and down Brae's entire body.

"Saga Two, copy," came a strong female voice. Though Brae had never heard this one before, there was a strange familiarity about it. The shivers continued.

Before Saga One and Two cleared off, they took up positions on Brae's right and left wing in close fingertip formation. Brae looked at Saga One...wondering if what her heart was feeling was at all possible. The pilot lightened the tint of his visor, turning his head to look right at Brae as he did so. Brae's chest tightened, and her eyes ached with threatening tears. Daeson Starlore lifted his hand and offered her a sharp salute.

"Keep heart, Brae. You're strong, and you are able." The voice of her father spilled hope and courage into her soul. Tears began to well up. Could it truly be? Before she could even respond, Daeson pitched his Starstreak up and away. Brae heard the mic click on once more.

"I'll always be with you, Brae," the strong, calm voice said.

Brae turned to look at the Starstreak on her left. Looking back at her from the cockpit was the face of a woman she had seen a thousand times but had never touched.

"Mom!" Brae whispered, pushing her hand up against the canopy.

Raviel placed her hand against her canopy as well. "I love you, Daughter. Be strong," Raviel said.

Brae cursed the tears that were obstructing the clarity of her eyes. "I love you," Brae finally radioed.

Raviel hesitated then saluted. A second later, she pitched up and away to follow Daeson. Brae found herself drifting in the sky above Jalem, too numb to do anything else. She wanted those precious seconds back.

"You okay?" Bridger asked over the audio com link.

The sound of Bridger's voice shattered her moment of reflection.

When they landed, Brae ran to Jeshu. She didn't know what to even ask him.

"How…how can that be?" she asked, tears spilling onto her cheeks.

Jeshu took Brae into his arms and held her, his eyes tender. "There's so much I can't explain right now. My father has power over life and death, as do I, Brae. What you saw, no human outside the Ruah has ever seen nor ever will see again…including you."

Brae's shoulders fell. After another minute of being comforted, she took a deep breath and stepped back. "I understand. Thank you."

Rhett, Bridger, and Jaym joined them, visibly confused, but there wasn't time to explain.

"We must return to the others," Jeshu said. "The hour has come."

CHAPTER

18

A Death to Live

When Jeshu, Brae, Rhett, Bridger, and Jaym returned to where the other sectators were gathered, it was evident that something was amiss. Mazon, Salara, and Quill were still communing, but Shayde, Cilla, Kase, and Lubin had rejoined with their bodies. They looked shaken and afraid. A hundred yards away, an intense firefight was taking place near the bottom of the hill. Brae could see and hear blaster fire coming hard at the defending contingent, presumably Mazon, Salara, and Quill.

"Return to our realm," Jeshu ordered.

"We can help," Rhett protested.

"You're not equipped for a ground assault encounter," he reminded, pointing to their flight suits.

"But neither are you," Brae said, pointing to his own flight suit. She instantly regretted her words, realizing how absurd they were. Jeshu didn't rebuke her—instead he looked at her with compassion in his eyes.

"I'll be back. Join the others," he said, then he disappeared through the trees leading to the bottom of the knoll.

Brae, Rhett, Bridger, and Jaym rejoined their bodies, awakening to the apparently peaceful realm of humanity. It took Brae a few seconds to translate her mind from the war she had just witnessed and back to the peace of their existence. The Protector Jeshu had given her silently dissolved away in a milky wisp. She lifted her head, catching the gaze of Cilla, Kase, and Lubin.

Shayde came to Brae. "Thank Ell Yon you're okay," Shayde said, wrapping her arms around her friend.

Kase was sitting on a section of a toppled pillar. Rhett and Bridger went to him.

"What's happening?" Rhett asked, putting a hand on Kase's shoulder. He and the others seemed pretty shaken. The typically playful eyes of Kase were no more. All members of their contingent had the look of early veterans of war.

"They're coming, and we can't stop them," Lubin said.

"What does that mean here though?" Rhett pressed.

Kase looked up at his brothers. "It's not just the Torians that are coming...so are the Keepers, the Builders, and an entire contingent of Raylean Guard with them."

Brae glanced over at the kneeling form of Jeshu, perfectly silent and still. She then looked at Rhett. "They're coming for him...we have to get him out of here."

"That's not all," Cilla said. Brae and Rhett looked her way. "Dahj is leading them."

"What!?" Brae exclaimed. "Is he being forced?"

Lubin frowned, shaking his head.

Anger instantly ignited within Brae's heart. She saw the same fury fill Rhett's eyes. During the last few weeks, Brae had noticed a shift in Dahj's attitude, but the man normally kept to himself, so she figured he was dealing with some personal challenges. This past week seemed worse, however, as she began noticing subtle hints of discontent. But never in a thousand years did she suspect betrayal...not after seeing the power and the love that Jeshu had demonstrated across the planet.

"I'm going to—" Rhett began, but just then Mazon, Salara, and Quill returned and awakened out of the Ruah.

"Where is he?" Rhett pressed Mazon before he had fully recovered.

Mazon was breathing hard. He wiped his face with his hand as if narrowly escaping death. "He took on the battle so that we could escape," Mazon was finally able to utter.

Brae walked to the edge of the knoll and peered down the wooded hill. She imagined the sounds of an intense firefight in the Ruah. In the darkness of nighttime in her realm, she could just make out the distant flash of lights moving toward them both on the ground and above the treetops.

"We're running out of time," Rhett said, coming to stand beside her.

"Yes, but even if they come, he has the Protectors...they wouldn't dare, would they?"

The eleven sectators waited near the silent form of their master, each one exhibiting anxiety in their own way. After a long three minutes, Jeshu finally stirred, traces of blue arcing power shimmying up and down his two Protectors. He lifted his head to see the faces of his followers. Seconds later, two patrol ships flew swiftly into position above them, illuminating the area with brilliant spotlights.

"What do we do, Jeshu?" Bridger asked.

Jeshu slowly stood. In the thick of the rising threat, Brae gazed upon the regal form of the Son of Ell Yon—powerful, unafraid, silent.

"Stand down, sectators."

A few seconds later, thirty Raylean Guards and a cadre of Keepers and Builders all led by Fasa Kylos and Dahj exited the dark walls of the woods. The armed guards surrounded Jeshu and the eleven sectators with their plasma rifles leveled at their chests. Brae waited for Jeshu to activate his Protectors and put them in their place as he had done multiple times before, but he hesitated.

"Identify the anarchist," Kylos demanded.

Dahj stepped forward to point a finger at Jeshu.

"You traitor!" Rhett yelled, taking steps toward Dahj, but two guards stepped in front of the former sectator, jamming the tips of their plasma rifles into Rhett's chest. Brae pulled him back and away from the guards and their deadly weapons. One flinch from a nervous guard and Rhett would have a hole in his chest.

Jeshu held up his hand, and Brae expected the condemning fire of Ell Yon to rain down on their enemies. Kylos stepped forward, pulling the sleeve off his newly enhanced Protector. More than the previous Ruah-enhanced lattice of before, Kylos's Protector was now fully encased in a red jeweled frame of extremely powerful-looking tech. Jeshu's Protectors began to flash ribbons of blue power, and Brae found it difficult not to anticipate witnessing the justice of Jeshu.

"Not this time, you heretic!" Kylos shouted. He clenched his fist as his Protector blasted forth a confining beam of power at Jeshu. The moment the front lobe of the beam hit Jeshu, the blue arcing traces of Immortal power in his Protectors extinguished.

"No!" Brae exclaimed. "Impossible!"

"Stand down, sectators," Jeshu commanded as he lowered his arm in defeat.

"There were rumors that Kylos had acquired a more powerful Protector suppressor," Cilla whispered to Brae.

Jeshu glared at Kylos then turned his eyes to Dahj. He stepped forward to face his former sectator face-to-face.

"You used one of my own against me to accomplish your evil deed...Dracus," Jeshu said.

Dahj smiled in a way that sent chills up and down Brae's spine.

"Of course I did," Dahj said, but the voice was not his own. It was deep...dark. "But he was willing, and betrayal is the sweetest form of revenge."

Brae now understood. This was the faceoff between ultimate evil and ultimate good. But surely Jeshu was just toying with Dahj and Kylos. *Now, Jeshu...destroy them now!* she pleaded in her heart, but he did not move, nor did the

Protectors activate. Had Kylos actually succeeded in suppressing the power of the Protectors?

Without a fight, Kylos and his Raylean Guards took Jeshu, leaving the sectators alone in the dark, questioning all that they had seen and heard.

At the bottom of the knoll, Kylos tapped on the interface band on his left arm, a look of disgust on his face. He made a final tap then looked at Dahj.

"The credits have been transferred to your account," Kylos sneered, then turned his back to the man.

Dahj glared at Jeshu with dark vengeance in his eyes. Complete abject evil was ravaging the soul of the man. Then for one split second, Dahj appeared in his humanity, frightened and ashamed. It was hard for Jeshu to see the destruction of a soul in the hands of Dracus. He knew what Dahj's end would be. Dracus used, abused, and killed. The credits he had received in exchange for his betrayal would never be spent by Dahj. Before Jeshu could say anything, Kylos ordered the captain of the guards to take Jeshu aboard a waiting patrol cruiser. At the back of the ship, one of the guards struck Jeshu with the butt of his plasma rifle. This incited a succession of abuse to which Kylos conveniently turned his back. The ship launched, and the guards finally relented, leaving Jeshu bruised and bleeding on the cold steel floor of the patrol. Jeshu's journey to death had commenced.

Jeshu was just a lad when he was enlightened as to why he had come to the realm of humanity. Knowing such a purpose changed everything. He watched with amazement the fleeting grasps for power by men—a thing by which so many were motivated, from the bully of a gang of five boys to the prefect of an empire of billions. His actions as the Merchant had surprised, shocked, disappointed, and encouraged millions. As the hour of his calling approached, Jeshu felt the weight of a galaxy fall upon him. *Is there another way?* he wondered...petitioned.

The tether to this reality was strong, but it wasn't what was causing such enormous angst in this hour. In order for Jeshu to purge humanity from Deitum Prime, he must become Deitum Prime, absorbing the evil of Dracus to cure the galaxy. It was a frightful endeavor, and it came with a price...the rejection of his father while he devoured and destroyed the Deitum Prime of the galaxy. The horrific death to arrive was but a fraction of the torment of that rejection. As the minutes passed, plots were fulfilled, and the hour of humanity arrived to do with the Son of Ell Yon as their evil hearts desired—Jeshu quieted his heart. *As you wish, Father*, he whispered through the Protector.

When they arrived at the Jalem sanctum, Jeshu was made to stand on the platform in the oration chamber with his hands bound, his face swollen and bleeding. He scanned the chamber, taking in each face as they taunted and rebuked him. On this day, the Keepers and Builders had convened a special council of judgment led by Preeminent Fasa Kylos and Master Builder Krisha Monae.

"Before you stands the heretic, Jeshu of Zareth." After each proclamation, the assembled Keepers and Builders shouted words of agreement for Kylos and rebuke for Jeshu.

"This man has beguiled our people, violated our sanctum laws, incited concern and undue attention from the Morian Empire, and has made blasphemous claims regarding our Sovereign Ell Yon!"

His fierce words riled the chamber members to a frenzy. Many stood and jeered upon hearing the accusations.

"He deserves death!" shouted many.

Kylos lifted his arm with the enhanced Protector, his face fierce with fury. He formed a fist, and the enhanced Protector unleashed a vicious beam of tortuous energy directed at Jeshu. Every muscle in Jeshu's body contorted under the power of the Immortal weapon. The searing pain was unbearable, but Jeshu didn't cry out. After five long seconds of horrific agony, Kylos released Jeshu and he fell to the ground on his hands and knees, trying to fill his lungs with air. Kylos stepped toward Jeshu so that the beaten and bowed figure was just two feet in front of the Preeminent

Keeper, his floor-length cape magnifying his power over Jeshu.

Glaring down at Jeshu with indignation, he pointed a finger. "Do you claim to be the Merchant...the Son of Ell Yon?" Kylos shouted for the entire chamber assembly to hear.

Though his body was still reeling from the attack of the guards and now from Kylos, Jeshu slowly stood to face his accuser. The 2,000 attendees hushed to silence, all anticipating the words of a self-condemning confession.

"I am, and you shall see me as Commander of all Malakians standing in power beside my father in the Ruah, and I will judge both the living and the dead."

Kylos's face turned red with fury. His neck began to bulge, and his muscles swelled as he threw his hand forward. The resulting energy release from his enhanced Protector blasted into the chest of Jeshu, sending him careening across the floor to the edge of the platform.

"Imposter!" Kylos shouted, his hand pointing accusingly at the prone form of Jeshu. "If he were truly the Son of Ell Yon, the Protectors he wears would have defended him, but see for yourselves how they are silent. Death to the imposter!" Kylos shouted.

This declaration incited an endless chant from the Keepers and the Builders...all except a handful who watched on in horror.

"Guards...deliver him to Subchancellor Pylok of the Morian Empire, where his insurrectionist activities will be duly judged."

Three hours later, Jeshu was standing before the most powerful man on planet Rayl, Morian regent council, Subchancellor Pylok. At first, Pylok refused to see Jeshu, but when Fasa Kylos appeared, he relented.

Pylok entered the Morian Hall of Judgment and appeared more than annoyed as Kylos, Monae, and six Raylean Guards escorting Jeshu waited. The elegant room was fashioned in such a way to intimidate whoever was being judged. Pylok's judgment seat was elevated with ribbons of light behind him giving him, a near god-like appearance.

"What is this about, Kylos?" Pylok demanded as he strode across the ornate floor and up to his judgment seat. "Why are you bothering me with an affair that belongs to your precious Keeper order?" Pylok asked as he spun about to sit in his elevated chair.

"Your excellency, this man is guilty of sedition against the Morian Empire," Kylos began. "We feel it is our duty to turn such a dangerous individual over to you before another insurrection occurs."

At Kylos's accusation, Pylok eyed Jeshu carefully. "And when has the Morian Empire earned such loyalty from the likes of you, Kylos?" Pylok shot back. "Where is the evidence of his sedition?"

"By his own mouth he claims he will rule the galaxy, and we know there is only one ruler of the galaxy. We have sworn our allegiance to him alone, First Leader of the Morian Empire Chancellor Krish."

Pylok sneered back at Kylos, then slowly stood. He stepped down the four steps onto the judgment floor near to Jeshu.

"By the looks of the man, you have already judged him." Pylok walked to face Jeshu, peering deeply into his eyes.

Jeshu gazed back at Pylok, knowing the man and knowing his thoughts. Here was a man in a position of authority with no avenue of escape. Caught in the stream of cataclysmic events, the river of humanity had placed him here in this position at this infamous time of judgment. As Jeshu considered the man, Pylok seemed to sense the silent power Jeshu held. Pylok's face softened—he swallowed hard.

"I will question the man in private. Leave us," Pylok ordered.

"But Subchancellor—" Kylos began.

"Now!"

Kylos looked concerned. He hesitated, then led Monae and their entourage out of the Hall of Judgment.

When the door to the hall closed, Pylok came close to Jeshu, eyeing him as if trying to solve a puzzle.

"I've been watching you for some time," Pylok began, his voice now sincere and absent of the demeaning tone he had used with Kylos. "My men have found no violation of our edicts by your followers or at the abandoned station you've inhabited. Why is Kylos so concerned with you...really?" Pylok asked.

Jeshu remained silent.

"Don't you realize that I have the power to release you or to execute you?" Pylok asked incredulously.

"The only power you have was given to you by my father. I have come from him and am here to bear witness to the truth."

"The truth?" Pylok demanded as he leaned in closely.

Jeshu felt the angst of the man, knowing that Pylok's hand was being forced by powers far beyond his own control.

"Do you claim that you will rule the galaxy one day?"

Jeshu glared at Pylok, allowing the man to see one fraction of a second of his Immortal power. "You say so, and it shall be."

Pylok's eyes opened wide with concern and alarm...then fear. He had seen Jeshu for who he was, and it clearly terrified him. He turned away, calling for his guards and for Kylos to return. When all were present, Pylok sat down in his lofty seat. As Kylos waited for Pylok's judgment, the Subchancellor fidgeted. Finally, he spoke. "I find no fault with this man."

Kylos and Monae were stunned by the proclamation.

"Subchancellor, if you set this man free, and he fulfills his promise to rise up and attempt to overthrow the Morian Empire, what do you suppose you will say to Chancellor Krish?" Kylos asked.

Pylok's face grew red with fury. "Are you threatening me, Kylos?" Pylok nearly shouted.

Krisha Monae stepped forward. "Not at all, your excellency. We are protecting you."

Pylok continued to fume, sneering at Kylos and Monae. After ten long seconds of fierce, contemptuous silence, Pylok stood. "His blood be on your hands, Kylos!" Pylok took one last look at Jeshu. "Deliver him to the executioner."

Never was a more innocent man sentenced to death than Jeshu Starlore. And the method of execution was to be the most brutal that had ever been invented...the ring.

The execution ring was reserved for criminals that demonstrated sedition and subversion or outright insurrection. The intent of such a public execution was to deter any future attempts by those foolish enough to contradict the Morian Empire. It was an extremely tortuous form of execution, inflicting pain throughout the six-hour process. For those unfortunates who endured the ring, death was anticipated as an end to the horror of their final hours of life.

Jeshu was escorted to an outdoor arena where serrated magnetic collars were clasped around his wrists and ankles.

"Remove those!" the lead commando ordered one of his subordinates while pointing at Jeshu's Protectors. One of the commandos attempted to remove the Protector on Jeshu's right arm, but it would not release. The man sneered and readied to pull harder, but then he yanked his hand away with a curse on his lips.

"It shocked me!" he exclaimed.

"Doesn't matter...he'll die just the same. Leave them," the leader growled.

Jeshu was then forced to lie down in the center of a large metallic ring while four Morian commandos stretched his arms and legs outward.

"Don't move, or your limbs will be torn from your body," one of the commandos warned with a smirk on his face.

They each then stepped back and out of the ring.

"Energize," one of the men ordered.

Pulsing ribbons of crimson light began to flow around the periphery of the ring. Then the electromagnetic engine engaged, pulling each of the magnetic collars outward with tremendous force. Jeshu felt his muscles, tendons, and ligaments instantly pulled taught beyond their limits. He felt multiple sets of muscles begin to burn as they tore, compounding the pain each new second upon the previous.

"Elevate," came the next command.

The ring's antigrav engine engaged, slowly lifting upright into the air, its captive suspended midair within the ring. Once vertical, the ring lifted another ten feet into the air. There, hovering above the elevated execution platform, Jeshu hung as the ring slowly rotated so that all could see his tormented face every few seconds. As was the Morian tradition for public executions, the event was broadcast across the planet of Rayl and throughout the Morian Empire. The crowd was cheering, laughing, taunting, and weeping. But this was just the beginning.

The four commandos went to a cabinet that was rising out of the floor. Each retrieved a stasis-field-lined, fluidic, metallic whip called a grissler, an instrument designed to inflict the maximum amount of pain via the cutting stasis field without cauterizing the wound each lash left. These Morian commandos were experts in the administration of the grissler, knowing exactly where the body would feel the most pain.

The first grissler lash landed across Jeshu's back, and the pain felt like a streak of searing hot oil had been poured from his right shoulder to his left hip. Lash after lash of the grissler was administered, leaving Jeshu's striped body a mangled mess of blood and torn tissue. The leader of the commandos halted the abuse just short of unconsciousness so as to maintain the pain for as long as possible. Jeshu's precious blood flowed freely from his body and onto the execution platform where channels were inset in the floor to carry it away.

For most victims of this torture, the Morian commandos would engage an added feature of the ring...an electric shock to keep its captive conscious. When they saw that Jeshu would not submit to unconsciousness, they engaged the shocking system just the same. The electrical energy assaulted his mind and body further...to the very brink of death. The horror of this execution was a poignant reality of how dark and evil the minds of men could become. And in this horror, Jeshu looked into the faces of his executioners and those that cheered them. He felt the wrath of his father begin to fall on these puny humans...fiery, condemning, righteous wrath. He also sensed the presence of thousands of Malakian warriors...weapons ready. He knew the power of both Protectors was at his disposal. Everything in his human existence begged for this torture to stop and there were a thousand ways to end it. But there was only one way to finish it—unconditional, unmerited, unrequited love for those who were killing him. He turned his eyes to the stars.

"Destroy them not, Father...forgive them for they do not understand what they're doing."

The torture continued for hours. At the front of the crowd of onlookers, a few of the sectators had dared gather to behold the torment of their master, ever hopeful that he would end the brutal torture and descend a victorious hero. But alas, this was not to be. Brae and Rhett fell to their knees in abject sorrow, weeping great tears of distress. With immense effort, Jeshu pulled in enough air to speak hope once more.

"Don't despair...I set the galaxy aright."

In his final hour, the mortal pain of Jeshu's body was about to be superseded by a pain no mortal had endured or ever could endure. His body had reached its limit, teetering on the edge of death. Millions watched as the man oracles had heralded as the coming Merchant, ruler of a galactic empire without end, hung alone in the Morian death ring.

In that moment, the galaxy changed forever—the two Protectors on Jeshu's arms began to pulsate with brilliant flashes of Immortal blue energy. The crowd hushed to silence as the Morian commandos retreated. The pulsing Protector energy flashes magnified until the display was frightening to behold. And then the final pulse of purging blue energy exploded outward with a power that no mere mortal could possibly comprehend. The wave of energy pierced through the bodies of everyone present and continued onward, accelerating with each passing microsecond. In less than two seconds it enveloped the entire planet of Rayl and continued onward into the space above, its power not dissipating as one would expect. Instead, it magnified, reaching the slipstream conduits. In just a few seconds, the wave of Immortal Ell Yon's power shattered the bounds of space and time to reach every soul in the galaxy, and then as quickly as it had accelerated, it retreated. And as it retreated, it pulled the essence of all Deitum Prime from the four corners of the galaxy along with it.

In the Ruah, C'fir Dracus screamed in rebellion against the force of Ell Yon's power, but it would not be stopped. Just as quickly as the pulse of power had expanded, it collapsed back into the body of Jeshu, Son of Sovereign Ell Yon, and with it came the burden of all the galaxy. The Protectors caused Jeshu's body to absorb all the Deitum Prime in a moment. Jeshu cried out against the molestation of his perfect soul, taking on the heinous crimes of the entire galaxy because of Deitum Prime.

"Father Ell Yon...why have you abandoned me!" Jeshu screamed in the lonely darkness of his sacrifice. Since time began, Jeshu and Ell Yon had enjoyed perfect communion one with another, and although Jeshu understood why his father had to turn away from him, the pain of such separation forced the anguished words from his lips.

When the absorption was complete, Jeshu looked upward, his eyes black and full of sorrow and pain. "It is complete," he uttered. Then he died.

Absolute silence reigned as the world...the empire looked on, and in that silence the Protectors on Jeshu's forearms fused the blood of Jeshu with the Deitum Prime he had absorbed.

At a molecular level, the cure for Deitum Prime was unlocked and stored within the Protector's core—unsearchable and unreachable by anyone other than Jeshu himself and his father. In his moment of death, the Merchant became the Solution for humanity, purchasing countless souls from the ravages of Deitum Prime. Even the evil seemed to perceive the reason for the epic silence that lingered but didn't last. The ground began to tremble as the Protectors on Jeshu's arms energized for one final event.

This time there was little warning. The Protectors exploded forth a wave of energy once more, piercing the minds and shattering the halls of the Keepers. In Jalem, it exploded through the Protector Vault, splitting the two-foot-thick doors as if they were made of chalk. Inside the vault, the enhanced Protector of the Keepers disintegrated to dust, as did every other Keeper Protector on the planet.

Every Crimson Rose on Rayl turned a magnificent luminescent white, never to be red again. In that brilliant burst of Immortal energy, the Protectors on Jeshu's arms fell silent and still then disintegrated to wisps of metallic molecular dust until they were gone. For the first time since Sovereign Ell Yon had bestowed upon young Daeson Starlore the initial Immortal tech over 1,500 years before, the Raylean people didn't have a single Protector to guide them.

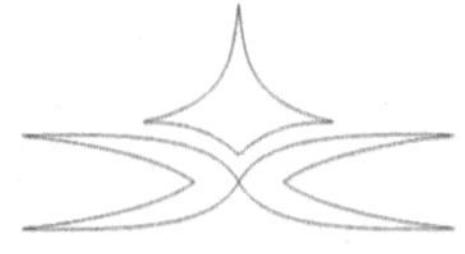

CHAPTER

19

Lost Dreams

Brae and Rhett held each other as the darkness of Dracus and his Torian Scourge seemed to envelop all of humanity in its grisly grip of death. In Jeshu's final moment, even the scoffers seemed muzzled by the terrible horror of killing the perfect man. The silence was broken only by the weeping of those who understood what humanity had done to its savior.

Brae lifted her eyes once more to the limp and bloody form of Jeshu suspended in the grip of the ring. First Daeson and now Jeshu. *Has Ell Yon lost? Does Dracus now own the galaxy forever. What hope is there now? What future for any decent soul remains?*

A figure knelt down next to Brae and Rhett.

"Surely he was the Son of Sovereign Ell Yon," Major Kamp said, placing a hand on Rhett's shoulder. "It's not safe for you here," he whispered. "Please come with me."

Brae felt Rhett pulling her from the ground.

"Come, Brae," Rhett encouraged, but she found no desire to do so. "You taught me to believe...to have faith," Rhett said. "More than ever, he needs us to believe in him now. We must go with Major Kamp...come!"

Rhett's words became emphatic, and it was enough to jar her into motion.

Before long, they were in Major Kamp's speeder, navigating through the chaos of Jalem ground traffic.

"I have a safe place for both of you," Kamp said.

"No," Brae said quickly. "Rhett, we need to get to our Spacehawks before Kylos or Terrok takes them." She hoped the other sectators had already done the same with their Spacehawks.

Rhett thought for a moment. "She's right, Major. Please take us to Olea Station."

Kamp hesitated. "All right, but for the record I think you're making a mistake. There was talk of post-execution directives, but I wasn't privy to them. You'll have to move fast. I've got a small transport at the spaceport we can use."

Thirty minutes later, Major Kamp was landing a small transport on a landing pad at Olea Station. The entire station was nearly abandoned.

"It looks like you're still in the clear," Kamp said, as he opened the side door on the transport. This would be a hot-drop where he kept the engines running. "Just do me a favor and get out of here as fast as you can."

Rhett thanked Kamp and exited the transport with Brae. The Major wasted no time in spooling the engines back up and launching. Rhett and Brae were still 200 yards from the main hangar where their two designated Spacehawks were located. Just as they started to run in that direction, all they had dreaded began to unfold before their eyes. A dozen Raylean Guard tactical soldiers appeared from behind one of the buildings to their right. Brae and Rhett froze. Out in the open, they had nowhere to hide and nowhere close by to run to. The soldiers were methodically clearing each building and they were now approaching the hangar. Brae and Rhett were cut off from their Spacehawks.

"What now?" Brae asked as she knelt down with Rhett.

Rhett's response was cut short when one of the guards spotted them.

"Run!" Rhett exclaimed.

They turned and made straight for the woods at the edge of the complex.

"Initiate your Spacehawk's AIFA to auto launch and track us to a rendezvous position in the forest clearing," Rhett said, as he tapped a sequence on the control band on his left arm. Brae tried to do the same, but it was a difficult task to accomplish as they ran across the complex in an effort to avoid the pursuing Raylean Guard tactical squad.

"Our Spacehawks will never get there in time for us," Brae replied as she tapped the final initiate button.

"AUTO LAUNCH SEQUENCE INITIATED."

Brae saw the message flash on her control band then focused on keeping up with Rhett as she drew her blaster from its holster. They sprinted for the edge of the forest, but Brae knew their efforts would be in vain, only delaying the inevitable. She hoped that the rest of the sectators and remaining Olea Station personnel had escaped. Although Brae and Rhett were in prime physical condition, they were no match for the pursuing tactical hover bikes and assault speeders.

"Halt, or you will be fired upon!" came the amplified order from their pursuers.

Somehow Brae outdistanced Rhett, but then she felt him reach for her hand, pulling her back. "It's no use, Brae," he shouted as two tactical hover bikes descended in front of them, cutting off access to the tree line just fifty feet away. All four of the hover bike's class-two plasma guns were targeted on them.

Brae slowed, desperately looking for an avenue of escape. "We have to try something!" she exclaimed, disappointed in Rhett's easy surrender.

"No, Brae," Rhett said pulling her close to him. "There's no place to go...it's over."

Brae became furious. "What's wrong with you? I'd rather die in a fight than surrender to these brutes!" She looked at Rhett, still stunned at his lack of heart. His face was sad but peaceful.

He shook his head, holding down her arm with the blaster in her hand so she couldn't take aim and fire at the approaching Raylean Guard forces. "I can't watch you die."

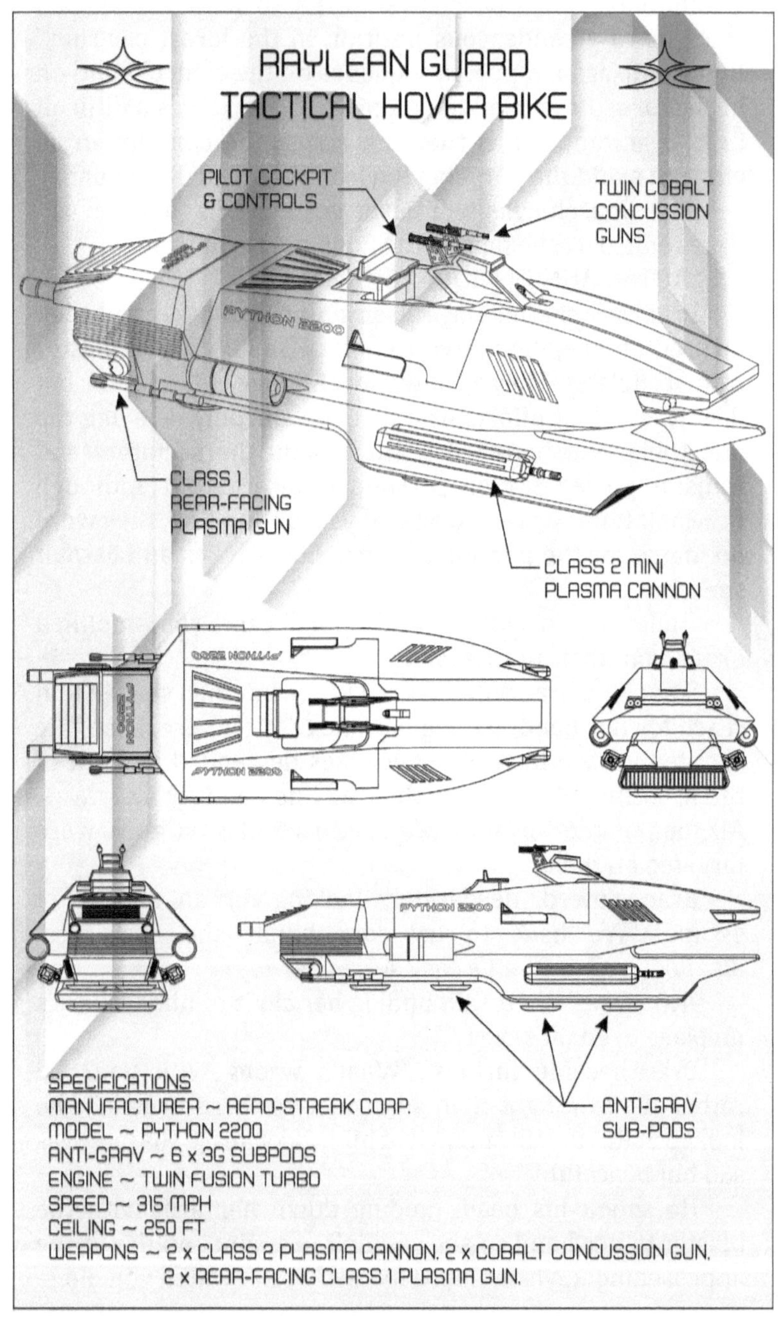
RAYLEAN GUARD
TACTICAL HOVER BIKE
PILOT COCKPIT
& CONTROLS
TWIN COBALT
CONCUSSION
GUNS
CLASS 1
REAR-FACING
PLASMA GUN
CLASS 2 MINI
PLASMA CANNON
ANTI-GRAV
SUB-PODS
SPECIFICATIONS
MANUFACTURER ~ AERO-STREAK CORP.
MODEL ~ PYTHON 2200
ANTI-GRAV ~ 6 x 3G SUBPODS
ENGINE ~ TWIN FUSION TURBO
SPEED ~ 315 MPH
CEILING ~ 250 FT
WEAPONS ~ 2 x CLASS 2 PLASMA CANNON, 2 x COBALT CONCUSSION GUN,
2 x REAR-FACING CLASS 1 PLASMA GUN.

In that simple statement, Brae understood just how deeply Rhett had come to care for her. Brae quit fighting him as she stopped and looked into his eyes. As the Raylean Guards began to surround them, Rhett whispered the words she had longed to hear.

"I love you, Brae."

"I love you too, Rhett."

In the chaos of an enemy's pursuit, Brae and Rhett gazed into each other's eyes, allowing those few precious seconds of intimacy to soothe the ache of lost dreams. Their confession of love for one another silenced the injustice that raged against them, if only for a brief moment. Brae submitted to her heart yet sorrowing for their unlived future together. Then the silence ended, and the forces of Dracus crushed their brief moment of peace. The Raylean Guard forces surrounded them with 30 blasters charged and ready to obliterate them.

"Drop your weapons!" the commander shouted as he and two dozen guards closed in.

Brae was still looking into Rhett's eyes, wishing they were on a different world and in a different time so they could live out their lives together and in peace. She felt Rhett drop his blaster. She dropped hers.

Is this the end that Jeshu had imagined? she dared wonder. *The Merchant brutally killed, the sectators scattered or imprisoned, Rhett and me seconds from being slaughtered by two dozen Raylean Guards?*

"Drop to the ground," came the sharp command.

Before Brae and Rhett could obey, one lone eerie bellow came from the woods behind them. The captain of the ground assault team glanced that way, trying to ignore it. Then to that one bellow was added a dozen more, and they became impossible to ignore.

"I know that sound," Rhett said, straining to look past Brae and into the forest. Brae glanced over her shoulder, but she saw nothing. Soon the air was filled with the deafening roar of the bellows of hundreds of ominous creatures. It unnerved every soldier there, including Brae. She turned about, capturing her first glimpse of the cause of the frightening sound. Stepping out from the tree line was a massive white zefflyn, its head lifted high and its pearl white fangs gleaming in the late afternoon sun.

Some of the soldiers moved the aim of their weapons from Brae and Rhett to the zefflyn. Then as the white zefflyn moved forward, the forest edge seemed to move with it. Hundreds of bellowing zefflyns emerged, slowly moving toward them. Fear swept over the captain's face as he witnessed something no one had ever seen before. The enormous, slender but muscular creatures slowly encircled the soldiers with Brae and Rhett still in their midst. The men began to panic.

"I know these creatures...if you shoot, you will all die," Rhett warned the captain.

Brae saw the captain swallow hard, his eyes wide with fear as the zefflyns completely surrounded them. The hover bikes were closest to the approaching zefflyns and one of the guard pilots began firing from his hover bike. But within seconds, five zefflyns leapt twenty feet into the air and tore the man from the bike, silencing him in a gruesome death. Nearly all the rest of the zefflyns immediately crouched to an attack posture.

"P-p-put your weapons down!" the captain ordered.

"But sir!" his sergeant exclaimed.

"Put them down now!" the captain shouted.

Slowly, all the Raylean Guards lowered their weapons then stood paralyzed in fear as the massive white zefflyn resumed his approach. There were still a hundred zefflyns bellowing their eerie cry, a warning to anyone who dared move against them. At last, the white king of the zefflyns approached the captain and his captives. Another eight escorting zefflyns were at his side, snarling and poised to eliminate any threat. The Raylean Guards nearest the massive zefflyn's approach slowly moved away from the creature that was as tall as any man present, clearing a path to Brae and Rhett.

As the white zefflyn cleared the way, the escorting zefflyns filled in behind, widening the path and protecting their king's access to escape. Inside the circle of guards, where Brae and Rhett were being held at the center, the white zefflyn walked a full circle about them, stopping at the captain. Fierce diamond-white eyes glared into the horrified face of the captain. Then the zefflyn opened its mouth wide, baring its long white fangs as it issued a guttural hiss at the man. The captain stumbled backward, falling against one of his men. The white zefflyn then turned to face Brae and Rhett. Brae wondered what this could possibly mean. *Will we all die in the jaws of these terrifying creatures?* she wondered.

The white king of zefflyns came first to Rhett, sniffing his tunic, its six-inch fangs pushing up against his chest. Brae squeezed his hand, having never let loose of him. Then the creature turned his attention to Brae. It sniffed her legs, pausing at the same spot where her wound had been then lifting its head to gaze its frightful eyes into Brae's soul. As terrifying as this encounter should have been, a calm came over Brae. She closed her eyes and bowed her head. The white zefflyn then mimicked her actions.

A moment later the zefflyn lifted its head high and bellowed a roar into the air that hurt Brae's ears. Instantly, every one of the one hundred zefflyns added their cry to their king's. The deafening sound caused all the guards to cover their ears. When it subsided, the white zefflyn nudged Brae toward an opening in the circle of guards, gauntleted by the escorting zefflyns. Brae and Rhett moved that direction. Surrounded and protected by the slew of zefflyns, they slowly exited the ring of Raylean Guards just as their Spacehawks were setting down 100 yards to the south. Brae walked that direction numbly, hand in hand with Rhett, still unable to process what was happening.

"How is this possible?" Rhett asked quietly as they came close to the perimeter of watchful and crouching zefflyns. "Will they let us pass?"

Brae continued holding tight to Rhett's hand, her courage waning. "I have no idea."

When they were within just a few feet of a dozen crouching zefflyns blocking their way, the white zefflyn behind them bellowed a command, and the zefflyns parted, opening a path for Brae and Rhett to exit. Carefully and slowly, Brae and Rhett made their way through the corridor of white fangs halted just inches from their bodies. Once through, Brae turned about to look upon the white zefflyn one more time. The creature's eyes sparkled in the bright sun, making them difficult to gaze into. The zefflyn held Brae's gaze for a moment then turned back to the paralyzed men and women of the Raylean Guard.

"Come on," Rhett urged, pulling Brae toward their waiting Spacehawks. They walked quickly at first then ran the remaining distance. Within a couple of minutes, Brae and Rhett were strapped in and launching into the air. As they departed, Brae banked her left wing to behold the uncanny sight of hundreds of zefflyns holding an entire squad of Raylean Guards hostage. Brae had no idea what their fate would be, and she didn't stick around to find out.

"Navi Two, initiate cloak," she heard Rhett say over the com. A second later, Rhett's ship disappeared.

"Copy, Navi One," Brae said, as she tapped the panel on her right. She caught a glimpse of her right wing just as her cloaking system engaged. It flickered then disappeared from sight.

"Where to, Navi One?" Brae asked over the com.

"To rendezvous with the other sectators," Rhett replied. "Or at least those that made it out. Sending coordinates now."

Brae received the coordinates, entering them into her nav system. Although Rhett was cloaked, her visor display showed a rendered image of his Spacehawk just a few hundred feet in front of and to the left of Brae. She replayed what had just happened, still aching from the rush of adrenaline it had caused. *How could it possibly be explained?* She was certain that their deliverance from the Raylean Guard squad would be a mystery forever. That Ell Yon was behind it all was certain, but it was still something she would ponder for a very long time.

In the great oration chamber of the Sovereign Sanctum in Jalem, the Keepers and the Builders gathered to discuss the process for reestablishing order and their authority for the Raylean people once more. Preeminent Keeper Fasa Kylos looked regal and at peace for the first time in three years. On the platform with him were six of his chief Keepers, the masters from the other sanctums on Rayl that had each hosted a Protector. Kylos stepped up to the glass podium, his full-length cape and Preeminent Keeper uniform punctuating his power and position once more.

"Fellow Keepers and Builders, we have persevered through a most difficult time. Upon our shoulders rests the noble and lofty responsibility to preserve the authority of our orders for the good of all Rayl and for the establishment of Sovereign Ell Yon's purpose for our people."

Most members of the assembled body of Keepers and Builders nodded and audibly affirmed Kylos's opening statement with enthusiasm. Kylos held up his arms, motioning for all to remain quiet so he could continue. His forearm was distinctly bare of even an enhanced Protector.

"Our time-honored orders were threatened by this man of heresy, but truth has won out. Now comes a time of rebuilding and regathering. Sovereign Ell Yon has confirmed our preeminence and right of authority through the death of this blasphemous man."

More audible affirmations and even shouts of approval rippled across the audience until one man stood up in the middle—Codemus. All 2,000 Keepers, Builders, and their associates hushed to silence. Kylos was visibly offended.

Codemus lifted his gaze to the preeminent Keeper, dauntless in his violation of chamber etiquette. "Have you all gone mad?" he asked, anger lacing his tone and countenance. "The things we saw him do...that all of you saw him do could not be done by any of us. Good things! I personally saw him destroy the works of Dracus in the minds of many."

"Sit down, Codemus!" Kylos shouted.

"I will not!" Codemus shouted back. "Are you all blind? Every single Protector we have has been destroyed. Though most of you don't know it, I have firsthand evidence that every single omeganite collector has been destroyed as well. What now shall we keep? And with what now shall you build?"

Codemus turned about to look into the petrified faces of every other Keeper and Builder in the chamber. As he did so, Sephner and Tazra stood with him.

"We brought false witnesses against him to condemn him, and he bore it in silence. We turned him over to our archenemy, the Morian Empire. At his death, our sanctum vaults were split open, and our so-called enhanced Protectors destroyed. Who then is guilty of heresy?"

"Enough!" Kylos screamed. "Sanctum guards, detain this man! You will be expelled from the order of the Keepers."

The two guards on the platform began moving toward Codemus.

"There is no need," Codemus shouted above the clamor as he removed his Keeper cape from off his shoulders. He held it high for all to see then threw it on the ground before him. "I renounce my position as a Keeper."

Sephner and Tazra did the same. "As do we." Five more Keepers and two Builders stood to proclaim the same.

Kylos fumed in anger, eyes red with rage. "You will regret this day, Codemus...all of you will!"

"The only thing I regret is not following Jeshu, the Merchant and Son of Sovereign Ell Yon while he was yet alive." Codemus looked about at the members of the chamber once more. "This is the beginning of the end of the Keepers and the Builders. Hope has been reborn for those courageous enough to follow."

The few seconds of silence after the intense exchange were palpable and interrupted only by Codemus and the other brave members of their rebellion as they exited the chamber. They passed by many that bore the same hatred and condemning visage as Kylos. They passed by others that wore the look of fear and dread. Some would not look them in the eye, while a select few seemed hopeful and eager. For the first time in the history of the orders of the Keepers and the Builders, there was a great division, for the truth of Jeshu divides many.

The final wave of power from Jeshu's Protectors pierced all of creation, including the dormant and dead circuits of a rebuilt android at the abandoned Olea Station. Within the first few microseconds of consciousness, the positronic mind was confused, attempting to reconcile memory, processes, new mobility actuators, power systems, and a variety of new sensors. It took another 120 microseconds to reconnect the new network in an order and functionality that worked. Once that was complete, Rivet opened his eyes. Although his body felt new, something was different. He replayed the moments with Daeson Starlore leading up to his liege's death and his own destruction. The deep sense of loss and failure was difficult to process. His last memory was that of lifting Daeson into his arms and then looking toward Brae Starlore as she sprinted toward the Starcraft. *Danger, Brae Starlore...stay away!* The message had processed, but in the fraction of a second before he could speak the words, death came on the wavefront of two powerful plasma cannon rounds. One microsecond of pain, then darkness.

Why am I alive now? Rivet asked of himself. He lifted his arms, rotating and testing the dexterity of each of his fingers. Though different, all seemed functional. A different body, but the same mind. *I've been rebuilt...is Brae Starlore all right? I must find out.* Rivet performed a full self-diagnostic check while searching the corners of his mind. In his search he discovered a single data portal unlike any other—its source unidentifiable. Rivet queried, but the portal refused access. He attempted to firewall the portal, but it seemed to have override authority and rejected the attempt. After 100 attempts via different methods and protocols, Rivet submitted, feeling...vulnerable.

Should I reveal this system integrity breach? the bot wondered. It had taken many years to win the trust of

Daeson and Raviel Starlore. What would this mean now? He thought he had left his kind behind, the AI androids of Mesos, for they had fallen to the whims and devices of Ell Yon's enemy, Dracus. *Is this some vestige of my former existence, or is this a pathway into the Ruah of the Immortals? The data from the portal seems to influence my thoughts. How much so?* he wondered. So many unanswered questions.

Rivet spent an eternity of 5.3 minutes processing this new existence. There was much to discover...much to learn. The galaxy was different now and so would its future be. *What part will I play?* asked the ancient android from the world of Daeson and Raviel Starlore.

ABOUT THE AUTHOR

Chuck Black graduated from North Dakota State University with a degree in Electrical and Electronic Engineering. After traveling the world as a tactical combat communications engineer for the United States Air Force, he was accepted into pilot training and served the nation as an F-16 fighter pilot. He is the author of twenty-two novels, including the popular *Kingdom Series*, *The Knights of Arrethtrae* series, the *Wars of the Realm* series, *The Starlore Legacy* series, and *Call to Arms: The Guts and Glory of Courageous Fatherhood*. *Kingdom's Dawn* was on CBA's top ten best sellers list twice in 2008 for all Christian Youth Literature.

Chuck is also an entrepreneur with sixteen patents and is currently the president and general manager for FlowCore Systems, a chemical injection automation company in the oil and gas industry located in Williston, North Dakota.

Chuck is a believer in Jesus Christ as Lord and Savior and in the Holy-Spirit-inspired, infallible Word of God. He is devoted to his wife, Andrea, their six children and spouses, and numerous grandchildren. It is his desire to inspire people of all ages to follow the Lord with zeal and to equip parents, pastors, and youth leaders to accomplish the same through his allegorical and Scripture-based novels, seminars, podcast, and published articles.

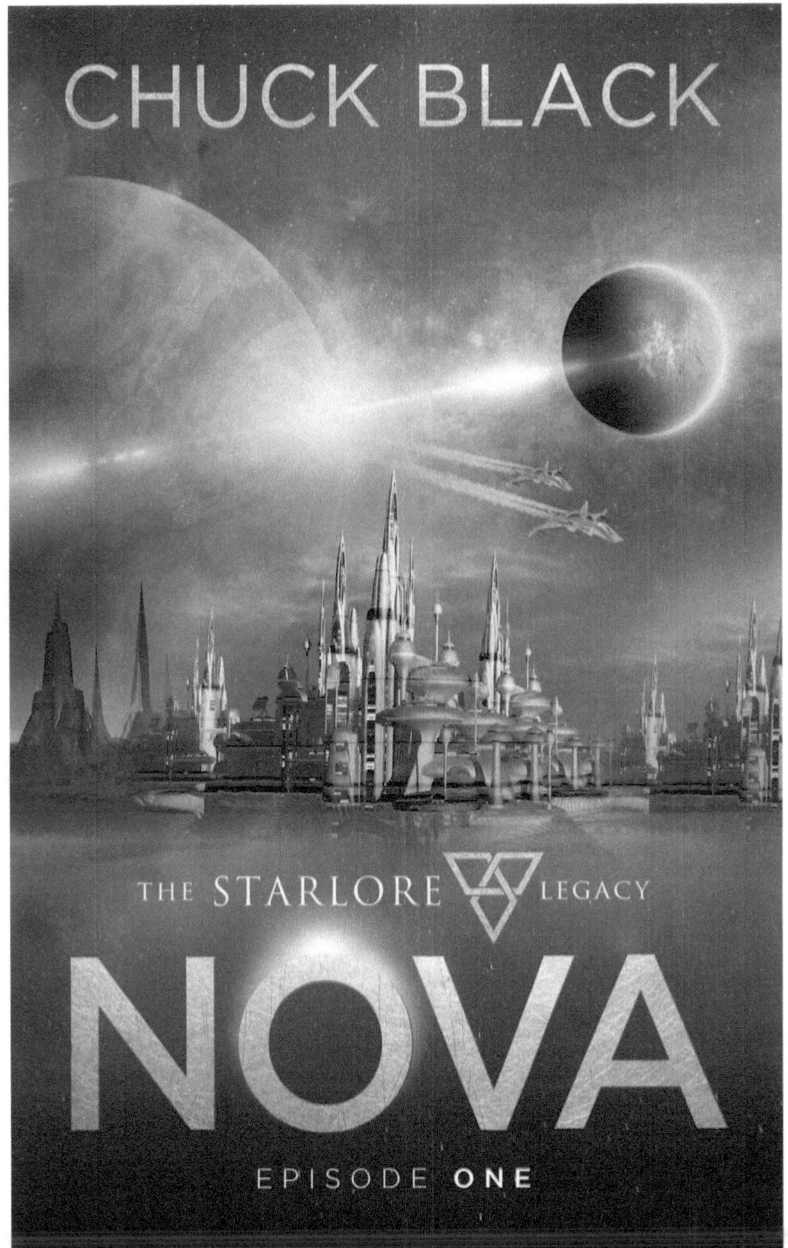
CHUCK BLACK
THE STARLORE LEGACY
NOVA
EPISODE ONE

THE STARLORE LEGACY
NOVA
A mighty empire. A lowly slave. A galaxy to save.
Will a hero rise?
Daeson Lockridge was born of royal blood, and all of his plans are falling into place now that his performance flying the legendary Starcraft at the academy places him as the second ranking cadet in his class. Only his cousin, Prince Linden Lockridge ranks higher. But a chance encounter with a lowly Starcraft mechanic shatters his perfect plan. The mysterious Raviel intersects his life and everything he thought he knew about himself, his family, his planet, and his galaxy seems a lie. Exposed as a fraud and with no one to trust he must flee the mighty Jyptonian fleet and search for the truth... a truth that will change his life and the future of the galaxy forever, for the Immortals are watching.
Published by
Perfect Praise Publishing
Williston, ND
ALL RIGHTS RESERVED
PERFECT PRAISE
PUBLISHING